An

Green-Field Library Selection

"This is a deeply moving novel that touches upon love, creativity, and memory. It is the story of a musician who develops Alzheimer's disease, yet continues to struggle with her craft. The author is a passionate and gifted writer who understands the nuances of memory and Alzheimer's disease."

—Dr. Bruce Miller, Director,
UCSF Center for Memory and Aging

"The strength of this novel resides in the author's intimate knowledge of music as she conducts the compositions flowing through it, much the way the concerto is divided into movements with new motifs, altered tempi, and distinctive prevailing moods."

—Laurna Tallman, author, *Listening for the Light*

D1551447

A Minor

BY MARGARET ANN PHILBRICK

© Copyright 2014 by Margaret Ann Philbrick

ISBN 978-1-938467-99-8

Published by

◤ köehlerbooks ™

210 60th Street
Virginia Beach, VA 23451
212-574-7939
www.koehlerbooks.com

Publisher
John Köehler

Executive Editor
Joe Coccaro

A Minor – A Novel of Love, Music and Memory
MUSICAL SELECTIONS

Thomas Chisholm, William Runyan,
Great is Thy Faithfulness ‡ — pages 16, 217

Frederic Chopin, Prelude in E minor * — page 20

Pyotr IlyichTchaikovsky,
Piano Concerto No. 1 in B-flat minor * — pages 40, 199

Johannes Brahms, Intermezzo in A Major * — page 43

Frederic Chopin,
Piano Concerto No.2 in F minor * — page 52, 198

Robert Schumann, Traumerei † — page 62

Ludwig van Beethoven, Pathetique Sonata * — pages 65, 216

Ludwig van Beethoven, Sixth Symphony* — page 109

Alexander Scriabin, Etude in B Major * — page 191

Johann Sebastian Bach,
Prelude and Fugue in B-flat minor * — page 192

Johannes Brahms, Waltz in A-flat Major † — page 204

*Visit www.koehlerbooks.com/dropbox/aminor
to stream these musical selections.*

* Licensed from UniqueTracks Production Music Library (www.uniquetracks.com)

† Public domain
Performance copyright © 2014 Margaret Philbrick, performance by Janna Williamson

‡ Copyright © 1923, Ren. 1951 Hope Publishing Company, Carol Stream, IL 60188.
(ASCAP)
Words: Thomas O. Chisholm
Music: William M. Runyan
Arrangement and Performance: The McMakens (www.themcmakens.com)

Also by Margaret Ann Philbrick

Back to the Manger –
A Treasure Hunt for the Nativity

margaretphilbrick.com

A MINOR

A Novel of Love, Music & Memory

Margaret Ann Philbrick

VIRGINIA BEACH
CAPE CHARLES

For Caleb and Dr. Karol Sue Reddington,
my inspiration.

The Piano

Softly, in the dusk, a woman is singing to me;
Taking me back down the vista of years, till I see
A child sitting under the piano,
in the boom of the tingling strings
And pressing the small, poised feet of a mother
who smiles as she sings.
In spite of myself, the insidious mastery of song
Betrays me back, till the heart of me weeps to belong
To the old Sunday evenings at home, with winter outside
And hymns in the cozy parlour, the tinkling piano our guide.
So now it is vain for the singer to burst into clamour
With the great black piano appassionato. The glamour
Of childish days is upon me, my manhood is cast
Down in the flood of remembrance,
I weep like a child for the past.

D. H. Lawrence
(1885–1930)

CHAPTER 1

Overture—A piece functioning as
an introduction to a dramatic work

Applause can be deceiving. "Over five hundred concerts, three hundred and fifty-seven encores, fifty-two premieres, and I'm still trying to figure them out. You'd think I'd be over it by now," Clare said as Nero opened the door to the back of his city car. Heading home to New Hampshire after another raging success in Boston's Symphony Hall, Nero couldn't believe he was about to endure another post-concert critique session. *How many premieres? How many drives have I listened to this? Clare ranting on, reliving every encore, picking apart every note, heartfully considering the audience's response and caring nothing about mine. When was the last time she asked me what I thought of the performance?* He couldn't remember.

"The Chopin was good. Seiji Ozawa is a marvel. Did you hear the resonance in the basses in the second movement? And what he did with the percussion? It was so subtle, yet strikingly clear. To me, the cadenza was weak. Did you notice it? My articulation was off." On and on it went, Clare writing her own review as Nero drove in silence.

"Clare, let's pull off in Gloucester for a bite," Nero suggested. "I think we need to talk about something more than the music."

Nero could see as he glanced at Clare in the rearview mirror that she was still back in Symphony Hall, moving through the measures in her mind, oblivious to his hunger. They held to their tradition of stopping in Gloucester to eat at Jacob's Wharf, the midpoint of their trip back home to the farm. This spot had provided solace from the crowd. They wound their way through the docks, taking in the late-night descent of peace, the lapping water against the skiffs at rest. As they walked toward the single yellow porch light, Nero saw Clare was beginning to come to. So often after a concert, she lived in her own musical space for hours, sometimes even days, before coming back to him. Maybe a beer and a bowl of seafood chowder would fortify them for the remaining four-hour drive, he hoped. Clare reached out for Nero's warm hand as they ascended the crumbling flagstone steps. Nero withdrew, forcing his clamped fists down into his pockets.

Inside the restaurant, Nero slumped against the torn red plastic booth and reached for the coffee-stained menu. He knew what he wanted: New England clam chowder and a divorce. *Putting it that way keeps things simple; no need to get bogged down by too many words. Maybe I could tell the waitress in my order and Clare would get the hint.* Nero looked over his left shoulder and raised a hand to flag the server's attention. *She's a fresh-faced new addition here.*

His mind flashed back to Satchel's Coffee Shoppe, where they first met in their New England Conservatory days. *Even with the taffeta ball gown and jewelry, she doesn't look much older than the afternoon of our first shared cup of coffee almost thirty years ago.* He watched her study the menu with her typical piercing intentionality. She ran her left hand through her frosted hair, causing her golden bracelets to shinny up her elbow. It was going to be hard to let her go, he knew. After drawing in a breath so deep he felt like he was preparing to jump into a frigid Adirondack lake, he released the words.

"Clare, I can't do this anymore. I need a break, an intermission from all of it. I've given up everything for your career, and what am I? I'm nothing more than your driver, your accomplice without a life. My own art doesn't exist. We bought the farm so we would both have a home to create in and be artists together. Remember?" Clare looked shaken, startled, and Nero watched her visibly shiver, like a cold draft had overtaken and disarmed her. She methodically put the menu down on the laminated pine table.

"Well, the farm is nothing more than a place for me to grow tomatoes and park the car. I haven't created anything. We haven't created anything. *We* thought we'd make art or children together. Instead, we have a scrapbook full of you, not us."

Clare sat stunned, attempting to steady herself in the face of his accusations. Nero could see that she was not going to formulate a hasty defense. She grabbed hold of a salt shaker and tapped it on the tabletop while staring out the darkened pane of glass. The streetlight cast a distorted shadow on her profile that appropriately captured the duplicity of their relationship. She looked like one of Picasso's "weeping women," her face broken into deranged segments. He tried to burn the image into his memory by closing his eyes, hoping to render it later in sculpted form.

"Clare, are you all right? Do you have anything you want to say?" Nero asked.

"I'm trying to remember when we went wrong," Clare responded, refusing to turn and look into Nero's eyes.

Ж

"Is someone sitting here?" Looking up at the young man with dark curls almost to his shoulders, how could Clare say anything but no? Without waiting for her response, he settled into the overstuffed brown leather chair of Satchel's Coffee Shoppe, as comfortable as an unwanted uncle coming home for every holiday. Smiling, the young man said, "I heard you last night, at Tanglewood. You were in total command. How do you do that?"

Clare, frustrated at being torn away from her immersion in the Schumann score, was caught off-guard by his direct intrusion. Unsure of how to address the question, she introduced herself instead. "Hello, I'm Clare Graham and you are?"

"Nero Cardiff from West Chester," he replied.

Nero, she wondered. *Who would name their child Nero?*

He shook her hand. "I'm serious. How do you take command of your art, your music, like that?"

Clare didn't appreciate the disruption from the score she had been reviewing. As he sat across from her at the carved wooden table, his eyes took hold of hers. They were penetrating eyes, almost black and outlined with a hazel edge, the look of darkness on the edge of morning. She found it hard to look away. Taking in his evident artistic interest, she ventured a partial answer. "I give myself to it."

"How?" Nero wanted more.

"Why do you want to know?" Clare countered, annoyed but intrigued.

"I am a potter. I make things with my hands. I feel my way through it. If it doesn't feel right, I can always start over, but you can't start over. You're up there on stage, and you own it. If you make a mistake, no one can see it and you go on. They might hear it, but they can't see it. I guess I want to know what it is to create something without the backup plan of starting over. As you said, 'You give yourself to it' fully and unbridled. I want to learn how to do that."

He leaned forward, almost looking into her soul, and said softly, "I want you to teach me."

Clare smiled as she studied his rumpled khaki appearance. He looked more like a shabby TV detective than a potter, but his earnest charisma was irresistible. "I am a pianist. We both make things with our hands. It really isn't that different from what you do."

From that day forward, Nero moved in with Clare and her career.

X

It was all so easy in the beginning. Nero wanted to attend all of Clare's concerts, the openings, the premiere parties. He even read the reviews aloud on the plane as they traveled from New York to London or wherever the next concert was scheduled.

At some point, I didn't change, he did, Clare thought. But in a small way, Clare knew Nero was right. He was distinctly absent from their scrapbook of married life. *Does a life of music make a person selfish?* This thought caused a jab of pain in her core, which she guiltily pushed away.

Clare looked up at Nero sitting across the table in Jacob's Wharf Café, and the memory of their beginning hung in the air like the wafting fog over the fishing boats. Studying Nero's craggy, aging face, Clare knew she had failed him. *What have I taught him about art, love, or life?* Initially, they had traveled the mountain peaks of her career together, hoping for the day when things would settle down, when they could actually stop and take in the view together.

Nero had grown impatient waiting for the *day*, while she waited for the next booking.

Have I given him anything as an artist? Is there anything fruitful between us, or was our relationship all for the audience, for those outside? Clare didn't want to let go. If she could just live differently, they could make it work. She ventured an offer.

"I understand. You feel like nothing more than my servant, but I didn't want it to be this way. I'm sorry. My music has given me such a rich and rewarding life, but at the expense of us. This wasn't something I planned, it just happened as we spent less and less time together. What if I take a break from concertizing and stay home for a while, work around the farm with you? You could teach me how to harvest the apples this year. I admit, I'm a farmer's daughter who doesn't know the first thing about farming, but I can learn."

Clare could see that Nero was growing impatient over her delayed responses and unrealistic suggestions for a last-minute fix. He turned his head sharply toward her and leveled a condemning retort.

"I appreciate your interest in the farm, but we've been here before. It's quite funny, actually, thinking of you suspended on a ladder picking apples while your mind is off in Vienna pounding out Chopin's *Fantasie Impromptu*. You left the farm a long time ago, Clare, your parents' farm and our farm. No. It's best you go entirely away because I need time to live my life without you in it. Once we've had a break," Nero reasoned, "then maybe, we can reevaluate."

Clare didn't want to press him for fear of provoking his anger. Admittedly, finding meaning and connection in feeding goats and picking apples seemed unlikely. "Nero, where are you proposing I go?"

Clare never *really* went home again after she left Mother and Daddy in Nebraska and went to the conservatory in Boston. It was all about achieving what she was born to do in their eyes, pushing through the beginnings of her career alone, until she met Nero.

"You've always been behind me 'achieving what I was born to do,' and unlike my parents, you've always been there for me. Now I feel like I'm losing you too. Why?" Clare knew Nero became stronger when her vulnerability entered the conversation. She had experienced his abusive side in the potting shed at the farm, and she didn't want to be confronted by his outbursts in a restaurant. Trying not to let her voice tremble, she whispered, "I feel like you are sending me away, like they did."

This time Nero raked his hands through his dark hair in frustration and rubbed the emerging lines of his forehead with his fingertips.

"They did not send you away. You know their choice and the sacrifices they made were intended to make you stronger, to prepare you for greatness. Madame Cardiff and all that," he added with a mocking bow. "Many young people with your gift don't make it because they're weak and unprepared. Try to look at my request in the same light as what your parents did all those years ago. In fact, I believe I'm being merciful by not asking for a divorce. You are not alone, Clare. You will always have your music, and the pious, proper Bethany and Tim. Their spirituality could go a long way in refining your character." Nero smirked.

Clare began to imagine herself in the Chicago area keeping busy until Nero finished his midlife crisis experiment. Perhaps teaching at the local college would bring about a refreshing change. "I could go visit Bethany and Tim in Chicago. There are teaching opportunities there that I have never explored, and I wouldn't be so lonely, surrounded by family. We can see how it goes. You could try working without me around, which might be more productive for you." Clare hoped Nero would find the appeal of work agreeable given he had only spun out tourist trinkets lately rather than pursuing the more refined pottery and sculpture he was capable of.

"Working without you around is something I've done for a long time, so spare me the false pathos of trying to do something unselfish."

"Sorry. It was just a suggestion." She could see his black eyes simmering beneath the surface of his obvious angst. "Nero, I am only trying to help, to come up with a solution that works for both of us," she continued. "Let's talk more in the car. I'm exhausted."

✕

The harbor's gentle lilt steadied to stillness. The hollow night sky surrounded them. As they walked to the car, the distance between them grew, to the point of rendering each silhouette enveloped by a shroud of foggy blackness. Propelled by aching, sandaled feet and still in her limp taffeta ball dress, Clare reached for the car door while Nero climbed in on his own side. For the first time in her memory, he did not open the door for her.

Clare paused with her hand clinging to the moist steel of the car handle. She determined to make it on her own. *I've been well trained. I'm at the top of my career. I don't need anyone.* While sprawled out in the backseat, she waited for Nero to start the car. He was looking at her through the rearview mirror, his eyes waiting. His isolated gaze made her uncomfortable, and she looked around the parking lot to see if any other patrons might be walking to their cars. They were alone in the lot.

"Nero, let's go home. There's nothing more for me to say." Clare could see from the angle of his profile that he was smiling, but in the half-light it appeared to be a twisted smile.

"Oh, I could think of a few things," he said, turning the engine over.

As the car turned onto Route 10, she peered out the back window and watched the yellow porch light of Jacob's Wharf fade into the night.

CHAPTER 2

Ars Nova—The new art

"You, a suburban piano teacher?" Bethany quipped over the phone. "I can't picture it. Well, I guess you could live here while you get yourself together. Maybe you could even teach my kids. You do remember, I have five of them."

Clare felt the familiar prickle of hair rising on the back of her neck with Bethany's suggestion she wouldn't remember how many children she and Tim had. Her grip on the phone tightened. When talking with Bethany she often felt confronted by the reality that her sister possessed the "good" life of a home bursting at the seams with children, while Clare didn't have any.

"Beth, I haven't forgotten how many children you have. I haven't been away that long and I don't need to move in with all seven of you. I'm looking to get some distance from Nero for a short time. He needs it as an artist. We need it as a couple." Clare took a deep breath. "I'm taking a break from touring to try something new, a change of venue, but nothing permanent. Something that keeps me plugged into the community, but at a distance. It would be good for me to share what I've gained from these years on stage. I'd rather it not be too intense and only for a brief time. Afterward, Nero and I will regroup and I'll probably return to the farm. Who knows, maybe he'll move out to the Midwest."

"Having you out here is hard enough for me to get my mind around, but Nero—impossible," stated Bethany. Clare tried to picture rumpled, flannel-shirted Nero wandering around Bethany's tony suburb of Brookline, smelling of organic manure and dirt. In her mind he looked like an impoverished landscape worker amidst the throng of buttoned-down commuters.

"I'll scout out some apartments for you," Bethany offered, "but I really believe it would be best if you lived with us at first, just to get started. When can we expect you?"

Hesitating, Clare took a deep breath before she answered, "The beginning of next month, September. The leaves will just be starting to turn."

After hanging up the phone, Clare tried to remember the last time she went to visit Bethany and Tim. It had been a long time ago, by her choice. They often invited her and Nero to holiday gatherings, but Christmas usually found her playing with the Boston Pops and it was more difficult to say no to those concert opportunities than it was to say no to Bethany. *Once you start saying no to bookings, you become replaceable.* And Bethany's life was so predictable and small, captured by that third-of-an-acre lot she rarely escaped from. But that's how she always wanted it to be, and how could she help it? Bethany had fought for and now owned what she considered the perfect life—a home on West Street with a Victorian front porch and a swing where she could sip lemonade and read good literature to her five blond-haired children. Her husband, Tim, walked down the sidewalk for *The Wall Street Journal* each morning and then caught the train into the city. He worked eight hours as an editor and came home in time for dinner the same way, day after day. As a family, they even walked to church on Sundays and sang hymns together in their front *parlor room,* as Beth called it.

Clare knew their well-planned life was steady, reliable, and practiced, and Bethany and Tim considered these as virtues, symbols of their success and God's grace raining down on them as a family. Clare regarded them as stale and petite bourgeoisie, but she needed Bethany now and this was not the time for personal judgments to get in the way.

)(

The next morning, Bethany heard Tim jog up the stairs after his morning workout at five and turn on the shower. This was her daily wake-up call—time to start getting the kids ready for school—but today she decided to lie in their sun-drenched four-poster for a few extra minutes and plan out her conversation with him. *Tim likes Clare well enough, but he is not a fan of Nero so that should make the news go down easy. Keep it short and sweet. He doesn't like to think about anything heavy before downing his coffee and peanut butter PowerBar.*

After wrapping up in her favorite fleece robe, a handmade Mother's Day gift from their daughter Sophie, she headed for the bathroom in which Tim had recently completed an authentic Victorian renovation. She took a seat on the edge of their newly installed clawfoot tub after bestowing a morning kiss on his already smooth face. She decided to dive in with the news. "Clare is going to come out and stay with us for a little bit. She and Nero have had a falling out, and Clare wants to get some space."

Tim glanced up from his morning preparations. "A falling out? Well, it's about time. I've always wondered how much longer their sycophantic syndrome could last. Serve Clare this, drive Clare here, bring Clare that. She isn't bringing your mother's piano, is she? That would mean she's moving in."

Bethany was quick to counter Tim's calloused observation. "Mother's piano is staying in New Hampshire at the farm. She might send for it later when she has her own place."

"As much as I hate to say it, I'm glad to hear this," Tim admitted. "I've always wondered how long Nero could give up his entire life for Clare. Really, Nero's nothing more than her servant, and real men can't live that way. When is she coming and how long is she staying?"

"After Labor Day weekend, I'm going to help her find a place, and she should be out by the end of the month. She will be able to give piano lessons to the kids." Bethany knew Tim needed a cost-benefit analysis to justify his investment.

"I hope we don't have to pay for that," Tim said sarcastically as he admired the perfect Windsor knot reflected in the mirror. "As long as it's just Clare and only for a few weeks, there shouldn't be any problem. We can give her the girls' playroom in the turret. We always have room for one more, right?"

Tim flashed a wry, familiar smile, which Bethany knew meant *one more*, as in one more baby for them. An aftershave kiss and Tim was bounding down the stairs for his newspaper ritual. Watching him stride through the white picket gate, then turn to close the latch, Bethany raised her hand in a grateful wave, knowing Tim could handle Clare for a while.

Ж

Leaving Nero and their New Hampshire farm initially seemed like a good idea. Nero's disappointment with his life was discoloring her work, and her success was stifling his. Clare felt guilty and cornered by his unfulfilled expectations. As she wandered through the raised beds of butter lettuce and kale, surrounded by quince and plum trees, she began to wonder.

Suburbia? The very word made her shudder. *Streets loaded with kids playing, bikes racing, women gossiping over the fence with no way to escape. Tim with his perfect hair parted in neat and tidy rows.*

Suburbia? Nowhere to be messy and grow. Definitely can't live there. Need to find a place right away. But where? Near Westdale

College could work. Mentoring a few piano performance majors might provide some quick income, and besides, it might be good to be near Bethany. Predictable Bethany. After these last few months of upheaval, a dose of her could go down better than expected. Clare's bare feet caressed the patchy, late summer grass.

"Come on, Clare. Let's go," yelled Nero. "What are you doing out there? We need to get going. You know traffic can be murder around the airport."

Her chest tightened, and she tried to relieve her shortness of breath by bending over for a last sniff of yellow chrysanthemum. "I'm saying goodbye."

As Clare approached the rusty pickup truck, she could feel Nero's eyes on her. Even from a distance the abyss of his eyes cut through her, leaving part of her soul exposed. He had the ability to look inside and see her wounds since their beginning in Boston. It was a skill that he'd honed over time like a sculptor sharpening his chisel. She knew he was watching for the first glisten of tears, and she steeled herself into the rigid posture needed to hold them back. "I'm saying goodbye to everything but Mother's piano."

"That means you'll be back?"

"Perhaps, or her piano will come to me," Clare replied ruefully, wondering how long she could live without the feel of her mother's piano beneath her fingers. There was originality to the sound of their mother's Bechstein that Clare traced back to her beginning, like a long golden note held across the borders of time.

Taking one last look over the fading fields of their New Hampshire farm, Clare felt captured by memories of her childhood. Instead of the sight of ripening apple trees down by the Sugar River, she saw the wide-open, empty palette of the Nebraska plains.

She saw her tiny mother, Emily Graham, who was the first to recognize that weekly piano lessons would be her daughter's ticket away from corn-crop subsidies and potluck dinners at the Lutheran church. Closing her eyes, Clare remembered her mother taking off her apron and sitting down at the piano to soothe her tired soul with her end-of-the-day hymns. In that present moment of saying goodbye, Clare wanted to flee to her mother's lap and take hold of her comforting hands as she pounded out **Great Is Thy Faithfulness**. Emily Graham was not a trained pianist, but she believed in Clare's raw talent. Almost as if by muscle memory, Clare soaked in the hymns by following her mother's hands and listening. Emily knew Clare could feel the music. Mr. Stanislav had told her so.

Mr. Stanislav, the only Russian piano teacher in all of Omaha, assured Mrs. Graham that Clare could not only feel the music, she could learn and remember it by hearing, like Rachmaninoff had been able to do. "So gifted was Rachmaninoff's ear and memory that he deftly played the matriculation composition of his best friend at Saint Petersburg Conservatory, ten years later for his good friend in Missouri. That is a true story, Mrs. Graham. Rachmaninoff only heard it once and he could play it from memory ten years later! An ear with a memory to hold on to what it hears, seemingly forever, comes along less than one every hundred years."

Amidst the singing of the barn swallows, Clare strained to hear her mother's voice encouraging her to go on, only to be interrupted by the throbbing of the truck's horn.

"Clare let's go. You aren't missing this flight if I can help it!" Nero hollered.

"I'm coming, Mama. Just one more minute, please." It had slipped out. "Mama. Just one more minute, Mama." A single statement she often said long ago to avoid leaving the piano when her mother called her to go to bed. A plea uttered countless times growing up. The pull of memory, so strong it impacted her speech, rendered her confused for a split second. In the distance she could see Nero, waiting in the driver's seat. The image of her mother, accompanied by the sound of her voice, vanished. Heading down the caliche lane in their pickup, Clare glanced back in the side mirror at their little cedar shake house on the hill, all the windows open for lack of air-conditioning because Nero always had to have the *natural* air. She refused to turn around and look back. The memory of her teenage departure from the family farm in Nebraska for New England Conservatory flooded her mind with the force of a sforzando. Her grandmother always told her, "Don't look back. It's bad luck." Back then she resisted the impulse to turn around and wave to her mother one last time as her father gripped the steering wheel of their own rusty pickup truck, bound with determination to deliver their daughter to the appointed palace of musical dreams. Little did she know it would be the last time she hugged her mother before she vanished from the earth, overtaken by a sudden heart attack while cleaning up the supper dishes.

The eerie familiarity of the scene pinpointed the pain of memory. Her mother's late-night piano hymns were forever silenced that afternoon, banished in the rearview mirror with the dust kicked up as they ambled down their long driveway. Why couldn't she forget this memory? How many nights had she been awakened by the image of her mother standing on the front porch in her apron, waving goodbye? She hoped this departure from Nero would not produce the same end. Certainly he would not die without her. He was too stubborn to die. On top of that, he was convinced that by separating he would be gaining his artistic freedom.

Clare knew she was leaving an unkempt part of her soul in the garden of Nero. Perhaps something in the grid of Chicago would bring a balance to their lives, something she could transport back to the raised beds of the farm that would germinate. Seeing Nero's sharp chin hard set to the west confirmed he was impatient for her to go. *A life without the pain he causes could bring newfound freedom, but what impact will it have upon my life as an artist? Pain gives birth to art.*

※

"Let me get that one for you. I can't believe you brought all these suitcases of music and boxes of books out here. This break from Nero must be for real." Bethany searched Clare's face for a clue to the cause of her sudden departure as they unloaded an endless caravan of Hartmann Luggage from the trunk and prepared for the journey up to the tower bedroom.

"Kids, come out here and greet your aunt and help us," Bethany ordered. Clare said to her sister, "Here come the von Trapp family singers from *The Sound of Music*," as she smiled and watched the orderly line of five blond-haired children emerge down the front porch steps. She half-expected Bethany to blow a whistle, inspiring the tribe to march down the stairs, single file in sailor suits.

"Aunt Clare, is it true you are going to teach us the piano?" Sophie beamed. Hugging all together and then in assembly-line efficiency handing off the bags, they dutifully set about the task of moving Aunt Clare upstairs.

The white Victorian showed little sign of wearing its one hundred and seventeen years—fresh white paint, crisp finials recently repaired, the theme of *We're all together here* shouting from its walls. Clare loved the front parlor of Bethany's home. It had the familiar tone of their farmhouse in Nebraska, but without the piano. Instead, cheery prints of summer children in fields of daisies hung on carnation and ribbon wallpaper with a smattering of antique rocking chairs around the room. A parlor all ready for the next church meeting, Clare imagined.

"Where is your piano, Beth?" she asked.

"Oh, we moved it to the back family room for sound control. The little ones banging on it in the front room traveled up the stairs, and we couldn't get away from it."

"Do you still have the Kimball hand-me-down?" Clare asked with a bit of dread in her stomach.

"No, we upgraded when Jeremy started to show signs of getting serious. It's a Bechstein like Mother's, but not quite as fancy. You'll like it," Bethany declared. "Let me show you to your room."

Clare wound her way up the former servant stairs off the kitchen, suddenly recalling how these old Victorian beauties curl upward. *I feel like a snail withdrawing into its shell*, she thought as she ascended the steps, which led to a long, central hall with small bedrooms on either side for the children. As expected, all their beds were made. Glancing in Bethany's room, she noticed the brass bed their mother and father slept in, but with a chintz duvet coverlet, so bright in comparison to the dingy lace their parents once used.

As Bethany opened the three-paneled door with its long creaking sound, a rush of hot air hit Clare's face. "Don't worry. There's an air-conditioning unit up there, so you won't expire," Bethany assured. Another creaky, curving staircase wound them up into the "attic," which was actually the top of the turret off the front of the house. The staircase's tiny windows seemed to speak with the sound of red oak leaves rubbing against them, their crinkling edges muttering back and forth.

"I don't think I've ever seen this room, Beth. Has it always been finished?"

"No, we recently remodeled. It was Sophie and Genevieve's doll room, but Tim built them a tree house in the backyard. They tell us they've *matriculated* their family out there. Matriculated? How do kids come up with these words?"

Bethany opened the door, and Clare found herself standing in a round room. The small desk looked out toward the street but seemed to be floating in the trees. Clare scanned the circular shape of the room, which caused her to feel dizzy. As she reached for the bedframe to steady herself, Bethany saw the first glimpse of a chink in Clare's armor.

"I know it's a bit of a climb, but you'll be out of the kids' noise and get some time to think up here. Maybe even pray or compose or meditate or whatever you do to restore yourself," Bethany said, trying to promote the tight quarters.

"I think I'm just worn out from the packing up and the trip out. I'll be fine."

Sitting down on the bed next to Bethany, Clare felt the familiar bond of strained sisterhood. "Do you want to talk about what happened with Nero?" Bethany asked.

"Not really. He thinks I'm hindering his work as an artist. He says he doesn't make anything anymore. Just drives me around. I've tried to include him, bringing him to scintillating dinner discussions at Maestro Ormandy's Philadelphia brownstone or benefits honoring the new works of a contemporary composer, but he doesn't engage. He doesn't care. All he wants is to be alone with me at the farm, to keep me there, locked up like Anne Boleyn. It's creepy."

"Well he certainly loves you, there's no doubt about that," Bethany answered with confidence. Clare remained silent.

Bethany stood and walked to the door. "Let me leave you to your quarters. Living with a family will be an adjustment for you, but there are benefits. I do all the cooking and Tim does all the cleaning up. We know you're used to your space, so I'll try to make sure the children honor that boundary. Do plan on joining us for dinner at six, which is the time we try to eat dinner every night. Tim will be home and all the children will want to spend time with you. Your bathroom is at the opposite end of the hall downstairs, with the periwinkle blue towels."

Listening to the quiet with her keen ears, Clare was surprisingly pleased. No ambient noise, almost soundproof. *Feels like the tower Yeats wrote in at Thoor Ballylee. Workable until I find what I need. A Bechstein. Excellent. How Bethany's tastes have improved since Jeremy started taking piano. Comfortable bed, albeit a bit lonely.*

Closing her eyes and still listening, Clare saw images of flowering quince floating within the measures of Chopin's ***E minor***

Prelude. She mused over the memory of her bare feet caressing the patchy late-summer grass of the farm.

𝕏

Taking a deep breath, lying down, and releasing a mountain of memories into Bethany's lily-of-the-valley patterned pillowcase, she could see Nero in her mind clutching the steering wheel of his pickup truck, looking just like her father the day they drove off to New England Conservatory. But Daddy never forced himself upon her with the possessive grip of Nero, who wanted her so desperately and yet today dropped her off at the airport with nothing more than a handshake. "I'm saying goodbye," Clare remembered with the lonely recollection of so many goodbyes spoken in the past, first to Mother and then to Daddy and now Nero.

The quiet of the turret brought rest. Sleep closed in, but Nero came to mind in a haunting melody accompanied by the almost palpable feeling of his dirt-encrusted hands clutching her neck, pulling her hair, locking the door. Tightening. Releasing. Falling asleep.

CHAPTER 3

Caccia— A two part cannon, to hunt or chase

"Clive, how was Mr. Koussevitsky today? He called here to say you were late for your lesson. Why were you late? What did you two work on?" Julia Chevalier Serkin pounced on her son as he came in the door after school.

Clive appreciated his mother's rare appearance at home, but he did not need or have time for the interrogation. "We worked on the Brahms," Clive stated without elaboration.

Julia pressed, "How's it coming? When will you have it ready?"

"I'm not sure, Mama. Right now, I have some work to do on a music appreciation outreach that we're bringing to the kids at Orr tomorrow. I need the computer, so I'll be up in my room."

Watching Clive head for the stairs, Julia called out, "Wait, Clive. What do you mean 'kids at Orr'? What is Orr, and why were you late to Mr. Koussevitsky's today?"

Clive respectfully returned to the room, attempting a quick response. "Orr is a high school in the inner city. A group of us are bringing a presentation to the kids there who don't have music in their school because the school board cut almost all of their arts funding. We decided to share what we have with them, building bridges through music with kids who don't have much."

"How laudable. I can see the headline now in the school newspaper: *Brookline Teenagers Reform Gang Members with Beethoven Sonatas.* Your desire to help people is admirable, but your music is more important. Papa is thinking of entering you in a high-level competition that would be a tremendous opportunity for you. Your elective time needs to be going to your music rather than kids in the inner city."

Clive looked at Julia and saw a mother who wanted results, a good performance first and his heart second, so he took the opportunity to remind her, "Mama, this project is about my music."

As Clive made his way upstairs, he held back a sigh of frustration at his mother's unwanted intrusion into his life. *Why can't she be more like Grandma Chevalier back in France?* His grandmother had an important job—teaching school with a schedule that allowed her time at home after school every day, not once a week. Somehow she managed to do it all. She worked and raised her children well. *Mama tries to do it all, and Anna and I usually get left out.*

)(

"Claude, I have a meeting out in D.C. in the morning. Can you drive Clive to his piano lesson tomorrow?" Julia Serkin spoke from the midpoint of her desk—central command as she called it—bracketed on both sides by computers and framed within the voluminous bookcase behind her. All of these she needed to navigate her job when she worked from home.

Claude Serkin studied his wife from the wingback chair opposite her desk. This isolated spot allowed them a moment of conversation while she finished up the day's work, without disturbing the children or any of the medical reports, which were arranged in towers about the room. Ever since she accepted the job as Chief Media Officer for the National Institutes of Health, she traveled more and was home less.

"My rehearsal starts at nine thirty and should take a good part of the day. It's Mahler," Claude responded to his wife's request. "Julia, Clive is a big boy now. He just turned seventeen, for goodness sake. After school, he can walk alone to his lesson or drive the car himself. Either way, he'll cut through Westdale College and take the shortcut."

"I know he's a big boy; I just prefer he not have the car all day while you're at rehearsal. Please. You know how much time he loses walking to his lessons from school, stopping for coffee, or taking a side trip into town with Anna for some junk food at Zehnders. Think of what he would do with the car and besides, Mr. Koussevitsky called today to say he was late to his lesson."

Claude Serkin assessed his wife's concern and doubted its merit, but gave in anyway. "Fine, I'll drive him, but please do not engage me in the discussion about his need for a new piano teacher. Mr. Koussevitsky is wonderful. I have nothing but respect for his insight and methods. If Clive brings it up again it's nonnegotiable. The answer is no."

"Claude, I respect your musical input into Clive's life completely, but I have noticed lately that he seems a bit listless about his music. He's lacking that joy and zeal we saw in him as a little boy when he would parade around the kitchen singing Grieg's piano concerto, you know the one he loved so much, which one was it?" Claude smiled, "Yes, the A minor, his favorite and on pitch too. I agree. He seems a bit off-balance, more brooding than allegretto. I think I'll talk to Rabbi Sherveen about it. He'll know what to do with teenage angst."

The following morning, Claude Serkin stepped into Symphony Center, and Mahler's *Titan Symphony* greeted his ears, but his mind returned to thoughts of his seventeen-year-old son. His assistant, Amanda, raced down the hall with an update for the day's rehearsal, extracting him from his thoughts. "Mr. Serkin, everything is ready to go. Mr. Still can't make it to the rehearsal today, a family emergency. Otherwise, everything else is in order."

Relieved that the current outbreak of influenza had not infected half the orchestra, the conductor raised his baton to hear the first strains of the violin tremolo, while anticipating the clarinet entrance and the beginning of the woodland dance. All thoughts of Clive were wrested away by Mahler's first symphonic notes of genius.

)X(

Brookline Academy sits atop the only hill in this otherwise flat Midwestern suburb. The edifice is dedicated to the cultivation of the talented and gifted. Red granite towers bookend each corner of the building, proclaiming permanence and the timelessness of art. Students stream down the hill and out the building, in uniform at three thirty, advancing to the next discipline of their day in ballet schools and rehearsal studios. Here, futures are granted and lives broken by pressures, expectations, and unfulfilled parental dreams. Tuition paid is worth every penny of hope for a place in the pantheon of the gods of art. On the outside, Clive and Anna Serkin's lives, chiseled from these granite walls, look very much like those of any other fortunate Brookline student. Anna, sixteen, is a promising biology student with an early passion for neuroscience. Her brother Clive, a pianist. Both have grown up in a world of protected, privileged encouragement and its accompanying demands for performance.

Anna streamed down the hill with the skipping freedom of being released from school. "Hey, are you going to Mr. Kooksevitsky today or could you go into town for some coffee?" Anna asked in her typical nosy fashion.

"Unfortunately, I must go to Mr. Kooksevitsky, as you insist upon calling him. My lesson is at four thirty. Why do you call him that anyway?" Clive looked at his effervescent sister's auburn hair in the fading sunlight and was surprised to see that she looked older than her sixteen years. *Older, but not wiser*, he thought.

"Because by all that you've told me, he is a kook. Isn't that right?"

"No, he is your typical old, gray-haired, Bach-obsessed piano teacher, living in an old gray house with the smell of bad breath and stale cat litter filling every room," Clive clarified.

"Oh, that sounds delightful. What a lovely place to hang out. Why don't you blow it off today and come with me?"

"You know I can't. Besides, I've made progress on the Brahms *Intermezzo* and he might actually be able to bring something to it today. On my way, I'm going to walk through Westdale and look at the music bulletin boards. You want to grab coffee there?" he countered.

Clive saw Anna stop, tilt her head to the right, and tap her index finger against her lips. *She's assessing or obsessing. I've seen that look before.*

"Are you up to something? Why are you walking through the college and looking at the music boards?"

"I just want to see if there might be something new on them."

Anna took note and elbowed her brother. "Well, if you are hatching a plan for a new piano teacher, I can't wait to be a part of that conversation. You know they both love Mr. Kooks."

"Mama does not love him as much as Papa, but I don't love him at all. I'm getting bored. Anyway, I'm just going to have a look," Clive declared. "Now you run along and be about your triple-advanced AP Biology homework, which you never seem to do but still get an A on every test. You are such a nerd."

"Okay, fine, I'll see you at home for dinner. I think Mama is actually making dinner tonight rather than her usual Chinese carry-out. Love ya." With a quick kiss, Anna turned and ran to catch up with her friends waiting at the corner.

Clive considered this walk one of the best parts of the day. Cutting through the conservatory on the way home from school allowed him ten minutes of free time to wander down the halls, peek into practice rooms, and listen. Behind those wooden doors with their tiny mirrored windows, every instrument was playing in freedom, all kinds of music—jazz, jive, gospel, and opera.

As Clive climbed the stairs, he eavesdropped on students' conversations, following along behind them. Occasionally, he'd go all the way up the stairs to a professor's office, even stand outside the door and press his ear against it to hear a movement of a Beethoven sonata and the teacher-student discussion afterward. *Oh, to have a teacher to talk music with, rather than just listen to,* Clive thought. He longed for the opportunity to learn from someone with whom he could actually converse, outside the realm of his parents' design for his life. Why did he have to be born the son of the great conductor Claude Serkin, with every step of his musical life planned out for him?

Scanning the piano department bulletin board, a lavender invitation written in calligraphy caught his eye.

Piano Students by Audition Only
Fall Semester Only
Call 847-696-5985

Not only did the color and formal lettering jump out at him, but also the stealthlike conveyance of its invitation. The picture of Scriabin in the background sealed his desire to think about making the call. Alexander Scriabin had been one of his favorite composers since he was a little boy. He was a pioneer, even to the point of using lighting effects with his music, which had never been done. He broke the mold. Clive wanted to be like Scriabin. *Give them more than something to listen to, give them something to see in the music,* he thought. Clive wrote down the phone number and walked quickly to Mr. Kooks's, while basking in the warm glow of hopefulness that comes from hatching a secret plan.

)(

Saul Koussevitsky's house smelled stale. Half-drawn, dirty yellow blinds, not cleaned since his wife died some thirty years ago, shrouded the front room. It was a modest house on Temple Street, a block away from the synagogue, the first bungalow he and his wife Rachel bought after they married under the chuppah. All the uncovered windows were stained with smoke.

Mr. Koussevitsky, a friend of Claude's since he taught Claude at the conservatory in Haifa, had forever been dear to the Serkin family. In the eyes of Claude Serkin, Mr. Koussevitsky was a teacher, master, and friend. Theirs was a relationship of biblical proportions, like David and Jonathan.

Back when they lived in Haifa, Mr. K's methods were new. He and his students would smoke cigars for hours together, listening to recordings of Uncle Rudy playing Beethoven. Then it would be the chosen pupil's turn to sit down at the old Bechstein and play his own interpretation of the *Pathetique*, working toward refining the poetic idea of ictus, what the composer is stressing or accenting in the music. Back then this was a novel idea.

Mr. K was considered a good musician and a devout Jew by his few, loyal friends, even though he did smoke cigars, which he tried to keep hidden at home. He loved going to synagogue and often mixed music with his faith during lessons. Music with Mr. K was explained through the lens of Judaism. Studying the Torah was what he had always believed should come first, in addition to music. *Maybe today we can get through the lesson without a religious reference,* Clive wondered. Pronouncements such as, "Yes, Clive, now that fortissimo is like Moses and the burning bush. Yes, that's what we want, give us fire," were a common encouragement.

Clive stood on the crumbling front porch for what he was sure was at least the seven hundredth time. He had been studying with Mr. Koussevitsky since he was three years old and this waiting moment on the threshold became a little more painful with each passing year. He didn't want another lecture on the God-given attributes of the music. Less than a minute after the bell rang, Mr. K's pointy face peered out from behind the lace curtain, the top of his head barely reaching Clive's shoulder.

"Ah, my boy, my boy, come in." A yellow, toothy greeting emerged from behind the peeling paint of the front door. He was wearing the same suit he wore when he immigrated to America. *This must be the only suit he owns. He probably still has his wedding suit hanging in the closet next to Rachel's wedding dress.* "How is my boy? Sit down and listen to my new recording of Menuhin playing Paganini's *Violin Concerto*. It is brilliant. I know you will love it."

Despite living in the twentieth century, Mr. K walked over to his phonograph to put a vinyl recording on the turntable. *Hasn't he ever heard of CDs?* Listening together, a foundation of the Koussevitsky method came without the old country tradition of sharing cigars. "It's just unacceptable nowadays. Children don't smoke like they used to," Mr. K said.

"Come, Clive, let us take some of that depth of sound, that singing, and put it into your piece." After two hours of refinement on the Brahms, Mr. K said some *holy light* was beginning to emerge. "Yes, there needs to be light and shadow, sun and shade, shading especially in this section here, Clive. You must transcend the notes."

Transcend the notes? Holy light? Religious references again. Come on, Mr. K, my bar mitzvah was four years ago.

"The holiness of God must be communicated through the music, even if it is Brahms, who didn't believe in anything. That's what Dvorak said in his letters, 'He believes in nothing!' Nonetheless God created Brahms so He is the master creator of the created."

Creator, created, does it really matter? Why can't we just focus on the music and not on what's behind it?

After his lesson, Clive walked home and counted the squares in the sidewalk while he thought about reaching for the ragged slip of paper in his pocket. *What was that number? 847-696-5985. Why wait? Mama and Papa don't have to find out. I could study with both teachers, using my prize money to pay for a new teacher.*

The pay phone on the corner of Temple and Third Street was the closest place to make the call. Clive reached for the stainless steel handle and pushed the door aside. Inside the silent box, he stood, staring at the receiver for a full minute before making the call. *Maybe I should call Anna first and ask what she thinks of this idea. I can trust Anna. Her instincts are good and she's more adventurous, but what if she says not to do it?*

Three rings and, "Hello, I'm sorry I'm not here to take your call. Please leave a message and I'll return your call as soon as possible." *Hang up. Hang up.* He exited the phone booth.

Leave a message? It was a woman's voice. *A female piano teacher?* That explained the lavender paper. He'd never had a female piano teacher; *How terrifying. Would this be dishonoring Papa if I just left a message? After all, he does want the best for me and my music.*

Clive listened to the competing voices of reason in his head, accompanied by the Brahms he'd been working on.

Mr. K's not so bad; he's just old, but Papa adores him. If he did take on a new teacher it would be best to try out the arrangement for a little while without telling anyone. It might not work out, and then he could go back to Mr. K full-time. *No one would even know.*

He stopped along his walk home to look out over the lawn of Westdale College. The unmistakable sound of Copeland's *Fanfare for the Common Man* poured out the open windows of a conservatory practice room. The music sent forth a challenge, a call to action, for the common man to reach beyond his grasp, to step out upon a new frontier. *Could it be a sign?*

He always wanted to learn Copeland. *Mr. "Kooks" isn't interested in teaching me modern music, even though Copeland isn't even close to modern. Papa always talks about how much Leonard Bernstein adored Copeland. This music must be a sign, calling for change. One phone call won't make any difference.*

Clive headed back to the pay phone. This time, with hand shaking, he made the call again. After hearing her voice on the answering machine and trying to picture what her face might look like, he said, "Hello, this is Clive Serkin. I saw your ad on the bulletin board at Westdale Conservatory. I'm interested in an audition. I'll call you again another time. Thank you."

)(

Dinner at Bethany and Tim's house was usually family-style, similar to Clare and Bethany's days back in Omaha. Somehow Bethany managed to herd a family of five children to the table at six o'clock sharp, with steaming hot food ready.

"Genevieve, would you pray, please?" Tim directed from the head of the table, still in his suit and tie. Everyone in the family simultaneously bowed their head and clasped their hands, as a 1950s family might have done in a Norman Rockwell painting.

God is good and God is great and we thank him for our food. By his hand we all are fed and give us Lord our daily bread. Amen.

A familiar prayer offered by Genevieve without a breath between the words. Clare couldn't remember the last time she prayed, let alone thought about praying. *What difference did it make? Did we pray before dinner back in Omaha? When did Bethany's family start praying before dinner? It must be something they do here in the Midwest.*

"Welcome, Aunt Clare," said Tim. "Everyone raise your glasses to Aunt Clare, who will be staying with us for a little while." Even the sippy cups got raised and shared in a clunky clink.

"Aunt Clare, what are you going to do while you are living with us? Are you going to give piano concerts in our house?" Devon inquired.

"No, no. I'm not going to be performing for a time. I'm thinking about doing some teaching and a lot of listening."

"Listening to what?" wondered Jessica from behind her still-smudgy gardening face.

"Listening to some other voices. My world back home is full of musical voices who tell me what to do and where to go."

"Oh, you mean Uncle Nero, don't you? He's bossy," piped up Genevieve.

"No, Uncle Nero does not arrange my schedule, and yes, he can be a bit bossy. He lives on the farm and spends time working there. He wishes I would spend more time living and working there too."

"Then why don't you?" asked Genevieve, with the honesty only the youngest child can be bold enough to deliver.

"Genevieve, that is not your business, young lady." Tim silenced her with a firm, correcting glance over his glasses. "Sorry about that, Clare."

"That's all right. Hers is a valid question. Uncle Nero loves my piano-playing, but he also hates it because it takes me away from him."

With a smile on her face, Genevieve said, "Sometimes I spend so much time with my favorite doll, Nessy, that Mommy says the other dolls might get jealous. Do you think Uncle Nero is jealous of your piano-playing?"

"Perhaps, but it is a bit more complicated than that. Let's talk about something else, shall we?"

"Yes, let me tell you how we came upon our new piano, Clare." Bethany jumped in to stop the children's questions from getting too personal for the dinner table. "You remember that we had the Kimball, which I'm sure you thought was awful. It wasn't that bad, but we could never keep it in tune. We placed an ad in the newspaper to sell it, and a nice man in town bought it for his wife. She had decided to learn how to play the piano as her fiftieth birthday gift to herself.

"When he came to pick it up, he asked us what we were going to be using for a piano. I said that I had my eye on a refurbished Steinway in Sophie's ballet studio, which they were looking to replace with an upright. He mentioned that his neighbor was moving to Seattle and he knew she had a grand piano to sell, so he gave me her name. Apparently it was a big piano, a concert grand, and much more expensive than he was looking for.

"I called. A darling woman named Maranatha said she was moving out to Seattle to take care of her sick mother and couldn't afford to move her piano out there. I asked her what kind of piano, and she said a Bechstein. I almost fell off my chair! Can you imagine just randomly getting the kind of piano we grew up with? So I went to see her, such a sweet woman whose mom needed in-home healthcare; but of course, her insurance wouldn't pay it."

Bethany's enthusiasm increased. "Entering her front room, I tried to keep my expectations low. There in the dark corner, kept out of the light, was a stunning sable-colored piano with elegantly carved legs. I could tell it was old and probably needed a lot of work. When I uncovered it, I saw all the ivory keys were in good shape, so my anticipation for the sound improved. I played as best I could, you know, one of the Bergmuller exercises I learned when I was little, which was embarrassing because I couldn't remember it exactly.

"She sat on the couch and cried, just hearing the sound of her piano being played again. Her tears, she later told me, were from a mixture of gratitude that I had come to play it and sadness because it hadn't been played much since her daughter married and moved to Georgia. Her daughter was a piano major at Westdale, but she didn't want such a big piano in her new apartment."

"That was not nice of you to make the lady cry, Mommy," Genevieve complained.

"Hush, Vivvy, let Mommy finish the story," Jeremy said.

"When I asked her how much, she asked me how much I could afford to pay. I know these old Bechsteins are worth a great deal, and I didn't want to steal it from her, so I offered her ten thousand and she accepted immediately. Can you believe it? I've priced them through various dealers and it really is worth much more than that. Wouldn't Mother be thrilled?

"As I was leaving, I asked her how she came about such an un-usual name, Maranatha, which from my own Bible study I know means *praise*. She told me her mother was a musician and play-ing hymns in church was her favorite kind of playing. Can you imagine, just like our mother. I felt like singing her praises for practically giving us this gem, which meant so much to her. And I felt a little guilty only paying ten thousand for it, but Tim talked me out of my guilt immediately."

"Yes, no need to feel guilty about that price," Tim said.

"Perhaps you could play it for us after dinner," Bethany asked. "Would you play for us, Clare?"

"I would be honored to play. I would also like to hear Jeremy play since he is the one taking lessons on it." Clare turned to look at him. "Would you play for me if I play for you?"

"Aunt Clare, I can play my favorite piece for you. I've just learned it and it's really hard. What are you going to play?" Jer-emy smiled with the anticipation of hearing his famous aunt play in his own home.

Clare hesitated a moment, unsure if she really wanted to play. A breeze came through the dining room, catching the sheer curtains and ruffling them toward her, beckoning her. The draft brushed over her, and Clare felt a calming coolness under her palms, like an unseen presence encouraging her to play. She often wondered if the spirit of their mother rested with her at the key-board, infusing her playing with the power of memories.

As her mind drifted back to the sound of Emily Graham's late-night piano hymns, Clare lost track of the thread of conver-sation swirling around the dinner table. It felt as if her mind was functioning in overlapping time periods, the current moment in-tertwined with the past. Looking down the table toward Bethany, she saw a woman who looked and spoke like her mother.

"Clare, don't be so skimpy with the potatoes. You need those to build your strength, to keep you healthy this winter." Mama looked so pretty tonight, but she forgot to take her apron off for supper again. In the background were the voices of many children. Where were all the children's voices coming from? Mama and Daddy were there, seated before her at the table.

A strong tug on her sweater jarred her away from the past, bringing clarity. "I can play the *Honey Bee March*, Aunt Clare." It was Jeremy, drawing her attention back to Bethany and Tim's dinner table.

Clare remembered how her mother had taught her to play *Flight of the Bumblebee* as a child.

"I can play a bumblebee song too, Jeremy. It's by Rimsky-Korsakov. You go first and I'll follow your lead. Let's try out your fancy piano." Rising from her seat and turning to look at the sheer curtains still billowing in the window frame, Clare wanted to lean out the window and peek down the alley to see her mother blowing on the breeze. Resisting the impulse, she made her way to the needlepoint piano bench, which was so familiar. Their mother had created it as a gift for Bethany's tenth birthday.

The Taylor music room came alive with the notes of the dueling bumblebees. Jeremy listened with reverence to Clare's command of each buzzing phrase, and the whole family beamed at Jeremy's talent despite the comparative simplicity of his selection. Even Clare was pleased with the quality of her playing, given the tricks her mind was playing on her at the dinner table. Fortunately, when she sat down at the keyboard, her memory was usually crystal-clear.

After all the children had been tucked into bed, Bethany followed Clare up the curving steps in the turret. "You played beautifully tonight. I'd forgotten how good you are. Having you here will certainly inspire the kids to get serious about their piano. Would you have any interest in teaching them?"

Clare knew this question was unavoidable. Not wanting to upset the rosy applecart of Bethany's gracious hospitality, she said, "I've been thinking about whom I should teach, and I've applied for an adjunct position at Westdale College. I can't teach young children. You know it would be too tedious for me. I've asked them if they will let me take it a semester at a time, and they seem very interested. Please don't be hurt, but it will be good for me to work with aspiring students who have ambitious goals and are much further along. They also have a studio available in the conservatory on the top floor, so I would be out of your way during the day until I find an apartment."

Bethany sensed that Clare was already pulling away from them and setting up her cocoon. She thought her sister acted a bit odd and distant at the dinner table for their first reunion together in over a year. She wondered if she was retreating from life into music too quickly, something Clare had done since childhood.

"Clare, that sounds like a blessing, but why don't you teach there and live here? Don't you think living in a family might be helpful and somewhat grounding after all you've been through?"

Bethany saw Clare flinch slightly. "What do you mean, 'all I've been through.' You have no idea what I've been through."

"Well, that's true because you haven't told me anything. For you to leave Nero and your touring is a big departure from the life you've created for yourself. So I know something significant must have happened. Do you want to talk about it?"

Clare's room in the turret looked and smelled like lily of the valley. Bethany sprayed it on her sheets, hoping to evoke happy memories of their childhood. She wanted to create the comforting atmosphere which Clare needed to let her guard down and confess what she had been through. Clare stared at the painted floor with a pained expression and seemed to be struggling to keep her composure. She began humming a familiar melody. Bethany recognized it as Faure's *Requiem*, and she wondered if this was a means by which Clare was trying to convey a message to her, without words. She waited in silence, unwilling to give in to the urge to hum the tune along with Clare, for that would push her further away from sharing any real content.

"All I can say right now is that Nero became overly possessive," Clare began. "He tried to keep me on the farm. He would delete messages on our phone to keep me from potential bookings. He became a bit violent in his own charming way. I began to grow afraid of sleeping on the farm because it was so isolated; no one would hear me scream if need be and there were times I wanted to scream but suppressed it. This drove me to play and tour more often to stay away from him, but while I was playing, I began to forget things. Nothing significant, but I noticed the difference. I forgot where I left my car in a parking lot. Yes, I know everyone does that, but at times, I couldn't remember what city I was playing in or where I was staying that night when I climbed into the cab, even though I'd been there for a week."

"I'm sure the stress and distraction of living with Nero was causing it," Clare concluded. "You can imagine how sad I was, and yet I felt relieved when he said one night, 'I need a break from our relationship.' I couldn't believe it. It felt like he had reached his limit, and out of his own fear for what he might do, he needed to be free of me."

Bethany waited for Clare to tell more of the story, but she had dissolved back into humming. She sensed Clare longed to hug her but didn't want to dissolve in tears, so she resisted the sisterly impulse.

Bethany reached out. "I really think you should stay with us for a while. You need some time to think and to heal. I don't think it would be good for you to be alone."

Her compassion began to irritate Clare. It never failed to happen. Whenever she shared something personal with Bethany, she always felt like she was covered with syrup when she finished, slimed by her sister's overwhelming sweetness.

"I'm just wondering when you started using words like *heal, blessing, pray*," Clare said. "Genevieve prayed before dinner tonight. Why? You were never a person who talked like a suburban church woman before. Where is this coming from?"

Bethany sensed that Clare felt threatened. "I hope it doesn't make you uncomfortable. If it does, let me know. As I've lived with Tim, I've learned that there is more to worship in life than the music, than what is here, now. I want our children to be aware of this reality. All our lives have transcendent value. There is so much more to it than what we see and hear right in front of us."

"Of course, our lives have transcendent value. We know that from Bach, from Bruckner. *Te Deum laudamus, te Dominum confitemur. Te aeternum Patrem, omnis terra veneratur.* Those were Bruckner's last words before he died. I know this. Just because I'm not as religious as you are does not mean I don't understand these things. Remember, I played the *Te Deum* with the Wagner Choral in Berlin." Clare threw herself back on the bed, appearing to retreat from her defensive retort. "Beth, I appreciate your sincere and warm hospitality, but it would be best for me to find a room of my own and move on with my life."

Move on with what life, wondered Bethany. No children. No husband. No adoring audiences she had known her entire life and then the problem of forgetting things. How bad was it really? Letting Clare start over alone didn't seem like the safest and best course to pursue. "Clare, even though you were always the apple of Mother and Daddy's eye growing up, I don't love you any less today than I did back then. You are my only sister and I want what is best for you. Although I don't know all that has happened, I think you need to move slowly. Get your feet on the ground a little bit at a time, don't rush into teaching a studio full of students."

"Thanks, Beth. I'll think about what you've said. I have been feeling a little strange—no, not strange, just different—since I arrived here. I won't be taking on a studio full of students or rushing into anything, maybe one or two students. I'm not sure I'd even be up for teaching your entire family piano. Five kids is like having twenty-five as far as I'm concerned, to say nothing of the noise. I need some peace and quiet to grow into my new life.

Please don't be offended."

Bethany studied Clare for a moment and she could see she was speaking from the heart with all the depth and sincerity she could muster. Reaching out her hand to Clare, Bethany pulled her up from the mattress and drew her in close as they sat side by side on the bed. She watched Clare making a connection in her mind as she turned to look at her. Perhaps she was remembering the fleshy hug of their mother's arms enfolding her. Without sharing another word, they found comfort in knowing they had each other, and with that long-buried and locked-away comfort, Clare had the freedom to cry.

CHAPTER 4

Cambiata—The name given to the adolescent male voice

Clive counted his way up several flights of stairs. Counting in silence kept him calm. Any Westdale Conservatory teacher would be an improvement over Mr. K. *And any studio would be a welcome change from his stale yellow parlor,* he thought. He approached a single office door which seemed to be alone on the floor except for the restroom and some instrumental storage rooms. The door was without the usual conservatory satirical comics stating pithy musical phrases like, *Go for broke, play Baroque.* Instead, the entire front was covered with a hand-painted Japanese landscape, Mount Fuji against a sunset backdrop. Not what one would expect from a Westdale piano professor.

Hanging above his head in front of the vent, a tiny wind chime sprinkled delicate flecks of sound as he knocked. Listening beyond the little chime, he could hear the familiar melody of Tchaikovsky's ***Piano Concerto No. 1***. Clive knocked again, louder this time. The music stopped, and it seemed like an hour before the door opened. In a flourish, the door flung wide, revealing a diminutive, attractive woman in a burgundy sweater, khakis, and wooden clogs, thrusting her hand forward with determined enthusiasm. "Greetings, I'm Clare Cardiff. You must be Clive."

Still holding his hand, Clare ushered Clive into a swirl of color and sound. Opalescent curtains were blowing in the window, with finches twittering outside. There were shelves upon shelves of books, but without the stale, musty smell that permeated Mr. K's studio. Instead of a studio full of composer statuettes, framed musical manuscripts and posters of various engagements adorned the walls. *Did Clare performed at those?* Carnegie Hall—1964. La Scala—1979. The Vienna Opera House—1984.

A rush of recognition overwhelmed Clive as a chilly sweat beaded on his forehead. He knew of Clare Cardiff. As they sat together on the red velour couch, which was neatly tucked into the single available corner, he said, "Yes, I am Clive and I think I know you. I can't believe I'm sitting here."

Sweat was dripping from him now—he could feel it trickling down his sides—and he was barely able to swallow, let alone speak. Clare was much smaller than when he had seen her onstage. There, she looked enormous at the keyboard. *How she commanded the piano when she soloed with Papa's orchestra. I must have been fourteen at the time. Was it Rachmaninoff's second piano concerto?*

He remembered that she wore a bright pink gown with earrings shimmering direct beams of light. They crested on the heads of the first few rows of listeners, particularly during the second movement. Her hair, a potpourri of blond and brown streaks, moved violently as she played, causing him to wonder how she could see the keyboard. He also recalled that she wore soft-soled clogs with her gown. Most unusual, but he guessed it had something to do with her preference for the feel of the pedals, meaning she preferred a connection more distant than most. Seeing her today, she was a mixture of the refined with the artistically disheveled, sparkling and yet dark.

Caught up in his memories of that night, he sat silently for a few moments. Clare called him back. "Really and how might that be?" she asked.

Clive tried not to stare. "I heard you solo with the Chicago Philharmonic a couple of years ago. My father is the conductor. It was the *Rach. 2*, I believe."

Now Clare was the one staring straight into Clive as if instantly mapping his DNA. "Wait. Your father is Claude Serkin," she said with the tone of a proclamation rather than inquiry. *Yes*, she thought, *he looks like Claude, with those burning Jewish eyes and that long, thin frame, but otherwise more delicately featured—he looks European and Jewish.* "Why didn't you bring your father with you? I would love to see him again."

Clive felt a prick of dishonesty against the nape of his neck, like an annoying itch that he didn't dare scratch.

"Well, Papa doesn't know I'm here. I have studied for many years with the teacher of his choosing, a kind, elderly gentleman from the old country. He's like a relative to us. Papa would not approve of my being here today.

"It's a bit like cheating on your uncle. I have thought it through, though. I will be able to pay for my lessons from competition money that I've saved, but now that I know it is you, I might not have saved enough," Clive admitted.

Clare smiled compassionately. "Oh, you must have saved quite a bit of money in your piggy bank. But don't worry about the money. Teaching is something I am doing just for a short time, to give a bit of myself away. We can work out the money later. Play something for me, and let's see where you are with your pieces."

As Clive sat before the upright Kawai—clearly Westdale College property, for he knew Clare would never choose to play on this type of piano—he realized that his sweat had transferred from his brow to his hands. *I'm never nervous. I can't believe this.*

Breathe. With a dramatic rising of his hands, suspending them in the air for an instant, he dropped them and fell into the Brahms **Intermezzo in A Major**. In a moment, he was lost. Clare was gone, and he was floating along the banks of the Seine on a languid, summer day with all the Parisians enjoying their Sunday picnics.

Music always gave him pictures, almost like a tour of the sound. Mama once told him that George Balanchine was famous for saying, "See the music. Hear the dance." Clive saw the music every time he played. This time, he moved from the *Intermezzo* and then played flawlessly through all the *Rachmaninoff Preludes*. He knew Clare had a fondness for Rachmaninoff, judging by her own impassioned performance of it. Long past an hour, he looked up to see her inquiring face as she sat unmoving on the red velour loveseat.

Hoping for a word of affirmation, he instead received a question. "What do you want to do with your life, Clive?"

He knew his answer would determine their journey forward, if there was to be one. Clive began, "My whole life has been set upon the path of the concert pianist. It is what my parents believe I can become and what I have always worked toward." He stared at the keyboard as he spoke. She sensed his emotional detachment from his response.

"Yes, but what do *you* want to do with your life?" Clare pressed.

He knew. Clive had always known, but he never had the courage to tell anyone and no one ever cared to ask. "I want to give my music to people who desperately need it. They are not in the concert halls of the wealthy, signed up for yet another concert series and the occasion to dress up and doze off before the recapitulation. I want to give it to those who can't live without it."

Clare recognized his passion. She had seen it in Nero during their first conversation in the old coffee shop in Boston, and she'd seen it in the early days of his sculpting in the potting shed.

Clive's response brought forward the painful recognition of so many missed opportunities to work together with Nero, the artist. Back then, she was selfishly and entirely focused upon her own career and her goals, barely noticing Nero's creations. This time, perhaps she could redeem herself with Clive. She would pay attention this time, taking him to the level that she knew he could achieve, and then set him free.

"Let's start every Wednesday, immediately after school," Clare said calmly, trying to hide her excitement. "I won't tell your parents, but your father will probably find out I'm here at Westdale. I've managed to keep a low profile so far, taking only a few students, not playing concerts, and not going out much. Although, I'm not sure how long it will last. You need to be prepared to tell him and your mother when the right time presents itself."

Clive felt his heart leap in his chest, but he concealed his joy by offering a deep bow, as he had been taught to do in deference to her standing as an artist. "Respect the artist and his craft, Clive. Show your appreciation with your whole being," Papa often extolled him. The prospect of a new teacher, let alone Clare, brought him to the edge of wonder and with it, to a precipice of fear. *She is actually going to take me on. Clare Cardiff. Maybe Mr. Koussevitsky is right. The God of Israel does care about my life.*

Clive knew he would need to work even harder, smarter, more efficiently, and yet secretly. He had never hidden something of this significance from Mama and Papa, but it wouldn't be hard. They would both be impressed with his rejuvenated commitment to the competition works. That would keep them from getting suspicious. Meanwhile, Mr. K. would be pleased with the progress and get all the credit. *Perfect!*

Looking at Clare, Clive realized he towered over the five-foot virtuoso, which felt good, given that musically she was a giant in comparison to him. "Madame Cardiff, if I may call you that, what would you like my focus to be as I practice this week?"

Clare, amused by his formality and more than slight shyness, studied his long, angular features, which gave him the appearance of a determined heron about to take wing. "Much of it is there, but focus on getting your fingers beneath you. Get inside yourself, put your full weight behind it, and then let go."

"Thank you, Madame Cardiff. I'll look forward to seeing you next Wednesday." He thought to bow one more time but decided the title of *Madame* was enough. The juxtaposition of his youth and adult formality made Clare laugh as she showed him to the door.

"Clive, someday you will surpass me. You do not need to bow to me, and for heaven's sake, do not call me Madame Cardiff. Since I know your dear father and what he would have you call me, you may call me Clare."

After the latch quietly closed, Clive turned back, stood still, and touched the painted door with both of his disproportionately large hands. He leaned forward, pressing his head up against the door-front image of Mount Fuji at sunset. He had been given a gift, a ray of light in the darkness, someone to follow who could take him to new heights and unforeseen vistas. Even her painted door was speaking this message to him. *She knows so much more than me, and what's even more frightening, she's beautiful. Those blue eyes.*

At Brookline most of the girls looked the same—dark hair and dark eyes. Clare's eyes danced when she spoke, like the hottest part of the fire, the blue flame. It made it difficult to look directly at her without staring. He wondered how much smaller she would be standing beside him, tucked into the crook of his arm, if she wasn't wearing her clogs.

CHAPTER 5

Lacrimoso—Mournful

The top layer of the ground froze early in New Hampshire that fall, so early that Nero wondered how he would get his bulbs planted before the blanket of snow silenced any hope. Then again, spring bulbs without Clare, did it matter? The rare occasion that Clare would be home in the spring, she rejoiced over every snowdrop, seeing even the delicate green striping on their petals and their polka-dotted centers. Now it was his turn to see the details—alone.

Nero thought his artistic life would experience a rebirth without Clare, but instead he stared at his frozen potter's wheel and blankly gazed out the window of his studio for a new muse. Nightcaps and women were clouding his vision. Sylvie down the street on Harcourt Lane had been kind enough to bring cheese-smothered casseroles, but her eyes were empty, black holes, nothing there. Katrina from Riley's Drug Store in town was interesting, but too accessible. Yet, maintaining contact with her was essential. She gave him what he needed to get through the day and, sometimes, the night.

Since Clare left the farm, his life became moribund. In some aspects, dying a slow death felt gratifying. At least he had ownership of the process, and that was a welcome change. He concluded that there is a certain amount of freedom in controlling your own death rather than being killed by someone else who was never there.

"Hey, Katrina, this is Nero Cardiff. Yeah, I'm good, but my prescription has run out. Do you think you could stop by tonight for a drink and bring me a refill?" It was so easy to get Katrina where he wanted her. Clare was never where he wanted her, and when she was, she was often somewhere else.

Silence. If willing, silence can take over a soul. The silence at the farm filled every bookcase, pantry shelf, and empty bud vase. The Clare Graham family piano was the main orchestrator of the silence. Its dominating, black presence in the living room jeered and cried out to him, daring him to break the stillness. It compelled him to do so, despite his own impotence at the keyboard. This cry of the piano, he obliged. While watching the sunset over the quince trees, he spent many pleasant evenings throwing empty highball glasses at the side of the piano to hear the silence shatter. It was a pleasing melody. The glasses would hit hard enough to rattle the strings, causing the piano to moan for its master, a fruitless cry, lacking in euphony. In the morning, Nero would see small nicks in the finish, which he filled in with a black permanent marker. *She'll never notice.* The inside of the piano matters most.

Not a word from Clare since she left. He was the one in need of space between them, so why should he be the first to call? She could at least care enough to call and see how he was getting along, he thought. Since Clare's departure, Nero was disconnected and unplugged as he walked through his days. There was no need for multiple phones to keep track of her whereabouts and plane arrival times, or to receive messages from her agent. All he kept now was the old rotary wall phone, which he only used to call for groceries or other necessities to be delivered by Katrina.

During the day, Nero escaped to his potting shed. Beginning as a shed for gardening tools and terra-cotta pots worth saving, Nero expanded it over the years. Now the potting shed was also the potter's shed, with his wheel and pottery tools, and a gallery stood out front, its rustic entrance framed by hollyhocks. "I'm surrounded by dirt, be it potting soil or potter's clay." That's what he would tell Clare, who could not imagine working in such an earthen mess. Wandering past the fading giants by the door, Nero gathered some hollyhock seeds into his pockets. *Black hollyhocks do look the most dramatic against the barn siding and appropriately funereal*, he mused.

Stepping into the gallery, he noticed cobwebs gathering around his dusty creations. It was time to clean this place up and get ready for fall tourists who come looking for foliage and a touch of rural America to bring home to their New York City relatives. The caravans arriving in search of windmills, lighthouse lamps, and leaf-stamped plates—all typical items which usually sell, but hadn't sold lately. The correlation was there. When he worked, things sold. When he couldn't work, no one came by the shop. This fall season would finally reveal the true value of his work. He would find out how much of the public's interest belonged to him and what portion came from merely snooping around to see where the virtuoso pianist Clare Cardiff lived.

Staring at the dust suspended in the sun's penetrating rays, Nero remembered how he had made love with Clare on the studio floor, with bits of clay, dirt, moss, and petals pressed into her milky skin, like Millais's *Ophelia* floating in the river. Those moments when he held her and she remained still were so few, so right. Spinning his creations on the wheel, with her music skimming over the tops of the garden and into the raised windows of his shed; her accompaniment to his wheel's metronomic rhythm. These were the flowers on the passion vine, fighting to be free of the bindweed that strangled their life together.

Standing in the shed, the earthy smell provoked a memory of how Nero once dragged Clare, practically by her hair, to the studio and locked her inside in a futile attempt to keep her there. He didn't want her to leave him for people she didn't know in places where he didn't want her to go. At first, he tried to be the dutiful artist by her side, but no one cared about him, his work, or his love for her. They wanted her all to themselves, and they fought for her. The agents and publicists thought they owned her. They took away the Clare he knew and loved. They took away their dreams as a couple, all they could have been and made together. They came like a thief in the night and claimed everything—even their child.

At first, Clare didn't know it was a miscarriage. She didn't recognize the warning signs. After a long European tour, he picked her up at La Guardia for a weekend reunion together in New York, but Clare wanted to go back to the farm. Immediately upon arrival, she plummeted into their bed completely drained. Waking early the next morning, he found her on the bathroom floor in a pool of blood, whimpering and clutching her abdomen. She claimed she hadn't even had a chance to tell him she was pregnant.

Their only child poured out upon a single square of white ceramic tile—unknown, unspoken, and unnamed. He struggled to pick Clare up off the floor and tuck her back into bed, but she was begging for a doctor, resisting him. He didn't jump at her request to make the call. Instead he sat on the end of the bed, staring at her in disbelief. She knew he had wanted a child for years. They talked about it, repeatedly. A little one racing around out in the garden, helping him water the seedlings, helping him not live alone. She could have called from Vienna and told him the blessed news or thrilled him at the airport. Why didn't she? No doubt, the fear of what a child would do to her precious career.

He could still see her lying there, as white and thin and empty as the tangled sheets. There was nothing there in front of him, nothing left. In the end, he did call the doctor. Clare recovered, but it was in this crucible of mistrust that Nero believed he began to lose her.

Now throwing a handful of clay on his wheel, he tried to make up for the loss. Forming a child upon the wheel might bring relief. Lightly pressing the pedal, working in an upward movement of water, smooth silt like afterbirth, coupled with the firmness of the clay. The gray beginnings of a figure began to emerge in his hands. He took the formless body off the wheel to look it over. Even at this early stage, it was more than a blob. After all, children are created in love and molded by the passage of time and the refinement of those who care and shape them—like clay. He reminded himself that he could make the form, but there would be no breath in it. Still, the clay took shape and resembled a log like a piece of smooth driftwood, tumbled soft by wheel and water. Perhaps a child formed on a wheel could bring Clare back to him anew.

He cradled the lifeless log in his forearms while moving over to his carving bench. The firm weight of its body reminded him of Clare. Holding it in his hands, he started to shape the face that he imagined their child would have had. It was a boy's face with moonlit eyes dancing upon tall tassels of harvest corn. As the sun moved across the espalier fruit trees of the garden, the bees hummed their working song. He trimmed the clay with precision while listening to all creation come alive with its final burst of effort before the winter stillness rushed in.

The timelessness of the studio overtook him. Before dark, he completed the clay child. Holding and gazing at him, Nero felt a familiar empty ache built by years of saying goodbye in airports, driving back home to the farm alone, the loss of their real child. He longed for Clare to see it, but at the same time, he wanted to hurl the clay body through the window. He carried it around the studio, even bouncing the baby in his arms to soothe the silent cries of his own heart and grow accustomed to the feel of its weight. Then he gently laid it back upon the potter's bat and covered it with newspaper so it could begin to air dry without cracking. Their child could not crack. He would decide the color of the glaze in the morning.

Watching the squirrels dart across the crab apple trees for their evening meal made him realize he hadn't eaten all day. Hopefully, Katrina would bring dinner tonight when she stopped by with his medication. *I think I called her this morning?* Turning for one last look at the child under its newspaper covers, he watched with false anticipation. Nero hoped the encroaching shadow moving through the studio might create the illusion of movement, allowing him the privilege of seeing it come alive. *The kiln will help*, he thought. *A touch of fire can bring about a life-giving complexion; too much fire and the piece would be ruined.*

Nero knew what it felt like to be burned on the inside and crack on the outside. If the child survived the kiln, he would have to name it. What would he and Clare have named their little one? She would pick the name of a favorite composer, and he would want to name it after his influential sculpture teacher, Carmichael Brown. Carmichael sounded intelligent enough, but what if it looked like a girl coming out of the kiln? He couldn't imagine them having a girl, too sweet for their relationship.

Leaving on a night light in his studio, he crossed the terraced path back to the house just as Katrina's car tires ground the gravel into the earth.

CHAPTER 6

Camerata—A group of people who would get together during the sixteenth century to discuss the future of their art

"'Guns buried in flowers,' is how Schumann described Chopin's music. What do you think of that, Clive?" Clive tried not to imagine the possibility of violence lurking beneath the beauty of Chopin's compositions. He preferred to think about and interpret the colors of his music and not dwell on the negative influences, but the presence of each was undeniable.

"I understand there is so much power beneath the beauty of his compositions, but it is difficult to find the moment where the power gives way to the beauty," he replied. "They work so closely together and alongside each other. Power and beauty are intertwined in this movement from beginning to end."

Clare sat quietly next to him with her folded arms beneath her cream poncho, considering his answer. *She listens to me. Mr. K and I listen together to recordings, but she actually listens to me.*

Clive stood up and relinquished his seat on the piano bench. He waited patiently as Clare dropped into the piano and played part of the second movement of Chopin's *F minor Piano Con-*

certo. Clive knew learning this concerto was like taking a step forward into manhood. He had heard many great pianists—Alfred Brendel being his favorite—perform it with Papa conducting the Chicago Philharmonic. Mr. K kept this concerto from him, believing he wasn't ready. "There is so much to learn before you are ready for the Chopin concertos," he would say. In contrast, Clare had entrusted the work to him from the beginning, and it felt like a sacred trust.

"I have wanted to learn this for years, and now I'm not so sure," he whispered to her.

"Don't doubt yourself, Clive. Step into it. You can do it," Clare reassured. "Let me tell you a bit about this section. Liszt described this movement as 'radiant with light, full of tender pathos,' and indeed it is. Chopin admitted he was in love—his first love—with a woman named Kostancia Gladkowska, who was the inspiration for this movement. He described her as someone whom he served faithfully, without saying a word to her for six months. Then he left Poland and ended up dedicating the piece to someone else, a very beautiful countess, with whom he also fell in love. In fact, she was with Chopin when he died.

"So we have a heart captivated by love and pouring it out in poetic rainbows of color on the keyboard. Those colors and the phrasing allow you to distinguish between the power and beauty when it is needed in this section," Clare concluded.

Clive stared at her profile, with her disheveled, frosty hair swept up quickly into a clip. Her arrangement was so different from his mother's daily display of defined hair. Clare knew so much and offered it freely without reservation. *How does she do that?* She always had the perfect historical perspective to combat his doubts. He longed to ask her but held back, not wanting to appear too personal in this early stage of their studies together.

He hoped the day would come when he felt comfortable enough in their pedagogical relationship that he would have the freedom to ask her anything. Instead, he tempered the inquiry.

"How do you know so much about Chopin's life?"

"I have had valuable teachers along the way who gave these insights to me, and it is my duty, as a way of honoring them, to pass them on to you," Clare confided.

"But you remember so much; the compositions and all that is behind them. I don't think I have that kind of memory." He confessed his first fear to her—the fear of not remembering everything he would need to know.

"You are mistaken. You do have this kind of memory, but you need to develop your own methods to enhance what you have been given. We all have methods we use to aid our memory. You know, tricks to keep us focused. Mine is my Folio, and even with the Folio my memory has been known to slip," Clare revealed.

Clive watched as she crossed the Persian rug and climbed the old oak stepladder all the way to the top of a bookcase. Reaching for an unidentifiable beige box, she came back with the look of a child at Hanukkah gracing her face. Gently lifting the lid, she removed a manuscript book that was frayed at the corners and bound in scratched chestnut leather. The book had a golden treble clef engraved in the center, surrounded by a wreath of forget-me-not flowers. It looked Victorian, perhaps even ancient. He could see the edge of each page was finished in gold. Her care in handling this holy book reminded him of Rabbi Sherveen passing him the Torah, which he read at his bar mitzvah.

"Now that you are studying with me, you are part of a family," Clare declared. "You are a descendant in a line of teachers and performers dating back before Brahms. In fact, Johannes Brahms is now your great-great-great-grandfather in music. We are all part of the chain that binds us to the art of our predecessors, indeed to our world's history. Unfortunately, few can claim their lineage with proof."

As she opened the book, the smell of royal Viennese music rooms filled Clare's studio. She told him, "This book contains the personal reflections of composers, teachers, and musicians throughout their years of study. Their motivations, original ideas, personal thoughts, and historical insights are written inside. Professor Rosenblith, my teacher at New England Conservatory, gave this to me after my Carnegie Hall debut. I was very young, just a little older than you. There are even a few things about my career tucked into these pages. Here are the newspaper reviews from that concert."

Clive skimmed the reviews, hoping for a glimpse of Clare's past. *Miss Graham plays with uncommon virtuosity. The second movement literally wept from the page*, wrote Dean Reynolds, critic for *The Boston Globe*. "*... astonishing versatility of technique and depth of insight with a majestic Romantic style. On the shoulders of Eben Tourjee's vision of founding New England Conservatory at only nineteen years of age, Miss Graham's teenage artistry has left the practice room, leapt onto the concert stage and into our hearts,*" praised Reed Butler from the *Boston Herald*.

"This Folio links us to the great minds of our art. Now you, Clive, will have access to their wisdom."

It's like the Torah, an ancient book filled with wisdom but miraculously kept private, he thought. "May I touch it?" Clive asked.

Clare lovingly passed him the box, as if passing a firstborn son. "Yes, but I would ask that you wear the gloves in the box when you look at it or when you write in it. It is old and very fragile."

Stunned, he paused and asked, "When *I* write in it? What do you mean? I am no one. I can't write in this Folio. I am hardly worthy to touch this book."

Clare threw her tousled head of hair back, laughing in astonishment.

"You really don't know the depth of the gift you've been given. Hopefully, this book will help bring you another step forward into your own sphere and to a place beyond your famous father. Clive, my dear, these pages are now yours to consume. You are worthy of your lineage.

"Yes, you, a tremendously gifted pianist, have come to me by way of noticing a subtle invitation posted anonymously on a conservatory bulletin board. This is not by chance. My sister, Bethany, believes that things happen in our lives for a reason. In this case, I believe she might be correct.

"This Folio will help you in your quest to become the musician *you* want to become. Not the musician of your parents' design. I am giving it to you, not them. May you have joy in discovering its secrets and in sharing your own insights."

Clive could feel the tips of his ears heating up as she said the words *my dear*. It was a term of endearment that separated him from everyone else. He leaned back away from her to prevent her from seeing the blush on his face. Every moment in Clare's presence made him feel like she was seeing inside his shell and enticing him out of it. In a single conversation, he gained a new family, a holy grail of parentage. Putting on the gloves, Clive opened the book with reverence. In front of him was a hand-scripted entry of Johannes Brahms, with an English translation tucked between the pages:

May 7, 1853—Robert and Clara joined me today in town for a Franz Liszt concert. After meeting me, he offered to play my Scherzo in C minor, which I've just completed. Sight-reading the piece with such sincerity and deftness and with an utterly incompetent violinist, I knew at once that he was destined for greatness. A master in our midst.

Tears filled his eyes, which Clive held downcast, hoping not a drop would fall onto the precious page. How could he keep this from Papa? Not sure why he was crying, he looked at Clare and said, "Papa would give anything to see these pages, but I want to keep them for myself. Is that wrong of me? If he knows about them, the whole world will know."

Clare reached out and touched his shoulder. Her hand felt like a burning wick, searing through him, bringing warmth to the core of his being. "Clive, these pages are for your musical growth.

They are meant for you. At this point in his career, your father does not have need of them like you do."

Her gentle hand softly wiped the tears from his face. Her touch brought the tender feeling he imagined, but rarely received, from his own mother. He wanted to reach for her hand and hold it against his cheek as a gesture of gratitude, for he had no idea how to thank her for such a gift.

"I will try my best to honor these pages by learning them and more than that ... by digesting them like food. When I am ready, perhaps I will write in this book. Will you want to see what I write?"

His heart hoped she would say yes, but his mind wanted her to say no. "This is what you need it to be, Clive." With a bow, he left with the box hidden in his valise.

Leaning her forehead against the chilled pane of glass, Clare could see through the window Clive's dark, thin figure, striding beneath the white oak branches. He had taken off his coat and wrapped it around the box for extra protection from the rain. *He thinks he's holding a treasure chest, but he is the treasure. Why do parents have to make such a mess of their gifted children?*

She felt compelled to offer a prayer to the gods of music, those in their family line, which Clare and Clive would now share together. He was becoming her son in a symbolic, yet almost literal, way. "Fathers, protect Clive. Give him the knowledge from your words and creativity. Help him to become all he can be through your teaching and mine. May he use our holy book to grow into all you desire him to be."

From the moment he first played for her, Clare could see and hear his heart pouring into the music. He had all the essential technical facility, but even more, he played from a place deep down, buried in a burden. She didn't want to know his burden, but now that he had the Folio, she would if he chose to share it. She had never shared the Folio with anyone, not even Nero. He might have defiled it out of some irrational jealousy of musicians and composers long dead, or he might have tried to auction it off at Sotheby's, pocketing the money and not telling her. There was no doubt; Nero was capable of such insanity. Besides, it was her sacred book ... her past, her present, and now in Clive's hands, her future.

CHAPTER 7

Affabile—Gentle

"Another strand of lights and this Christmas tree will be the prettiest we've ever had," Bethany proclaimed each year. The number of new strands kept pace with the number of last year's strands lying dead on the floor, like a graveyard of plastic green wire. The Taylor children raced about the house in their pajamas, with red candy-cane mouths, their sticky fingers plucking out *Angels We Have Heard on High* on the Bechstein. Their noise escalated to a pitch that would send everyone to bed without a Christmas story if Bethany didn't soon end this family project.

"Tim, would you get the phone? I'm stuck on the ladder finishing the last strand of lights."

As he cut through the children's darting robes and slippers like a running back, Tim answered the phone and heard an almost unfamiliar, sedated voice, imperceptible in the chaos of holiday prep work.

"Nero, is that you?"

There was an elongated silence before he heard, "Is Clare there?"

In the months since Clare had lived with them, Nero did not call or send any word. Tim believed it was over. Since she moved into her apartment, Clare never uttered his name when they were all together, which blissfully indicated to Tim and Bethany that she was getting over him.

"No, Clare doesn't live here. She has her own place now. Nero, how are you doing? Are you getting ready for the holidays?" Tim thought a touch of Christmas cheer would be good for him.

With that, the line went dead.

Seeing the confused look on Tim's face, Bethany inquired, "Who was that?"

"Typical friendly, polite, upbeat Nero, the perfect uncle as usual," Tim recalled, shaking his head in disgust.

"What did he want?" Bethany asked with concern.

"He was looking for Clare. It might have been Nero, but his voice sounded different and far away. Perhaps he's overseas. Do you think we should tell Clare that he called? I don't want to set her back. I'm not even sure it was him," Tim reasoned.

The thought of Nero reentering Clare's life now that she was somewhat settled disturbed Bethany. "There is no need to say anything. Best not to dig up old wounds," she said.

For the first time in her life, Clare seemed to be creating a kind of routine, participating in a place and investing in the community, albeit in small doses. She had only taken on a few students, but the ones she taught, she spoke of them—one in particular—with much fondness. Despite her initial reluctance, she came to their house once a week and taught the Taylor children in shifts. In exchange, Clare stayed for dinner and evening entertainment sessions, with the children playing and singing their choral music for school. She loved playing the part of their accompanist, using tricks at the keyboard to keep the kids laughing and engaged in clandestine practice sessions.

Bethany could not understand why she didn't take on more students or give concerts at Westdale. When asked, Clare said she was working on a "development project," which she wanted to keep confidential for now. She might be in the composing mode, which Bethany thought would be so healing and new for her, but composition takes energy and Bethany didn't think Clare had that much extra energy, although now might be the right season for it. She was a bit mysterious, but for the Taylor family, the savings of hundreds of dollars a month in piano lessons made room for her eccentricities. She and Tim tried not to ask too many questions.

"Mommy, now that the Christmas tree is done, what are you going to read to us tonight?" The perennial question, always asked by one of the children at the moment of maximum exhaustion.

"It will be short tonight because Auntie Clare is coming over after all of you head off to bed," Bethany replied.

"Oh, let us stay up for Auntie Clare. We want to hear her play. She could even read us our story," Jessica begged.

Bethany felt pleased by how attached they had grown to Clare in such a short time. She hadn't expected the piano lessons to work out so well, given her sister's initial resistance to teaching them and her penchant for guarding her time with the determination of a hawk. Thankfully, because the children were musical and related to her, Clare seemed to be giving it her all.

"Not tonight, kids. I'll read you *Santa's Favorite Story* and then off to bed. Auntie Clare wants to talk to us tonight without you monkeys climbing all over her."

"But we love climbing all over her; she's practically our size. She really is much smaller than you, Mommy," Jessica chided, to Bethany's chagrin. *No one stays thin after having five kids and Clare has never had any*, she rationalized.

While Bethany told the story of Santa and the woodland animals going to see Jesus in the manger, Tim finished the dishes.

Then he piggybacked the youngest ones off to bed, flouncing each of them onto their covers with a winged flourish at their journey's end. After kissing them goodnight, he and Bethany began their evening recap. Often their favorite part of the day, they talked about each child and then prayed for them individually. Bethany loved the thoughtful wisdom Tim brought to this time together. She could see him for the person she dearly loved and married, without the trappings of the business world weighing him down.

"Wisdom that is pure; then peace-loving, considerate, submissive, full of mercy and good fruit, impartial and sincere." The wisdom that James talked about in the Bible was the wisdom she saw and loved in Tim, especially during their late-night meetings. This intimate time together was a solid rock upon which they could unpack their burdens, as the chaos of their household swirled around them on any given day at a forever-trying-to-catch-up pace. Without this moment of quiet, she didn't know how she and Tim would survive.

How did Clare live without faith in the Lord? Bethany often wanted to ask her, but she knew music was the spiritual compass Clare allowed to be her guide. They had just finished praying for Jeremy when the doorbell chimed. Clare blustered her way inside as the snow billowed behind her.

Bethany could see Clare eyeing the Bechstein. Knowing the children had been tucked into bed minutes before, she sat down to play some of her favorite lullabies from Schumann's *Kinderszenen*, finishing with **Traumerei**. The children loved this moment and Bethany relished seeing her sister send them off into their dreams with her version of a prayer.

"Clare, keep playing. You'll put them all to sleep in a blink. I want to pull together a little nightcap for us to enjoy while we sit and talk." Bethany headed down the hall toward the kitchen.

Turning from the piano bench to address Tim, Clare took in the newly decorated Christmas tree and the tired eyes of Bethany's dutiful yet annoyingly put together husband. She felt grateful for all they had given her during these months of transition. Their home, valuable time, and precious children were foundation stones in her initial life away from Nero and the absence of touring. Clare wondered how they always had room to offer time for one more person at the end of the day. So many times, she came over and an old friend from out of town had stopped over, or a missionary visiting from New Guinea on furlough, or some other esoteric person would be staying with them. They lived such full lives, but somehow there was room for more life to be poured into the top of the glass.

She marveled at their openness and compassion for others. For Clare, it had been so important to guard her time, to keep each valuable practice minute under lock and key. She couldn't dream of indulging in their kind of freedom, yet she appreciated it. Was it freedom that they had in abundance as compared to her solitude and servitude to the keyboard?

"To what do we owe the honor of this late-night visit?" Bethany inquired, bringing in hot cocoa in snowman mugs.

"Well, I wanted to ask your advice about something. For a few months, I have been teaching Clive Serkin, a brilliant student. Perhaps you've heard the last name?" Clare inquired.

"Is his father the conductor of the Chicago Philharmonic?" Bethany asked.

"That's right. Back in September, Clive responded to my advertisement on the Westdale Conservatory bulletin board and ended up auditioning at my studio. I jumped at the chance to teach him, but he refuses to tell his parents for fear they will be incensed at his betrayal of their chosen Jewish teacher, someone named Mr. Koussevitsky. Clive has paid for all his lessons with his competition earnings and has continued studying with both of us. I want to enter him into the Tchaikovsky Piano Competition, but because he is under eighteen, I must have parental approval to do so. He is delicate and I don't want to hurt him or force him to tell them, but I don't think he should continue this charade. I don't want to pry either. We are at a point now when I need his parents to know what's going on."

"Is this why you haven't performed any concerts since you've been here, in order to protect Clive? Good for you, such a protective and unselfish act. You must care deeply for him," Bethany affirmed.

"Yes, I have a close relationship with him and I don't want to betray his confidence. I figured since you are parents, you might have some ideas."

Bethany looked at Clare intently. *Close relationship*. Clare had looked away when Bethany spoke. Clare had never worked with children until now nor had any of her own. Could she be physically attracted to a seventeen-year-old or was she simply attracted to the idea of being like a mother to him? While Bethany was still reasoning through the possibilities, Tim took a risk and asked, "Clare, how close is your relationship with Clive?" He could see her bristle and straighten up her spine on the needle-point piano bench.

"Our relationship is strictly musical. We don't talk about family matters," Clare declared. She hated this about Mr. Perfect Tim. He had a knack for asking the tough questions. She wanted to cry out, *He is becoming the son I've never had*, but she wasn't ready to reveal her heart to them or anyone else. They really knew so little of her life and the world around it.

"I think you should tell Clive of your plans for him and then instruct him to tell his parents," Tim stated. "This boy needs to take responsibility for his own career and decisions. It's not your job to intervene."

Tim gazed at the keyboard, considering. "Could it be a personal issue, also, a matter of your own reputation? How does that work in the music world? Esteemed conductor's son studying in the closet with concert pianist. I mean, people don't really care about the students a famous pianist takes on, do they? I see commuters read *People* magazine on the train and there aren't a lot of articles about concert pianists in there."

"No, this isn't about my reputation," Clare said. "It's about the boy and doing what's right for him. Because Clive is who he is and the family is Jewish or at least part Jewish, the depth of loyalty is different, probably beyond what we all understand. Certainly the dynamics of loyalty are beyond what I understand, given his reluctance to tell them."

"Ultimately, you want an honest working relationship with Clive, so you will need to take the lead there, regardless of the consequences," Tim continued to counsel. His voice dropped, his caring side becoming more obvious. "You know, you might lose him. His parents may not let him continue studying with you."

The Christmas tree lights began to blur as Clare stared at the tree and digested this reality. *I could lose him.* A knot began to tighten in her chest as the possibility simmered in her soul. *I really could lose him, first Mother and Daddy, then Nero, and now him?* With tears brimming and about to spill over, Clare recognized that Clive had a partial hold on her soul. He was filling in a crack created by painful losses in the past. She didn't want the crack to become a canyon.

"I'll think about it. He is precious to me," she whispered.

The melody of Beethoven's **Pathetique Sonata** flooded into her mind as she stared at Tim and Bethany, who were studying her every move. Bethany could see another chink in Clare's armor, so she seized the opportunity to stretch Clare beyond her known comfort zone. "Why? What is it about him that is so precious?"

Bethany and Tim waited in silence. Clare knew her sister already knew the answer to her questions. It was because she didn't have any children of her own and Clive was filling a void. As if by her own design she was molding him and shaping him into what she'd never known, but she didn't dare share that with Bethany, who would have some pious retort she didn't want to hear.

Seizing the chance to bring a Godly intersection to Clare's

vulnerability, Bethany took a risk of her own. "We always end our day in prayer. Can we pray for you?"

Lost in her own thoughts, Clare almost didn't hear the question. "Pray for me? Why? If prayer helps you two, then good for you. I have everything under control. Thank you for your thoughts tonight. I'll consider talking to Clive."

With that, Tim helped Clare put on her black velvet cape, complete with military-style epaulets. As they showed her out, Bethany tried to hug her. After their conversation, Clare appeared to be reachable in a new way. Maybe this Clive was changing something inside her for the better, softening her up a bit, she hoped. But Clare appeared to rush. Before Bethany could touch her, she slipped on her clogs as fast as she could and headed down the front porch steps, without looking back. Her tiny footprints were immediately erased by drifting crystals of snow.

CHAPTER 8

Agitato—Harried, excited

Anna Serkin made her way through their large, empty house in need of an after-school snack. Having Mama and Papa at work or out of town most of the time had its advantages. Reaching for a bag of chocolate chip cookies instead of the pita chips and hummus Mama had left out on the kitchen table, Anna made her way upstairs to their bedroom corner of the house.

What is with Clive lately? He is acting so weird, like he's avoiding me. He never wants to get coffee after school, and he's always off, alone in his room.

Anna loved Clive's brooding, furrowed brow and his artistic nature, which he let go of intermittently around her, like a minor key transitioning to a major key when they were together. She was the only one in the house who could bring him out of his piano mood, a singular skill upon which she prided herself, but lately she hadn't been able to. Ever since the fall began, he would go up to his room after dinner and lock the door. There was a strange musty smell too. *He is definitely up to something,* Anna thought.

Anna tossed her backpack on top of her desk and turned to look down the hall, facing Clive's bedroom door, wondering if she should investigate. Her brother also seemed to be taking more piano lessons with Mr. K, and he didn't complain about his teacher's yellow teeth or chalk breath anymore. He was even showering and changing his clothes before some of his piano lessons, which just wasn't Clive. He had preferred to go to school day after day in his version of a school uniform: ripped jeans and the same T-shirt, the black and white one with Chopin sneering on the front. When Anna asked him about this new routine, she would get a snide, little response. "I'm a big boy now, Anna. I need more than one shower a day." Her brother had just started showering every day, and using shampoo every day too, about a month ago, and now he acted like he'd been doing it his whole life.

Mama and Papa are oblivious. At home in the evening, they mostly sat and listened to Clive play, heaping praise upon his renewed energy and devotion. "Your interpretive abilities are growing, Clive. The Brahms is a good challenge for you," Papa complimented. Mama listened more than usual. The two of them no longer darted off to their home offices after dinner. Could they even notice there was something different about Clive? *They're so clueless,* Anna thought. As she sat, leaning back against the top of her desk, she listened to the quiet of the house. The only sound was the reliable tick of the grandfather clock downstairs, which once belonged to her grandmother Bubbe Serkin. She knew Mama and Papa would be home late that night, and Clive was at his lesson. It felt like the perfect time to have a look around Clive's room and see what he might be hiding from her. *Yes, no, yes, no:* the grandfather clock was helping her determine the right course of action. She easily rationalized that he would do the same out of concern for her. It was her sisterly duty to help him through whatever he was experimenting with before he found himself in real trouble. *Could it be drugs?* No. He looked too normal for that, actually even a bit better than normal. *Could it be pornography?* No, he didn't even think about girls, let alone look at them. She pledged to herself upon entering the room that if she found anything, she would never tell Mama and Papa.

Starting at his desk, Anna tried to trace the musty smell. There was nothing unusual littered about his desk, except a couple of guitar picks; Clive didn't play the guitar. She sniffed under the bed and as expected, found dirty socks and gym clothes he never wore. Clive managed to get out of gym to practice the piano in the choir room during his gym class, which she found infuriating. Before reaching for the closet handle, she paused to listen carefully to be sure no one was in the house. As she stepped inside, she encountered *the* smell.

Beneath the laundry piles was the scent of something ancient. It seemed to be coming from a large cardboard packing box which was secured with duct tape. Gingerly tearing off the duct tape and opening the lid, she came across stuffed animals from different eras of Clive's life. His favorite, Timber the Husky, was on top. *This is just the moldy smell of stuffed animals. Why can't he get rid of these?*

While reaching for the tape to reseal the box, Anna lost her balance and tumbled against it. The box barely moved. She tried to lift it up and noticed that it felt unmistakably heavy to be filled with nothing more than stuffed animals. Flinging out all of the animals revealed a book buried in the bottom of the box, but Anna didn't recognize it. She stretched her arms all the way down into the bottom and attempted to lift the book up and out of its deeply secured location. She guessed the book weighed about twelve pounds and appeared to be handmade leather and very ornate. *Some old music book, how typical. This is hardly worth locking the door for.*

The handwriting inside the book was legible, like calligraphy. She recognized a few names, like Brahms. *It must be some sort of music journal from years back.* Studying it did not reveal the author, but there were many different types of writing throughout the book, and dates all the way back to the early 1800s. *This should be in a museum. Did Clive steal this?*

Turning to the book's last page, she found Clive's handwriting, in cryptic messages without much content as though he were trying to conceal the meaning:

Cardiff—Welsh, Caer—stronghold, fort. Taer—flowing as in a river.

Clara—Latin origin—famous, brilliant. She is my stronghold: a fortress in which to run, flowing and brilliant.

Anna ran a hand down her face. *Could Clive actually have a girlfriend who he is writing about in some dusty old music journal? Now that is something juicy.*

The back door slammed. Someone arrived home earlier than expected. Jamming the book and the animals back into the box and replacing the duct tape with haphazard care, Anna kicked the laundry over the box top and ran down to her room, taking a seat at her desk. She heard Clive whistle his way up the stairs, still wearing his backpack, not even stopping for his customary snack. Halfway up the stairs, she heard him stop. "Anna?"

"Oh, hi, I'm in here studying." He walked past her bedroom door without saying hello or asking about her day. She saw him down the hall, again stopping as he entered his room—his tall, thin silhouette ominously stretching the length of the opposite wall. Calmly, he closed his door and locked it. She heard him in his closet and waited for the sound of the tape to tear, but it didn't. Silence. Anna held her breath, wondering if he would notice. Again, he called to her, "Anna?"

"Yes," she sheepishly replied.

"Could you come here?"

As she approached the closed door, Anna noticed a crack of light flowing to her feet. She entered his room and found that the light was coming from the closet. Reaching for the door handle this time, she felt sick. She had betrayed her only brother, her advocate and defender with Mama and Papa—her hero. Air began escaping from her lungs with such swiftness she thought she would either choke or faint.

She found Clive sitting on the closet floor in the midst of the laundry. He looked broken, cracked by the single lightbulb's tilted shadow. "Why did you do it?" There was calm, even a hint of serenity in his voice, as he directed this single question at his sister.

His simple lack of anger caused her to burst into tears of guilt and repentance. Anna cried out, "Please forgive me. You have never hidden anything from me or locked me out before. We've always been together and it felt like you were leaving me for someone else or something else. I had to find out what it was. Please forgive me. I didn't find out anything. I don't even know what it is. I won't tell anyone. I promise! I won't ever tell Mama and Papa."

Clive wanted to reach out and grab his younger sister by her dark ponytail. Instead, he hugged her as she collapsed to her knees on the closet floor. She had not learned much from the Folio. They could go on.

"It's all right. I forgive you," he said reassuringly. "It's only an old notebook full of music and thoughts by different composers. I hid it from Papa because if he knew about it, he would want to keep it. Then the Folio would become his and he would share it with the orchestra. It would leave me forever. I couldn't tell them." Looking at her tear-strewn face, Clive was moved by the agony she felt in her betrayal. Anna loved him more than he realized.

"Where did you get it?" Anna asked.

He couldn't tell her more, not yet anyway. "It was given to me by a colleague. It is valuable, priceless. You may not speak of it to anyone. Give me your sovereign word on this," Clive insisted.

The blessing of his forgiveness washed over her and she gratefully agreed. Anna did not tell him she had seen the name *Clara Cardiff*. Now was not the time to ask him about it. He had already confided enough. *Clara Cardiff. Welsh.* Somehow she would find out more about this mysterious Clara Cardiff. She certainly wasn't at Brookline Academy. Anna knew all the girls his age at Brookline, but he did cut though the conservatory often on his way home from school. She was probably a student at Westdale College Conservatory. *Clive, hanging out with a college-age girl-friend? I wonder what she looks like. Could she be Jewish? Would Mama and Papa approve? How old is she?* Her mind was racing with questions she was dying to know the answers to. In her own way and time, she would find out.

CHAPTER 9

Modulate—To change from one key to another

"Mr. Koussevitsky says I am ready to enter the Tchaikovsky Piano Competition," Clive declared to his father. "He believes I can win. I will be playing the Chopin *Concerto in F minor* as my concerto of choice and of course, Tchaikovsky's *First Piano Concerto*. I need your blessing and signature to enter."

The sound at the dinner table grew faint. Even Anna knew that careers were made and lost at the Tchaikovsky competition. Julia Serkin set down her soup spoon, appropriately off to one side on the plate, and stared at Clive.

"Isn't it a bit early for you to be considering this competition?" Julia questioned.

"The Tchaikovsky is different from other competitions in that it runs only once every four years." He could tell by their shocked faces and Papa's silence, they thought he was too young to compete. Clive studied all of their expressions, but particularly Papa's. All soup spoons were now quiet except Papa's. Everyone anxiously awaited his response.

Claude peered over the table at his son, who was earnest in his desire and belief. "How often have you played through *The Well-Tempered Clavier* as a warm-up?" he asked, not looking over his glasses and still eating his potato leek soup.

"I'm sorry, Papa. I'm not sure I understand the question."

"Before Chopin would play a concert, he would warm up playing through the entire *Well-Tempered Clavier*. Schumann referred to it as *your daily bread*. This was how he prepared himself. How have you prepared yourself for such a task?" Claude asked, continuing on without waiting for Clive's response. "You are my son, my son with great God-given talents. You must be prepared thoroughly to take on this competition." Another soup bite went down with an audible swallow. Claude wiped his mouth with the linen napkin and carefully set it down on the dining room table. His eyes focused on his son with intentional silence, almost meditative.

Clive knew his answer to this particular question could bring his father to accept or deny his request. He chose to be unspecific, for there would be no winning a war of repertoire with Papa. "I have prepared myself by listening well and giving everything of myself to the piece at hand. That has been enough up to this point. I have won many competitions with this approach."

Clive saw his mother stiffen in her chair. "Clive, your father and I want nothing more than to see you succeed. We want you in that seat when you are ready. No one at your age has gone there and won. You are a touch too young to be taken seriously. Perhaps you should work another year before you compete. Take your time and build your repertoire. This isn't something you can rush into, and there isn't much time to prepare. Isn't the competition later this year? I thought pianists readied themselves for years before they entered the Tchaikovsky."

"Mama, I can understand how you might think that way, but Chopin was only twenty when he composed the *F minor* and then performed its premiere shortly after."

"You are *not* twenty," Julia quipped.

Clive was relentless in his reply. "Mr. Koussevitsky says I am ready. He is what you have chosen for me because you believed he was best for me, and now he is saying I am ready. Why does it have to be about winning? Papa's question was about being ready."

"Your mother is right. Your timing feels a bit rushed. The competition is in the fall, is it not? I will talk to Mr. Koussevitsky and listen to his thoughts. You are working hard, Clive. There is a new quality in your playing, a kind of determined empathy and hopefulness. I will talk with him and we'll see."

X

Every time Clive approached the painted door of Clare's studio, he brushed the wind chimes to announce his arrival. He loved this about her, music playing at her door before he even set foot inside. He often arrived early so he could stand by her door and listen as she practiced the Brahms *Sonata. She thinks it needs refining. I think it's nearly perfect.*

Brahms seemed to be her preference, and he could understand why. He sensed in her a desire for order, but unwillingness to submit to it. Her studio floor reflected this oxymoron. Piles of music were strewn about, ceaselessly waiting to be *filed* in the library, but never quite getting there. This came in handy during their time together as she walked barefoot through the ordered heaps to find the perfect reference from another composition to explain a point she was trying to make. Order with color and fire, the Classical with the Romantic—those qualities defined her. After hearing a break in the movements, Clive took advantage of the silence and knocked on the painted door.

"Mr. Serkin, I presume, *buongiorno*," she said, flinging open her door. Italian greeting today, French on Monday, and German on Saturday. *I would love to speak three useful languages. My English and Hebrew don't go too far in the music world.*

Clive had passed the first semester test, so she agreed to continue teaching him through the second semester. The Tchaikovsky Competition would be later that year. He felt comforted, knowing that he could count on her getting him there, well prepared. His mind wandered to an even greater possibility.

Clive and Clare in Moscow. Clare speaking Russian, introducing him to everyone on the competition jury and people in every corner of the city. They could walk along the Moskva River together and talk over his progress, like Rachmaninoff did with his students.

Clive jumped at the sound of Clare's voice drawing him out of his daydream. "Let's start with the second movement today," Clare said, taking her seat on the little bench next to him. "This larghetto must sing like Chopin for his love, Kostancia. We have talked about this. He never spoke to her. So this movement was his message, the very words he longed to speak."

As Clive began to play, he thought only of Clare. *This is my message to her that I cannot speak.* There was so much he wanted to say to her and yet he knew she would think he was merely a boy, infatuated with his piano teacher and nothing more. So he, like Chopin, communicated through the keyboard. As he played the larghetto, he imagined walking hand in hand with Clare along the Moskva as trembling leaves took flight from their summer branches, drifting alongside them toward the water. With the closing delicate ascent of thirds to the final pianissimo, he surrendered to Chopin's language. Then he brought his hands down from the keyboard and waited.

Rarely did Clare affirm his efforts with a compliment, choosing instead to inspire him in his approach and spur him on further with a new idea. "Even though it is pianissimo, don't let the final note sound like evaporative, decaying mush. The final note must be clear.

"Overall, the gentleness is there, but it lacks humility," Clare continued. "There should be no pride involved, for you are a young man learning from Master Chopin. Schumann himself said of this piece that it is one which 'all of us put together would not be able to reach, and whose hem we can merely kiss.' They are bowing to him, Clive. You reverence him by your playing. Chopin is greatness, originality, invention, and purity of sound. We all bow to him. This humility must be there."

Scooting Clive off the bench, Clare took her place to play the movement for him. He watched her tiny hands and enormous heart fill the musical idea. The notes were crying out so intently that he could hear the yearnings of Chopin's heart.

After listening to Clare play the movement, doubt crept in. "Perhaps Mama and Papa are right. I am too young for the Tchaikovsky Competition," Clive moaned. "I have not lived long enough, not known enough sorrow to give this piece what it demands."

Clare waited pensively, then objected. "That may be true, but you have been given the talent to play it with your own voice. You have spoken to your parents about the competition, so you have told them we are studying together? This is true?" Her eyes alighted on him with the reflective whiteness of the keys, intensifying their blueness.

Clive could not lie to her. "No, I have told them Mr. K desires to enter me into the competition. I talked him into it. He is genuinely pleased with my progress, although he thinks it is because of his teaching. He does not know I have been studying with you, but he thinks I might be ready."

Clare could hear the last words of Tim and Bethany, "You could lose him," rumbling through her mind. Yet, she believed it would be best for Clive to face his parents and confess their private lessons to them. "Clive, it is time for you to tell your parents about our work. They need to know what is behind your growth and determine the path forward with you. Hopefully, Mr. Koussevitsky and I can work together to play a part in your development. Honesty is always best."

Clive knew his father would not take kindly to his musical betrayal and game playing, the false impressions he had cultivated, and the heaps of praise attributed to Mr. K for his improvement. He could lose Clare because of his own deceitfulness. He needed her to get through the competition, and in his heart he was beginning to believe he needed her to get through life itself.

"Papa has made every decision about my musical life from as far back as I can remember—who I would study with, what I might play, and what competitions I entered. He and Mr. K have a family relationship. He is like an uncle to us. Mr. K's father was the brilliant conductor, the great Sergei Koussevitsky. This is the musical bloodline in *our* family, which I can't go against."

Clare interjected, "You already have, by studying with me and not disclosing the truth."

"I am not ready to tell them. My parents might take you away from me. I can't take that risk."

He halted with the sudden admission of his feelings for her, embarrassed but relieved that it had slipped out.

With the awareness of his caged words being set free, he determined to go on. "I can't lose you. I've learned more in six months with you than in a lifetime with Mr. K. Please give me a bit more time. Papa is going to talk to Mr. K to determine if I can do the competition. If he says yes, we can enter and then I will think about telling them. Papa might understand at that point because if I enter and am accepted, he will see the benefit of my continuing with you, and the excitement of the opportunity ahead of us. Mama has wanted me to work with a different teacher for at least a year so I don't think she will be a problem. Please, just a little more time."

Clive wanted to take her small hand in his, but he waited. Clare could see Clive was willing to sacrifice his honor on her behalf, and she was flattered.

As if reading his mind, she clasped his hand between her two hands. The coolness of her tiny hands upon his burning fingers reminded him of Grandmother Serkin, how she cared for him when Mama and Papa were away and he was sick with a fever. The family blessing of a cool touch of reassurance was one he longed for and did not receive often enough. Clive could hear his heart pounding in his ears; the sweat of his hand was embarrassing, but he did not pull away. He longed for the moment to last.

"Clive, I don't know your mother, but I do know your father is a dear man. He is not a tyrant. He is a musician. He will understand. Tell him." For the first time, Clare held on to him like a son. She was giving him the advice of a mother, and as good mothers do, she was willing to sacrifice their relationship to see him grow into a man.

Clive drew close to her with romanticized desire. Her hand fit seamlessly in his as the black piano keys agree with the white ones. He let his eyes slowly move down to focus on her hands surrounding his, and he was stirred by a desire to protect her accomplished hands. Their hands could work together by design: four hands working, living, rather than two. Piano for four hands. He did not want to disappoint Clare. Yet his desire for her, for more time sitting next to her—and his eagerness to take all she could give to him—overpowered his urge to honor Papa by telling the truth.

"I will do what I have to do. They are my parents. Please trust my instincts," he said. Summoning all his courage, Clive impulsively reached out and hugged her. Their first hug felt awkward due to his enormous size overwhelming her small frame, and their position, seated side by side on the piano bench. He held her for a brief moment and was surprised by how childlike she felt in his arms. She was ominous, even intimidating, at the keyboard and only a fraction of that impression next to him. The juxtaposition encouraged his masculinity. He was bigger and stronger than he believed or knew, and her femininity brought definition to his realization. Without looking back at her, he grabbed hold of his coat and his escaping breath and darted down the stairs.

As Clare watched his tall, thin figure stride beneath the oaks, she knew she was treading dangerous water. Clive was falling in love with her and she was growing to love him, not with passionate abandon like she once knew with Nero, but with a nurturing tenderness. It was a new feeling and a restorative one, innocent and pure. Maintaining Clive's innocence would be paramount to his future. She remembered a line from Brahms in her Folio, "If only I could live my years as an adult, and could play with the innocence of my youth." She could not risk stealing an integral part of his musicality by taking advantage of him, but keeping her distance might be challenging. She sensed he needed a mature woman to fill in the gaps of his youth, but stepping into that cavern could produce consequences she did not want to bear. Perhaps his mother had been absent in some way during his formative years, or even now.

Clare sat for a while, pondering further. A diversion might be a good idea. The holiday season would be the right time to go visit Nero? Five months was long enough for him to learn what life is like alone. Clare was not sure if she missed Nero, but she missed the farm. Yet, if the Serkins allowed Clive to continue studying with her, it would be a privilege to see him through the competition.

All decisions for another day, Clare recognized as she sat down to play Brahms. Dropping into the keys, she made her way through the first section but found that at the Andante Espressivo, she completely lost the thread of the music. There was nothing except blackness, no images of the measures in her mind. The physical space between her ears felt like a black hole. Even going back several measures brought no refreshment of the music to her memory.

How many times had she told Clive, "Memory slips are due to learning the music wrong, not failing memory." But she had learned this music correctly and known it for years. Recognizing that blanking out is part of living a musical life, she pulled out the score, looked at it, and then put it back in the bench. Always keeping the music for the pieces she was currently working on in the bench helped keep things clear in her mind and prevented valuable time from being wasted searching through piles.

She began to play again with renewed confidence. When she arrived at the measure in question, she was able to go on and finish the piece. Thankfully, although she lost the music momentarily, it was all still stored in total, somewhere in her brain. The key was unlocking it when it disappeared.

With relief, she reminded herself, *You haven't blanked out playing a piece since college.* This episode was probably due to the stress and distraction of her prior conversation with Clive. Could he have caused this incident of memory loss? *Unlikely.* While she knew he affected her soul, Clare hoped it was not a physical effect as well.

)(

Claude Serkin climbed the steps of Saul Koussevitsky's front porch with the familiar longing for home. Their common heritage and love of Israel, their homeland, was something he shared with only a few in this suburban enclave. Claude and Julia had chosen to live in Westdale for Brookline Academy, the preeminent high school to foster their children's passions for science and music. According to Julia, this was where they would receive both the best education and semblance of a normal life. His thoughts often meandered into this perspective. While his wife was happy, their children knew nothing of their true home, which embittered Claude.

Julia, as usual, got everything she wanted. The family could have lived in a Jewish neighborhood, as Claude desired, but instead landed in a suburb, with its chemically sprayed lawns and tree-lined streets. Their children had never seen "home," the rock-faced landscape of the Kidron Valley. *They need to come with me the next time the orchestra performs in Jerusalem,* Claude determined.

Saul's tiny, ever-receding frame stepped into the foyer and embraced Claude. The older man sported his customary gray suit and tucked-in, thin-striped necktie with a clip. Squinting through his narrowing eyes, he conveyed his customary greeting. "Ah, Claude, *mazel tov*, please come in. To what do I owe this honor? You mentioned on the phone you wanted to talk about Clive and the competition. Please come in and sit down for a cigar with your old friend."

The front room remained as ever, since his wife, Rachel, died. Every piece of furniture rested in the same spot, down to the ashtrays and yellowing lace curtains. Claude began, "I want to thank you for your efforts and faithfulness to Clive. He is making excellent strides and shows great motivation these days. Something has changed in his understanding and commitment to the repertoire. Do you see it?

"Clive worked through the Brahms *Intermezzo* with a vengeance. He is now approaching the *Chopin F Minor* with equal intensity, but with other qualities and colors which I have not heard before. What do you think?"

Reaching forward to light Claude's cigar, Saul offered the telling smile of a master whose apprentice had surpassed him. "He is different. He is maturing. His technique and depth of understanding are working with the music, as opposed to one running ahead of the other. This is why I felt he could try the Chopin. He has wanted to, Claude, for such a time, and always asking, 'Am I ready?'

"One day he sat down right here and played the second movement for me. Imagine, he learned it without me," Saul admitted. "He simply came in and played it for me. And without my knowing, oh, such playing—he captured the longing and tenderness, the subtlety, with nothing forced at all. It was a wonder, even humble for his age and inexperience. I knew then it was time to let him try."

With each cigar breath directed toward the curtains, Claude could see Saul grow more enthusiastic. His own dream of nurturing a pianistic star might have a chance of fulfillment before he died. Claude could see that he could taste it with each inhalation of the disproportionately enormous Havana. He almost wanted to let Clive give it a try for his old friend's sake alone. "How often does he come to you in the week since you have begun this concerto?" Claude asked.

"Oh, just the same as ever, once a week. This is why I am so pleased. Nothing from my end has changed. It is all driven by Clive. He wants this, Claude. I can see the determination on his face. He has the best of you and Julia in this way—fierce, and a face like flint."

Ash falling on his jacket went unnoticed as Claude pondered the *once a week* reference. It seemed like Clive had mentioned attending his lessons more often, even two or three times a week.

"Are you sure just once a week? We would have to spend much more time than once a week if we were to undertake this endeavor. I do not want to risk it if he is not ready. I'm not sure the repertoire is there for him to make it through all the rounds, let alone get to the finals," Claude stressed.

"So what if he doesn't get to the finals?" Saul questioned. "At such a young age, he will learn so much by being there."

"You know, Saul, no one has ever heard about the man who came in second after Van Cliburn. Van Cliburn went home to a ticker tape parade in New York City, while Mr. Second Place, whoever he was, probably went home to become a high school piano teacher. This is nothing we would want for Clive."

"Ah, Claude, it is nothing you and Julia would want for Clive, but is it what Clive wants? You must let go of him, and this may be a good time to start. Release his life to what he and God have planned together. You might be surprised. It could be much more fruitful than what you have planned."

"I don't know if Clive is asking God what He has planned for his life," Claude said with a tinge of shame.

"Well, then, perhaps you should ask Him."

"Me ask God? Well, I do talk to Him, but maybe I should ask Clive first."

"Yes, you ask Clive and ask Clive to ask God." Saul winked, which acknowledged that asking God was something they all needed to do more of.

Claude knew Saul was right. Readiness, from his fatherly perspective, was not the most important thing. It was what Clive believed in that would determine his path. "Do you think he truly wants this? Do you believe he is ready?"

"My friend, we have been together all our lives. You are as close to me as my brother. I have never lied to you. Clive is as ready as a seventeen-year-old genius can be. If he wants this, you must let him try."

"It will take more work from your end and more travel. Are you up to it? You hate to fly."

"Ah, I am an old man, but Clive is like my son Rueben. At his young age, he goes places that we cannot go, like Rueben did at seventeen. Bless my adventurous Rueben. He is still climbing mountains, even now as a father. They bring their babies in backpacks or fanny packs or whatever they call them. Have you ever heard of such a thing? Babies go everywhere these days. But this is what we want for them, Claude. Although I cannot climb Rueben's mountains, I can be there to meet him at the bottom, and that means something. Yes, God will provide, and I will make the trip to Russia. Claude, will you accompany us?"

Claude knew late summer would be a perfect time for him to go, with the orchestra resting in their summer home, led by a series of guest conductors, but fall would be difficult. He could arrange to conduct the Moscow Symphony or lead master classes at the Moscow Conservatory. Somehow he would make it work. "Yes, I will be there, but I'm not sure Julia will be able to get away. We will see."

"Yes, yes, Julia. That is another thing, Claude. Forgive my boldness, but she should make the trip. Although Rachel's life ended far too early, she never regretted being there for her children."

The reference to Julia's absence from Clive's life hurt. She had long ago made the choice: work first, home second. He knew a good Jewish wife would never have made such a choice, but the jury was still out on the rightness of her choice, and the Tchaikovsky Competition jury could have some input into the success or failure of Julia's decision. Claude knew she should go to Moscow, but he couldn't force her. "Well, there's not much I can do about Julia. All is dependent upon her work schedule. My friend, I am counting on you to have Clive ready. Saul, give me your word." Reaching out his hand to take the tired hand of his old friend, Claude thought he saw a gratifying mist clouding Saul's eyes. This might be his last trip to Russia and certainly the last chance to take a student there.

To quell his emotion, Saul proposed a toast. "We must drink to our boy."

Crossing the shag carpet, following the direction of its worn path, he came to the breakfront, which was draped in his wife's lace handiwork, the cloths of years of shared Shabbat. "These Swarovski glasses—a wedding gift to Rachel and me—are from Russia. They will bring good luck."

Raising their glasses with a drop of brandy poured in each, the two men spoke in unison: "To Clive. *L'chaim.*"

CHAPTER 10

*Mixer—A device that makes a composite signal
out of two or more input signals*

February was almost over, but Nero's windowsills at the
farm and in the potter's shed were cluttered with empty
seed trays. Likewise, seed catalogues were piled up in the copper
bucket by the front door. By now, the lettuce should have been
started in the cold frame, but empty peat pots from last spring littered the frame and the sills. Their torn brown shells were repre-
sentative of Nero's heart; he didn't want to be reminded of Clare.
Dry, brittle, and torn—not the ideal soil conditions needed to
plant something new, he realized.

Sleeping with the statuette of their child brought some comfort, although Nero often woke up when his head knocked into
it during the night. Its skin was so cold and hard. He wanted to
warm it, so he found an old shawl Clare had worn in the garden
in the early spring and wrapped the baby in it. He guessed it belonged to Clare's mother by the old look of the creamy yarn and
antique style of crochet.

Nero had named their son Johannes. He looked German

coming out of the kiln, and Clare loved playing Brahms, especially in the spring. *What was the name of her favorite one? The Rite of Spring? The Four Seasons? Were those by Brahms?*

He couldn't remember any of them with clarity since she had left the farm.

Johannes was a few months old now and a good baby. He didn't cry. He didn't move. He didn't even spit up, and best of all, he looked like his mother. His face had the little slant like Clare's—everything a touch crooked from the nose down. Nero loved the distinctive angle of her face.

When Katrina slept over, Nero hid baby Johannes in the closet trunk to avoid an eccentric appearance. His pharmaceutical provider was an important thread of sanity for him. He had to protect Johannes, but Katrina as well.

The winter entrenched unremarkably. Snow crept up to the door. He often forgot to light the wood stove in his studio, so the potter's wheel waited for another day. If he held off from his Scotch and water until ten in the morning, Nero thought he might get something done. Sculpting a series of terra-cotta birds might be a new area worth exploring. Flying would be such a relief right now. Getting a pilot's license was an idea, but drinking and flying don't mix together well. Instead, sculpting birds might give him a lift.

Nero prided himself on how he had gone almost six months without calling Clare. Oh, there was that one little call to Tim and Bethany—the one he realized was a mistake as soon as Tim answered. *That man, such a disgusting loser, always trying to improve everyone around him with his good deeds and righteous outlook on life.* He had hung up immediately at the mere sound of Tim's authoritative voice. Willpower was not his forte, but Nero had to show Clare that he was getting along just fine without her.

X

As Clare came into the studio, she made a mental note to hang her keys on the key hook by the door. It was a Christmas gift, desperately needed, from Bethany's son Jeremy, who was her best piano student in the Taylor family. Lately, Clare had been finding the keys to her apartment in strange places, even the freezer. One day, she caught herself actually looking for her keys there. *Things can get so jumbled up in the mind when there is stress*, she thought. Stress, it was the evil bane and cause of all the world's health problems. But was her life really stressful?

The break from concertizing and subsequent foray into teaching brought refreshment. Working with Clive was proving to be an adventure into caring deeply about a young person for the first time. Not only was he obscenely talented, he was so sweet and vulnerable. Teaching him was not providing much income. Clare gave Clive discounted lessons because of his ability and the fact she knew he was paying out of his own pocket. She decided the benefit of cultivating such a musician was worth the lack of compensation. She saved plenty over the years, so a year away from the concert stage would not be a problem financially, although it wasn't exactly a career builder.

There was some stress in the way Clive held back the truth about their lessons from his parents. In the few seasons she had soloed with the Chicago Philharmonic, Claude Serkin was a gem to work with. He was a man of spirit and character. He, like Maestro Solti, brought that integrity to the music. He even kept the small supply of bonbons in his pocket that he, like Sir Georg, peppered into his mouth on the sly during rehearsals. There were similarities between the two maestros, who both treated her with honor and artistic freedom whenever they collaborated with her. The thought of her being the object of Clive's betrayal before a man of Claude's stature was somewhat distressing. Clare hoped the secrecy didn't continue much longer. What they could all accomplish working together on Clive's behalf was an enticing prospect, she recognized.

With an unforeseen exuberance, Clive burst into Clare's studio without taking the time to ring the chimes in advance of his arrival. "Papa is going to let me do the Tchaikovsky Competition. He said yes! His meeting with Mr. Koussevitsky went perfectly. The paper was signed in my presence. See, here it is; our plan has worked," a beaming Clive announced as he stretched it out in front of Clare.

"Congratulations. Tell me how your parents accepted the news of our partnership in this great endeavor?" Waiting, Clare could tell immediately that he had not told them.

Clive moved to the piano and sat down to work through his arpeggio warm-up without a response, as though the music could overcome their necessary conversation. Clare gently touched his hand to stop him, causing Clive to shiver and look away. "Clive, it is not *our* plan. It is your plan. Why didn't you tell them?"

"I have come to realize that I need both of my teachers to succeed. Mr. Koussevitsky has his own wisdom to bring to the work. Although he is annoyingly old and obsessed with the Torah, Mr. K is kind and knows well the breadth of my required repertoire. You give me, I mean, you give the music life. I take the nuts and bolts from his studio and bring them here where they are transformed into art."

"Well, then telling your parents is the next logical step. If you feel this way, they will understand. They simply need to hear this from your heart and they will listen. What do you think they are going to do, take you away from me?" Clare asked.

An ache came into his solar plexus at this thought. It was a physical response tangibly felt, like a flowing river dammed up inside of him. He could imagine the music being cut off without her, rendering him mute. He had to keep the current of Clare moving inside him. "I need a little more time to prepare them. They need to be ready to hear the news. I'm thinking of investing Anna in the task. She always gets her way with Papa."

Clare studied Clive's face. If she and Nero had a child together, he would look nothing like Clive with his elongated features, lanky body, and almost black eyes. Taking a bit of a gamble might be the best move at this point, so she issued an ultimatum. "I am approaching the point of discontinuing our lessons if you don't tell them. Shall we set a deadline? We all have to work with deadlines. The competition is six months away. The sooner we are on board together, the better your progress will be. You need to tell them all by week's end, including Mr. Koussevitsky. Let's move on with the Chopin, the third movement this time."

Instead of settling down to work, Clive found himself deep in thought about the Folio. It contained mysteries relayed by those experiencing them in their lives so long ago. Not only was he learning about the composers, their music, and their students, he was acquiring new life lessons. Keeping secrets—when absolutely necessary—was acceptable, even preferable, as told by Brahms himself in his writings about the relationship of Robert and Clara Schumann:

May 4, 1838—I have learned that Clara's father has forbidden her engagement to Robert and is taking them to court over the matter. Robert managed to pursue Clara in secret, so why did they not proceed with the marriage in the same manner? Why make way for this courtroom charade? Such enmity is fruitless. I am considering dedicating my next piece to them as a wedding gift.

In fact, much goodness came out of the pair's secrecy. They defeated Clara Schumann's father in court and went on to become one of the great musical collaborations in history. Perhaps he and Clare could do this someday. Maybe they could tour together. He could write music for her to perform or she could do the same for him.

"Clive, let's get started." Clare could see his mind was wandering and they had so much to accomplish in such a short time. "You must know that his two concerti are the only performed works from his early years. They are so different from the classical concertos of the day with their typical interplay between the soloist and orchestra. Here, the pianist is showcased with attention to detail rarely heard in a concerto. It is not about the structure. It is free verse poetry with the meter of a Polish mazurka. In other words, do not get caught up in the lack of structure or try to deconstruct it. Liszt said that Chopin 'did violence to his genius every time he sought to fetter it by rules.' Remember this and let go of the rules."

As Clive began to play, Clare found herself transported back to New England Conservatory, thirty years ago. She was discussing the same movement with Professor Rosenblith. "Not too much rubato there. You want the folks in the back seats at Tanglewood to recognize the music, but also to hear it for the first time. You need to take them there. Make this the dazzling finish it is meant to be."

Clare had proceeded to play through the entire Allegro Vivace without stopping. Afraid to look at Rosenblith, she glanced at the poster of Boston Garden on his studio wall and waited. She was expecting a searing critique, which always came after she initially completed a significant work. Instead, she heard Rosenblith clapping and laughing as he repeatedly said, "You are on your way, Clare." From that day forward, she began to believe in her ability to play Chopin.

"Thank you, sir. Thank you," she said aloud, startling Clive, who was coming to the middle of the movement. Surprised by her outburst and confused as to why she was calling him "sir," he abruptly stopped playing and looked at Clare.

"Forgive me. I'm not sure I understood what you said. Were you speaking to me?" Clive asked.

She looked at him blankly. Clare was caught off-guard by his question and the confused face before her. She had been speaking to Professor Rosenblith and now she was here with this stranger.

"Clare, what were you trying to say to me?"

The room suddenly felt close and colored to the extreme. Clare looked for the wall poster of the Boston Garden and instead saw a painting of some unknown gentleman with a beard. Standing up from her seat and walking over to the window brought an unfamiliar view of enormous oak trees and cars parked in neat rows below. Did she own one of those cars? This didn't look like Boston.

"I'm sorry," Clare apologized to Clive. "Let's take a break. I've lost something." For the first time, Clive saw a distance in Clare's eyes which was unfamiliar to him. Usually, her eyes were dancing with bright exuberance as she explained a musical image or idea, but here they appeared far away, disconnected from the present. "Ms. Clare, are you all right?"

Clive saw her stand up and walk over to the bookcase mumbling something aloud. "Professor Rosenblith gave me that book. He will know what to do."

Clive stood, stunned at the sight of Clare scanning the bookshelves for something completely unrelated to what they were working on. "Who is Professor Rosenblith?" Clive asked. But she ignored him, continuing to look into books for the answer that seemed to be escaping her. "Madame Cardiff, I think I better go now. We've done enough for today." Her mind appeared to be intent upon finding a bit of information in a large volume as she continued to pull vast quantities of books off the shelf. With confusion and concern, Clive turned at the door to look back at her. As if she were in a different room, apart from him, he could hear her repeating the same questions to herself, "Now where is that book? I know I have it here somewhere. What could I have done with it?"

CHAPTER 11

Recitative—A voice style in opera used to tell the plot and bridge the gap between arias

"Bubeleh, where are you?" Clive teased his sister as he searched the downstairs for her.

"Stop calling me that," she cried out from the kitchen. She knew she was Papa's "little girl" but he didn't have to rub it in.

"What else should I call you, my little *Havilah, Chava*?" Clive laughed, knowing she would hate that reference even more.

"We are not in *Fiddler on the Roof*, Clive." He began chasing his sister around the island in their kitchen singing, "If I were a rich man, a zee-ba-de-ba-zee-ba-de-ba-zee." The sight of Clive attempting to shake his almost concave torso made her laugh even more as she sprinted for the pantry. If she could just get the door shut before he reached it, she would be in a safe zone.

Clive cornered her in the pantry, and Anna thought he was going to put on Mama's apron and continue his Tevya rant, but instead he gave her a hug and grew serious.

"Anna, I need your help with something delicate. Are you willing?"

"How delicate is it? If it has anything to do with your laundry, my answer is no."

Clive smiled. "This is a tougher problem than getting the laundry done. Think internal dirty laundry, not external dirty laundry. My dilemma would benefit from some feminine ingenuity."

"Absolutely, especially if this is about your secret girlfriend," Anna said with a devilish grin.

"What are you talking about?"

Anna knew she had Clive's full attention. "I haven't said anything until now, I swear," she began, "but I learned about your girlfriend in your old, smelly book. Her name, Clara Cardiff, was written in there. I've been waiting and even hoping you would come and tell me. You know where to go for help. Sisters are always good for advice on women. Let me get my notepad and take a few notes. What seems to be the problem?"

"This isn't a Charlie Brown comic strip where I'm coming to Lucy with cold, hard cash to pay for a fix. This is real and difficult. It's not a joke." Clive's furrow was back, and she could see this was not the time to try and erase it from his brow.

"Sorry. What's up?" Anna asked.

"Do you remember when we would walk home from Westdale last fall and I would cut through the conservatory on my way to Mr. Koussevitsky? Well, I wasn't exactly doing that. I've been studying with another piano teacher along with Mr. K, for the last several months, and keeping it from Mama and Papa. Her name is Clare, not Clara. I didn't want to tell Papa because she is a famous concert pianist, on sabbatical at Westdale. Papa knows her. She has even soloed with his orchestra, so it would have been difficult to get him involved. You know, he would have taken over, moved my piano lessons to our house, and spent hours talking about the orchestra's new works with her over tea. I wanted to do something for myself apart from him, and she is helping me tremendously. Clare is nothing less than brilliant."

"OK, so don't tell them."

"I didn't plan to, but she is making me," Clive confessed. "She says if I don't come forward and level with them, she will cast me out. We would be finished. There wouldn't be any more lessons. I need her to help me through this competition, but even more than that, I want her in my life."

"What do you mean, *in your life*? Clive, are you in love with her?" She could not believe it. He had never spoken to her about a girl before. She always assumed the only relationship Clive had was with the piano. "How old is this piano teacher?"

"I think she is in her fifties, but I'm not sure. She could be in her forties. It's hard to tell."

"What? That is practically Mama's age. That's so creepy. You could be in love with Mama!"

"Stop it. This is different. She is my mentor and friend. Being with her gives me life, and that translates into the music. I can't lose her, so I need to tell them and I need you to help me figure out how to do it."

This had the potential to be epic, Anna thought. She had read Sophocles in school. She knew about the Oedipus complex, and this sounded almost as weird, with the prospective for a similar tragic outcome. She didn't want Clive getting hurt and ruining his future by ending up blind like Oedipus or, even worse, deaf like Beethoven. "What do you want from me? I can't tell them for you?"

"No, but you can go before me. Lay the groundwork with Papa, which will help with Mama. Tell him a few things to set him up for something really devastating. Then when I do tell them, what I have to say will be an easy pill to swallow, compared to what they were imagining. How about it?"

Clive continued, reminding Anna, "You are my beloved sister, and Papa's favorite. I know you can think of something. Plus, you're the drama queen. I'm asking you to create some drama in my favor."

X

As Clare wandered the parking lot looking for her car for what seemed like the fifth day in a row, she determined it was time to tell Bethany. She couldn't tell Nero for fear he would do something rash, but Bethany would be able to recommend a doctor. She knew everyone in town. Clare couldn't remember the last time she had a physical. It was probably nothing, but Mother always said, "It's better to be safe than sorry." All mothers say that. Thankfully, she, Clare, did not rifle trite little clichés at Clive. She'd hate to think he thought of her as an overbearing mother.

Walking through the gate and up Bethany's flagstone front walk, Clare noticed that Tim had the walkway snow shoveled to the point of looking sculpted. The snowman in the front yard was adorned with a red feather boa and felt beret … a fine Valentine's Day touch by the girls. *Once again, everything looking perfect out in front of the Taylors' today*, she thought. *Why am I always the bearer of depressing events when I come here? Why can't it be the other way around?* What was it about Bethany that allowed for her to have a seemingly full and anxiety-free life? Did she live differently? Maybe it was all those kids. Bethany didn't have time to even be aware of the things in life nipping at her heels. She was always moving too fast to feel it.

"Hi, Clare, come on in. I put the tea on the stove just now. Is Earl Grey okay with you? Here, try these blueberry and lemon curd scones. Jessica made them today from a recipe in her *American Girls Cookbook*. They are like tasting summer, delightful on a snowy day. I tell you, Jessica might be a chef someday. She is always tugging at me to make a new recipe from one of her books."

She certainly isn't going to be a pianist, thought Clare.

"So what brings you here at this time? There are no lessons today."

"I wanted to see the kids and ask you a question. I need a doctor recommendation for my annual checkup. I don't think I've had one in years, and I've been feeling a bit different."

"How different? In what way?" Bethany asked.

"I'm not sure. It's like my body feels strong, but my brain feels weak. It comes and goes. Some days, everything is firing on all cylinders, and a day later, it's like I'm somewhere else," Clare confessed.

"Welcome to getting older. We all have days when we aren't firing on all cylinders. It depends how many cylinders you're used to, doesn't it? You probably have an eight-cylinder brain and I have four, so you would notice a difference and need more tuning up. Your brain is immense, Clare. You have volumes upon volumes of music stored in there. Your mind is entitled to a flicker now and then, don't you think? Don't be too hard on yourself."

"This is more than just a flicker. I have moments when I literally don't know where I am and I find myself talking to someone who isn't there. When I snap out of it, I'm really confused. I've also noticed that I don't seem to be hearing as well as I used to. When my students are talking to me, I'm straining to hear them, even leaning forward on the bench like a tottering old lady in faux suede. I'm too young for this to be happening. What if I have a brain tumor? A tumor could be cutting off my hearing and strangling my brain. I want to find out right away and deal with it or I may never get back to the stage. I'm not interested in deceiving myself."

"Well, I can understand your concern, but there's no need to overreact. I know just the person who can take care of this for you," Bethany assured as she went to her office corner and checked her rotary file. She efficiently returned and handed Clare a business card belonging to Dr. Oliver Templeton, Neurosurgeon. "He is a friend of Tim's from college who has a thriving practice here. He will be a good fit for you. He majored in biology and piano when they both were at Yale. Give him a call. Now, if he is very busy like most good doctors are, and his appointment receptionist says he can't see you for a year, then tell her that you are a relative of Tim Taylor's. That should get you in the door."

"Thanks, Beth. I always seem to be coming to you with some crisis. I'm starting to feel like the gods are against me."

"Clare, it is not the gods, as you say. There is only one God and He is definitely not against you."

"You sound so certain, like you've talked to Him about it. How do you know?"

Bethany was pleased that God was allowing all these events to happen in Clare's life because it was causing her to think about Him. For the first time, Clare was beginning to experience life beyond her control.

"Well, to be perfectly honest, I do talk to Him about it. I pray for you all the time. You are my only sister and I want what is best for you," Bethany lovingly stated. "Sometimes what is best for us can be hard, something we don't choose, like your separation from Nero. He caused you to leave. Otherwise, you would have continued to take advantage of him and all he was continually doing for you, with nothing coming back to him in return."

"You have no idea what was truly going on with Nero. There is always more to the story," Clare shot back.

"I'm sure that's true, but God is moving the pieces of our lives all the time for His good purposes. He wants what is best for us, and sometimes that is different from our plan. It is our job to learn to love Him and his plan, regardless of what we want."

"The way you talk about God makes it sound so easy. Just give it all to Him and move on. That sounds a bit fatalistic, don't you think? What about our ability to choose? Do we lose that too?"

"Oh my no, you always have the freedom of choice. You pick which doctor to see, and you choose whether or not to love God. He doesn't force you."

Bethany sat peacefully composed beneath an enormous family photo—all of them pictured standing in a field of blooming wildflowers, dressed in pure white linen. Clare wanted to blurt out, "What do you know about hard things? Your life has always been perfect."

Instead, she left with her usual matter-of-fact expression of appreciation. "Thank you so much for your help. I will call Dr. Templeton, but I came here looking for the name of a doctor, not a spiritual counseling session. Don't try to change who I am. We're too far down the road for that."

Bethany smiled. "Clare, you asked the question. I simply gave you an honest answer."

CHAPTER 12

Animato—With spirit

Clive gently leafed through the musty Folio, studying the passages, feeling awed and humbled by the words. He was in the company of greatness, reading a sacred text, with its inspiration and warnings:

> *Chopin is unfortunate in his pupils. So many of them have died or given up their careers. G. Sand even believes he is in love with her daughter and has forbidden their continued study. Fortunately, I have had much better luck. Our relationship to our students may be a greater legacy than our compositions.*
> J. Brahms, 1840

Clive shuddered. He definitely didn't want to be one of those pupils like Chopin's. Clare deserved better. In her great unselfishness, she chose to give up the privileges of performing to share her knowledge and experience. Clive felt determined to help promote her name, even beyond her concert days. *May she be like Brahms, one of the fortunate ones with much better luck.* Winning the Tchaikovsky would bring acclaim to both student and teacher. Clare would be triumphant, celebrated, share the limelight. *I will make her name known beyond the virtuosity of her playing,* Clive thought.

But that incident in her studio the other day, what was going on in her head? *I need to get to know her better so she will have the freedom to tell me everything. Maybe I should ask her out to dinner after one of our piano lessons.*

Clive's wandering thoughts were abruptly interrupted by a knock on his door. "Clive, may I come in?" Anna asked.

Upon hearing Anna's voice, he hid the Folio for safekeeping, even though she knew about it. Entering with a triumphant look, she pounced on Clive's bed. "I have spoken to Papa and Mama. They bought it."

"What did you say?" Clive queried.

"I told them that I noticed you no longer ate your snack after school anymore."

"OK, that is a genuine genius observation." Clive wondered where this was going.

"I explained how I've been watching how little you're eating and I believe you're getting sick and we wouldn't want an anorexic pianist. It is slightly true. At dinner, you're moving your food around on your plate without eating it. After school, you never eat the snack that Mama leaves out for us. When we stop at the Westdale Café, you don't even finish your hot chocolate. What's going on with you and your eating habits anyway? You look like you're losing weight, which is something I need to do and you don't.

"This way, when you tell them about Clare, Papa and Mama will be relieved that it's only about her and not a serious illness. They will have to choose to help you out of concern for your well-being, rather than being furious over your deception. Pretty good, huh? Anna comes to the rescue of her tormented, artistic brother, once again."

Arms folded across her chest, he waited for her to clang her tin cup and demand payment for her services. "It might work. Thanks. It is something I can talk up when I tell them ... how the challenge of keeping this from them is affecting me physically. Not bad, Anna.

"I have something else to ask you, given that nerd biology brain of yours." Clive attempted to flatter his sister with the hope of getting some more information. "During a lesson with Clare the other day, she seemed to check out for a moment, float off, and then she said something to me like she was talking to someone else. This was more than daydreaming. It was like I wasn't even there. She was actually talking out loud to someone else. I think she said the name *Professor Rosenblith*, but I'm not sure. It was strange.

"I'd swear she didn't know who I was or where she was. She simply stared at me and went over to the bookshelf looking for something. She's never done anything like this before. What do you think could have been going on? Could she have had a stroke? A delusion?"

With the authority of the future doctor she hoped to become someday, Anna considered his questions. "The hippocampus is the part of the brain where memories are accessed. It is like a storage bin for our life experiences—where we've been and where we are. Clare may have some type of problem in that area, but there could be a million other causes. Is she having trouble speaking or getting words out? What else have you noticed?"

What he noticed more than anything about Clare, he withheld from Anna. Her hair illuminated by the sun coming through the studio windows, with its multiple colors of sable brown and frosted blond. How he loved the way her left pinkie curled upward when she played. He realized there could have been other noticeable symptoms, but his eyes focused mostly on her physical appearance, so he might have missed them. "This event was the first that stands out in my mind," Clive offered.

"Well, keep track of it by writing it down and tell me if anything else occurs. She probably should see a doctor, but I'm sure you don't want to suggest the idea to her."

Do I have that kind of relationship with her at this point? I don't think so. "No, it's not my place. She is my teacher, not my mother."

"She sounds like more than just a teacher to you."

"She is more than a teacher. Clare is more like a lifeline between the composers of the past, their music, and my future."

"Don't put too much stock in one person, Clive. This is your life and your music. If you had to do it without her, I'm sure you could. Now I need to get going on my homework."

With a quick high-five, Anna headed for her room, and Clive watched her bounce down the hall. He appreciated her smarts and creativity, but most of all her love. He truly believed she would do anything for him. Hopefully, he wouldn't have to ask her to do something extreme.

CHAPTER 13

Morendo—Dying away

D r. Templeton was unlike anything imaginable in a neurosurgeon. His waiting room made Clare feel as if she
was sitting in a Viennese salon. Tapping her heel to the beat of
Bach's *Partita in D minor* playing over the sound system, she
waited ... and waited.

"Clare Cardiff. Take a right and head down the hall, and then
take a right again into examining room C. Dr. Templeton will be
there momentarily. It won't be necessary to change your clothes.
Just wait to talk to the doctor," mumbled the nurse, whom she
recognized as the gruff, older one with too much makeup.

After previously completing the sterile parade of tests and
questionnaires, today's doctor visit would hopefully provide
some answers. "Take deep breaths. Everything will be fine," Clare
could hear Nero whispering before she walked on stage in those
early days. *Rest assured. Focus on the music.* Listen and wait, she
told herself as she closed her eyes and remembered.

In his blustering but gentle fashion, the corpulent, heavy-browed Dr. Templeton briskly knocked and entered, holding his stack of files like a textbook. Pulling out the sliding stool to sit down, he pushed his glasses higher on the bridge of his nose and looked up at Clare. He resembled a snowy owl stretching out his talons to retrieve his prey as he reached into the files. There was a long silence, except for the *Partita*, which had concluded at the exact moment he was about to speak, like an overture before the opening act.

"Bach wrote that toward the end of his life. He was only sixty-five. Such a pity he didn't live longer, don't you think?" Dr. Templeton asked.

Clare was never sure if this musical dialogue was for her benefit or perhaps he did this with all his patients. "How old are you, Clare? Was it fifty? You don't look a day over forty."

He had the medical charts and should have known her age. *False flattery*, Clare thought. "Well, I've seen this before in much younger people, but never in a musician of your caliber. This will be interesting," Dr. Templeton said, his voice tinged with a perceptible anxiety.

Clare waited, growing frustrated by his ambiguity. "Seen what before?" she asked, suddenly longing for the comfort of Nero's strong arms. She breathed in the stale air, hovering between the gaps in his words. As much as she needed to hear his diagnosis, she wanted the silence to continue and shield her from what Dr. Templeton was about to say.

"You are experiencing some memory loss. It could be early onset dementia, but I can't say with one hundred percent certainty. We are seeing it present in younger and younger patients these days. One of my most recent was only thirty-seven years old. I've even read reports of symptoms presenting as young as eighteen. There is much that can be done when it is identified at this early stage, so not to worry.

"You are in good hands here. There is a facility in the city at Central Memorial that has the most current memory care treatment center in our part of the country," the doctor continued. "The specialist there is a dear friend of mine. I will put you in touch with him. The bottom line is there is a great deal of hope for you to live a full life. Your music will help with that."

"I don't understand. *A full life*! What does that mean?"

"With early onset dementia, the disease progresses at different rates for each person. Let me explain a bit about what is going on inside your brain. Dementia is caused by a buildup of certain kinds of protein in the brain. The protein called amyloid turns into plaques that cut off and tangle the electrical circuits. This causes neurons to die off, often in bundles, so the brain begins to look like a highway with potholes and tumbleweeds all over the place.

"We are trying to learn what causes this plaque development. In your case, no one in your family has a history of dementia, so there isn't a known genetic contribution. We don't know yet why it happens."

Clare couldn't move. She felt cold, almost frozen and stiff, as though her limbs were steadily losing their life blood. "Does this mean I am going to die of Alzheimer's?" she asked.

"There is no need to jump to such a dramatic conclusion. We really can't tell if a person's brain has progressed to Alzheimer's unless we look at it posthumously. Although, a scanning technique for testing is in development right now. The research is moving so quickly, you should be very encouraged. There are new therapies you can undertake immediately. Your music is one of the best defenses against progression available to you. Music is not a cure, but it is an important part of maintaining the cognitive function you currently have."

Music as a defense? Clare imagined her mind as a battlefield, the basses warring against the treble clefs amidst the tumbleweeds, all fighting one another upon the score of her episodic memory. "How does my music act as a defense?" she asked, her voice cracking with nervousness.

"Cognitive and physical exercise both have a powerful impact on preserving those neurological connections. Music and memory work together in a way that recent research shows is lasting—and even healing—particularly for anyone who studied music in their younger years. To a degree, it is possible your music could save your brain. It could continue to bring you joy and meaning in life for a very long time, even when you might not be able to do other everyday tasks."

For the first time in years, Clare thought of her mother at the piano, playing those late-night hymns. She remembered learning how to play them while sitting on her lap. Even though she never practiced them, she could still play *Great Is Thy Faithfulness* to this day. The thought of only being able to play hymns, while her entire brain was rotting away inside her well-toned body, was making her shake slightly. "I want you to see Dr. Steinberg at Central Memorial. He is the authority on music therapy and cognitive function. He will put together a customized P.C.P. for you. Call him right away."

"What is a P.C.P.?"

"That stands for Personalized Care Plan. It is the latest approach in taking an offensive posture in the battle against memory loss. Not to worry, Clare. He's the best. He will take good care of you. You have much in your favor that many don't."

With a handshake and a wink, Dr. Templeton whisked out of examining room C with the lightness of someone about to embark upon a long-awaited vacation. There was no office music playing soothing strains of Bach at the moment. Clare wondered if the gruff nurse had turned it off to torment her even further.

Sitting on the examining table, immobilized and unable to get down, Clare thought of Nero. *I need to talk to him. He knows me. He'll know what I should do.*

Her heart beating in her eardrums seemed to get louder until the steady metronome of her own blood flow prompted the first step into her life as a statistic. She stopped to look at the poster of the old woman's expressionless face on the examining room wall. The poster read:

27 percent of Americans have a family member with Alzheimer's.

5.5 million Americans currently suffer from the disease.

That number will increase to 13.4 million over the next 50 years.

Have you been checked?

Without even thinking, she mechanically reached into her trench coat to put it on but then stopped. Rather than leave, she decided to sit for a few more minutes to digest Dr. Templeton's words. *If I just sit here a bit longer, maybe Dr. Templeton will wander in and say there's been a mistake. That diagnosis was meant for one of my other patients, Clare Thompson, not you. Please forgive me.* But after several hollow minutes passed, no one came into examining room C.

At the glass partition, the sunny young receptionist captured her attention. "Ms. Cardiff, would you like to make your next appointment now? Oh, I see Dr. Templeton has recommended you pay a visit to Dr. Steinberg. We can set that up for you, if you like."

"No, that won't be necessary. I'll take care of it myself. Thank you."

The walk down the beige hallway felt as though she were gliding across an airport's moving walkway. *The moving walkway is about to end. Please step off.* She could hear it in her head, the same message in the dozens of airports she had traversed throughout her career. Would she ever be able to fly again on her own? Or would she always need an escort—or nurse—to get her from one place to the next? *Am I going to be driven around in one of those confounded beeping carts like an invalid?*

Getting outdoors for air often had a mind-clearing effect, but attempting to remember where she parked the car took away some of the benefit. *What if I can't drive or cook? What if I won't be able to talk or read or make a phone call?* She took off her shoes to feel the pavement puddles and make sure she still had the neurological connection to her feet. Leaning forward, she gazed down into the gray, tepid water swirling around her toes. *Will I always be able to feel? Will my brain cut my body off piece by piece? What will be left?* Rain started pelting down as she aimlessly searched for the car. *I'm looking for a Honda. No, that was my first car. What car was I driving today?*

She checked her wallet for her driver's license and came across a picture of Nero. *I owe it to him to call. He'll be worried about me. He needs to know.* Written on a piece of paper in her wallet was the number of her license plate—WYJ 777. *Is that my license plate number? Seems easy enough to remember, but why can't I remember it?* The rain pounded as she realized she had left her raincoat in the examining room. She could come back and pick it up later. Finally, with the license plate visible, she made her way to the car. A mixture of rain and tears covered her cheeks.

Looking in the rearview mirror, she noticed her smeared mascara. *Will I look different? Will people stare and say, "Isn't that Clare Cardiff, the pianist? Oh my, look how she's changed."*

"Drive home the same way you always do. Turn on the wipers. Call Nero as soon as you get home," she said aloud. Talking out loud provided a sense of order behind the darkness of fear, which was determined to cloud over her.

The doctor had said there was hope for her to live "a full life." *Who will take care of me when I become worse? There is only one person who always has taken care of me.* "Just take deep breaths. Everything will be fine," Nero had reassured her before so many concerts.

Clare forced herself to listen to Beethoven's **Sixth Symphony** to calm down. While her quivering hand tried to get the music into the CD player, her mind was ringing with an infernal comingling of Smetana and Stravinsky. *Turn up the music. Drown out*

Smetana. Beethoven is what you need right now. Didn't Smetana die of dementia—or was it Stravinsky?

Pastoral strings were singing in her car. She could picture the audience at Carnegie Hall, already on its feet, welcoming Clare back for the encore. Her taffeta ball dress billowed in a creamy cloud before each step as she returned to the stage. Triumphant, she played *Rage Over a Lost Penny* while Nero stood, stage left, smiling and waiting for her.

CHAPTER 14

Accelerando—Becoming faster

After dinner, Claude returned to his study. Taking the score from his desk, he walked over to the antique music stand, placed it in the proper spot, and raised the stand to his preferred height. He reached for the remote and turned on the Berlin Philharmonic's recording of Dvorak's *Slavonic Dances*. Pretending not to notice that Julia had just crept into the room, he leaned over to cue the imaginary violin section. The Chicago Philharmonic would be performing several pieces by Dvorak as part of its Spring Concert Series, and it was Claude's practice to listen to the new recordings at home, well in advance. He knew Julia loved watching him conduct from behind, especially when he didn't know she was there, but this time he could sense her presence behind him.

During a break between movements, she teased him by letting out a cough worthy of a bronchial attack. Startled, Claude circled around and laughed, muting the music with the remote. How he hated those coughers during a concert, and his wife knew it.

"Sorry to interrupt. Claude, we should ask Clive about his weight loss," Julia began. "He isn't eating. What Anna told us is true. I've noticed it too. I have some friends at work who specialize in eating disorders and could offer some insight. But we should talk to Clive first."

"That all seems a bit farfetched to me. Boys don't get eating disorders. That's a girl problem, isn't it?" Claude surmised. "He's caught up in his music and preparing for the competition. He's too busy to eat." Mozart and many others suffered the same problem and survived. Claude was somewhat envious of a musical place so consuming that one forgets the daily round.

"He will be fine. No need to talk to your vigilante friends at the NIH. Let's not bother Clive with it tonight. He'll be practicing for at least another hour, and bedtime does not pair well with entering tender territory. I promise to keep an eye on his eating habits for the next few days and see if I notice any change."

With a click of the remote, Claude turned his back to his wife, but Julia had successfully distracted him from the music. *Does Clive have the stamina to endure what is ahead? He is already very thin, and we are just getting started. Anna can be a bit of an alarmist, but if a teenage girl is talking about severe weight loss, should I be paying more attention?* Claude forced these thoughts into the background and returned to dancing his baton in tempo with the Slavic folk driven strains of Antonin Dvorak.

)(

Assuming it was Katrina at this time of night, Nero wrestled his way over to the house phone with his glass of Scotch in hand. At first, there was stillness on the line and then a breath. Figuring it was a wrong number, he leaned forward to hang up when a small voice came across the line.

"Nero. It's Clare."

After almost eight months, she was finally reaching out to

him. He took his seat by the piano. "I hope you aren't calling to tell me you want your mother's piano, because you can't have it. I've been enjoying it too much."

Laughing, she replied, "Wonderful. Are you playing Mother's Bechstein?"

"You might say that. I play it at night occasionally." He leaned over to see if the permanent marker had concealed all the nicks from throwing his drinking glasses against the piano. "How are you doing, Clare?"

After a lengthy fermata of silence, Nero heard a deep sigh. "That's why I'm calling. I'm facing a bit of a challenge, and I'm wondering if you might be able to come out for a short visit."

"What kind of challenge?" Clare intimating she needed him indicated something was wrong. "Are you all right?"

"I'm holding my own right now."

"Tell me what is going on, Clare." Another long silence, but this time he heard music in the background. "Where are you right now? Are you in your studio?" He felt an impulsive rush to jump into his truck and drive to her rescue, but he knew better. Make her wait.

"No, I'm in my apartment. It's nice. Can you come and see me here?"

"It's been eight months without a word and you are asking me to come see you. Isn't that a bit melodramatic? Why now?"

She didn't want to tell him. Going from renowned pianist to mentally incapable during one phone call was too unattractive. "Have you talked to Bethany and Tim?" Clare asked.

"No, why would I?"

"I think they mentioned you called them over Christmas, but I'm not sure." After four glasses of Scotch on the rocks, Nero didn't remember calling them.

"Today, I received a troubling medical diagnosis." Clare didn't want to say too much over the phone. "When I was in the doctor's office, I wanted you there with me. I'm not looking to move back to the farm. I'm simply asking if you could come out for a weekend visit."

He paused to make her wait a little longer. There was certainly nothing keeping him at the farm. "I do have a lot going on with my work right now, but I could get away for a weekend. When were you thinking?"

Surprised to hear he was working, Clare tried to affirm his artistic endeavors. "That's great to hear you're working so our separation is going well for you? Is that right?"

"That's right."

"Well, I'm sorry to interrupt your productivity, but could you come out next weekend?"

"Let me check my schedule and get back to you. Is this medical condition life threatening?" Nero had to ask *the* question.

Picturing herself wandering around the farm after dark in her nightgown, completely lost and subjected to coyotes, Clare replied, "No, it's not life threatening. Let me know if you can come. Thanks." She hung up without waiting for a goodbye.

Nero couldn't begin to imagine the steely Clare ailing. He had only seen her suffering one day in all their years together. That was the morning on the bathroom floor after her miscarriage. Two days later, she was leading a master class at The Julliard School. Her usually collected voice sounded shaky over the phone. There was more to it than she was revealing.

On a personal note, he knew the separation wasn't working out. Sleep eluded him. There were more mornings when he had a drink in hand before ten in the morning, rather than a lump of clay. The house was unkempt and the maid was unreliable and unapproachable. She was a good-looking, strong Ukrainian, but a tad too muscular for his taste. At least when she came to the house, she cleaned the place like a tornado. Then, before he could convince her to stay for a drink, she would utter some lame excuse about having to get right home to her family and leave.

The silence of the house without Clare was a weight upon

him, like shackles holding him in a static state. Listening to CDs of her music made it worse. Her voice was in her piano-playing, but she wasn't speaking to him. She was speaking to them, and how he hated them. If Clare needed him for a short visit, as she called it, she might need him for a lifetime, depending upon her condition. *Worth a try*, he thought.

Going into the closet, Nero took the lid off the leather trunk and gently lifted Johannes from his nest of blankets. He cradled the clay child, so cold and still, in his arms. "I might be going to see Mommy. Would you like to come with me? She would be so delighted to see you. You must miss her. I know she misses you."

The lifeless baby's blue eyes stared blankly at him. Nero felt as one with the baby, united by emptiness and unfulfilled stillness, and at the same time, a longing for hope and a future with Clare. As they sat together on the closet floor and watched the moon rise high above the garden's dormant flowering quince and lilac, the moonlight cast a deep shadow into the closet. For the first time in many months, Nero slept in peace upon the cedar planks of the closet floor, Johannes nestled in his arms.

)(

"You will be proud of me. I'm making progress," Clive confided in Clare as they walked hand in hand down the brick street toward Sylvie's Bistro for dinner. His step was livelier, almost buoyant, for the feeling of her hand knitted into his.

Apart from intense collaboration at the keyboard, their Friday night dinners brought a freedom in conversation about his competition repertoire. Together, over lentil stew, they could explore ideas percolating in each other's mind without the piano keys for demonstration. This newfound freedom brought intellectual heft and depth to their relationship.

Clive had decided to take hold of Clare's hand the first time they went out for dinner. He wanted more intimacy, and this innocent first step was one he was comfortable with. They had already held hands in Clare's studio, upon her initiative, so he didn't expect a rebuff. His mind wandered to what it would be like to hold on to more of her, just a little bit at a time, moving from fingertips to wrists to ... He was so much bigger in size that he found himself intrigued by the idea of swallowing her up in both of his arms, enwrapping her. Clare's voice broke into his fantasy.

"The deadline for you to tell your mother and father about us is now past." She spoke the words with a stern gaze over her menu.

"I know this has taken much longer than you demanded, and I appreciate your patience with me. I went ahead and enlisted Anna's help in preparing the road with Mama and Papa. She has created the perfect framework for my telling them about us. I'm confident it's working. They are ready to receive the news about us studying together and should be receptive above all else. In fact, I'm thinking of telling them this weekend."

Clare didn't move, continuing to stare from across the top of her menu. Her blue eyes nearly matched the Mediterranean color scheme of Sylvie's Bistro.

"The Folio has been a great source of insight for me," said Clive. "I have read about Clara and Robert Schumann and how they moved forward in their relationship, despite her father's disapproval. Do you remember the copied page from Clara Schumann's diary on their wedding day? She wrote, 'My whole self was filled with gratitude to Him who had brought us safely over so many rocks and precipices to meet at last.'

"Isn't that interesting, Clare? She is expressing gratitude to God for bringing her and Robert together. Do you think our finding each other could also be from God? I mean, what are the chances of my seeing your small, colorful advertisement on a bulletin board in Westdale Conservatory? I haven't thought about God in a long time. Do you think it is possible He could be a part of all that is going on in our music and studying together?"

"My sister, Bethany, believes in God. She believes He cares about us so much that He governs what happens in our lives. We know that many of the great works were inspired by the composers' reverence of God. Look at Bach's *Saint Matthew Passion*, Handel's *Messiah*, *The Creation* Oratorio, the *Resurrection* Symphony by Mahler. No doubt these works honor the Creator, but does He arrange our day? I don't think so. There is too much tragedy in the world for Him to care about trivial things like a note on a bulletin board.

"I'm glad to hear you are ready to tell your parents. The time is long past due. We had our first conversation about this back in February, and look how long you have managed to avoid the inevitable. We are all responsible for our relationships, Clive, and as I've said before, honesty in all relationships is best."

Looking at Clare, in her short khaki trench coat and Afghani scarf, he couldn't help but believe there was something more to their relationship than the Tchaikovsky Piano Competition. Could he ever be in an intimate relationship with a woman who was so much older than he? Could he marry a woman in her fifties? Was that even possible?

The two of them never talked about her personal life. Clare didn't wear a wedding ring. There weren't any photos in her studio depicting close relationships. The only family member she talked about was her sister, Bethany, and her family.

As he read about her concerts from clippings in the library, it became clear that Clare's life had been entirely about music. There was nothing else. No husband. No children. Perhaps God had been saving Clare for a future with him.

Clive reached across the white paper tablecloth for both of her diminutive hands. How well they meshed. Her porcelain, bisque hands fit practically inside the palms of his. They were the black keys and the white keys together, and if God was arranging their musical union, as he did for Clara and Robert Schumann, it could be glorious. The thought of God having a hand in their relationship was a new revelation of hope, theirs being not only a musical relationship but a divinely ordered one.

This new insight electrified him. He wanted to lean across the table and kiss her but decided a public place would be inappropriate. Anyone in close proximity might recognize her. No, he would save their first kiss for a private moment where it would be theirs alone.

CHAPTER 15

Interval—The distance between two pitches

*T*he *New York Times*, a pot of hot coffee, and WFMT broadcasting the Metropolitan Opera from New York— usually Sunday mornings were Clive's restful time of the week, a solo respite when he and his family relaxed, enjoying each other's company. By ritual, the family had gathered in the library and stretched out in the sun like contented cats upon the floor pillows. It was their version of Sabbath, but Clive was about to ruin the mood.

With great respect, Clive softly broke the silence. "Mama and Papa, may I ask you a question?"

Claude and Julia looked up from their *Times* Sunday magazine. His formality caught them a bit off-guard.

"Have you ever been drawn into something so deeply that you forgot about your normal life in some respects?" Clive inquired.

Julia jumped at the topic. "Yes, when I was doing my doctoral work and studying for my oral exams, I lived on coffee and bread. I ignored the other food groups. I almost forgot about water until the coffee started dehydrating me. Then I expanded my unhealthy menu to coffee, bread, and water. It was dreadful. I'm lucky I didn't end up in the hospital. Let's hope you aren't doing something like that. Anna pointed out that you have lost some weight since you began perfecting your repertoire for the competition. We have noticed too. Are you feeling all right?" his mother asked with unusual concern in her voice.

"I have lost my appetite a little, but there's more to it than the competition." Clive took a deep breath. "I've been studying with an additional teacher, besides Mr. K. Her name is Clare Cardiff. We've been working together since last fall."

Like a bedsheet, Claude methodically folded his Sunday magazine and put it down on the coffee table. "Clare Cardiff, the pianist? She lives out east, in Boston I believe. I don't understand. How could you possibly know her?"

Clive's hands began to sweat with the coffee, the sun on his back, and his father's calm questioning. "She's been here on a sabbatical of sorts. I found her at Westdale Conservatory. I've been studying with her every week, in addition to my regular studies with Mr. Koussevitsky."

"Why have you gone and done this without consulting us? Does Mr. Koussevitsky know about this? His feelings would be deeply hurt," Claude said. "Your mother and I thought your progress was due to his excellent teaching. You were deceptive in leading us to believe this was the case, praising Mr. K yourself."

Papa's disappointment swelled. He wanted answers. "You have never gone behind our back like this, and clearly it's not good for you. You look like a skeleton. Is this due to your carrying on this deceit for months?" Then Mama chimed in.

"Yes, I am shocked. You have never hidden anything from us. How can this be?"

Clive soon realized he would not be able to tell them all he wanted to say. "Mama, Papa, all my life I have always obeyed your musical construction of my life, doing what you both wanted, which has been good for me. For some reason—maybe even a supernatural one—I saw an advertisement on the board at West-dale and was moved by everything within me to call the phone number.

"I swear I didn't know it was Clare Cardiff. Her name wasn't even on the paper, only a phone number. I can't explain it. It was like something other than myself stepped in, a movable force that made me investigate."

"Don't be ridiculous," his mother snapped. "We are all re-sponsible for our own actions. Nothing made you do it. Given the musician your father is, did you not think he would want to know about this and have some input? How dare you go behind our back, when we have given you nothing but the best your whole life. Was that not good enough for you?"

Anna weighed in, trying to diffuse the heat of the exchange. "Mama, don't look at it like Clive was going behind your back; try to see it as his way of giving you his best. He wanted to do this for you, not just himself. He knows how much winning this competition means to you."

Julia glared at Anna. "You stay out of this, young lady, or I'll excuse you from this room."

Clive could tell his mother's emotions were preempting a graceful finish to their conversation, so he appealed to Papa more directly. "Papa, Clare is a jewel. Her depth of knowledge of the Romantics is like nothing I have ever seen. She has firsthand ex-perience with the composers. It's special, secret knowledge hand-ed down by a genealogy of teachers, a family line going back to Brahms. I can't get that insight from anyone else."

"No one has firsthand knowledge of the composers but those living at the time. Many have third- or fourth-hand generational knowledge, but not first," Claude argued. "I am sad that you have gone ahead and done this without telling us, especially since Mr. Koussevitsky has always been a gifted musician and teacher for you all these years. To me, it sounds like you might be a bit too enamored with Ms. Cardiff. I believe it would be best for you to take a break from your studies together.

"It's time for you to work solely with Mr. Koussevitsky and me," he stated matter-of-factly. "We need to begin talking about the role of the orchestra in both the Tchaikovsky and the Chopin concertos. We should listen to recordings together and analyze the interpretations, Bernstein's 1949 *Deutsche Grammophon* being my favorite.

"Remember when you were a little boy and we would go to rehearsals together?" his father asked. "You would talk incessantly about the music in the car on the way home. We should do that again, before you leave us and go out on your own."

Clive felt confused. His parents didn't understand what was at stake. Clare was slipping away with the silent stroke of a baton in the master's hand, ushering in the violins.

"Papa, you talked to Mr. Koussevitsky when it was time to decide if I should do the competition or not. Will you do the same with Clare? Then you can hear how our work has defined me. Please get her professional opinion."

Claude looked into the hollow, pleading eyes of his son. "That won't be necessary. Looking at you is enough to convince me. Studying with Clare Cardiff is not the best for you right now, and I want only the best for my son.

"I look forward to working with you. We'll get started on Monday. Let's meet with Mr. Koussevitsky and formulate our plan for the remaining time before the competition. We don't want to waste one minute. We will trust you to tell Clare Cardiff that your meetings together have concluded.

"I do remember when she played the Rachmaninoff second concerto with the orchestra in the spring of 1989. Her hands were so small and delicate; they looked like fine china, but the power within her was immense. She was such a talent at that young age, and a fine musician. I know she will understand our decision."

With his thoughtful declaration finished, Claude reached for his newspaper, methodically unfolded it, and placed it in front of his face, a silent pronouncement that the conversation was over.

Without another word, Clive left the library and headed for his room. Locking the door and reaching for the Folio, he felt weakened, like he was unable to surgically stop the bleeding. His lifeline—to music and love—had been severed in a single, shortsighted assessment. *How could Papa disagree, knowing all Clare could offer him?* Then Clive came upon an entry of Robert Schumann's written as a fictional story by him as a teenager:

She rushed through the cemetery to read an inscription on the gravestone. 'Here lies a broken heart.' Smiling, she sat down on the grave. A skeleton came and sat down next to her, then threw its arm around her. 'You want a kiss?' she asked shyly. The skeleton laughed, gave her an icy kiss, and left. 'I must have sinned,' she cried out and went into the church where the skeleton was playing a waltz at the organ.

Here lies a broken heart. Clive wondered if this epitaph would be on his gravestone too. Should he go to synagogue and talk to a rabbi? Was his sin so great? Nothing serious ever happened between them. He did love her, and love is never wrong when conspired for the expression of a greater end.

Having read the Folio, Clive knew how Robert and Clara Schumann's love story ended. His own father was getting in the way, just like Clara Schumann's. He and Clare could not repeat their fate. For the first time in many years, he felt like praying or running away. Instead, he turned back to the pages of the Folio. Clive knew the answers were there to be found in what was his Bible. Robert and Clara Schumann did get married. They triumphed over Clara's father in court and won, so there was hope. She gave him the Folio so he could learn from it, to show him his way forward. *I can't afford to lose her.* With the manuscript under his desk lamp's dim glow, Clive read on, desperately searching within his musical family's colorful past for a way to keep Clare in his life.

CHAPTER 16

Dissonance—Notes that when sounded simultaneously
cause tension

Nero pressed the grimy white doorbell button. Cardiff #416. *This can't be her place?* Standing outside, he studied the landscaping. *A dump,* he thought, *surely Clare could afford something better than this.* There was a decent arrangement of serviceberries and hearty boxwood. The etiolated shoots of the daffodils were fighting their way through last fall's matted leaves, which had still not been raked. *At least some money went into what they've planted on the outside,* he observed.

Nero studied his image in the glare of the security camera glass. He saw the same old potter he had been looking at for the past several months, rumpled, faded, and alone. At least for Clare he shaved for the occasion. Ring the bell again. No answer. He told her what time his flight was arriving at the airport. She should be at home.

As a young student with a backpack came out the door, Nero quickly swept inside. Apartment 416 should be fairly easy to find. Ascending the stairs with alacrity, he hoped the mini-workout would put some blood in his cheeks and give him a healthy glow. To see him looking so well would no doubt please Clare. It was eleven thirty and he hadn't taken a sip of Scotch, an hour and a half past his first drink-of-the-day time.

Her front door had a wreath of dried rosemary on it. The Victorians believed rosemary was a symbol of remembrance. *How fitting*, he thought. Lifting the metal door knocker, he let it fall. The sound was empty, with no response from the other side. Clare had refused to give him her phone number. He was definitely not going to call Bethany and ask for information. The need for a drink suddenly began to tighten its grip on him.

Nero determined it would be best to take a walk around this quaint suburb and find the closest music school. He forced himself to resist taking a drink until he found Clare. Walking the streets with his duffle bag, he wondered how she could live in such a drab-looking place. Westdale was so plain and ordinary, surrounded by school buses and tons of students. All of them seemed to be holding paper coffee cups conveying profound quotations like, "Love is the gentle art of being." *How tedious*, Nero thought.

Turning toward the Westdale campus, he asked one of the coffee-cup-carrying students where the conservatory might be located. Nero figured Clare would probably be there. The student couldn't have been older than eighteen, but her whitened smile was extremely attractive against her olive skin. She pointed toward the colonial-pillared building at the end of the brick walkway. This building would be more in keeping with Clare's aesthetic tastes than the rest of Westdale. He imagined her in a small studio with a window view of the front lawn, bookcases overflowing with music and her collection of rare manuscripts and biographies.

Nero checked the faculty roster board, but Clare's name wasn't there. *No surprise*, he thought. Clare would be clueless about teaching piano and never expressed interest in doing so.

Still, there was a hint of Clare in these halls. Closing his eyes, he took in a deep breath, hoping to catch a scent of memory. It came to him ... New England Conservatory, where he and Clare first met.

As another student emerged from a tiny room with a single upright piano inside, he decided to try a little harder to locate Clare. "Is there a teacher here by the name of Cardiff?" Nero asked.

"Yes, she has a studio up on the top floor, in the rented section of the building."

How serendipitous it felt to picture Clare, the teacher, receiving her old, careworn pupil unexpectedly. Turning to the right at the top of the stairs, he saw the wind chimes she had taken down from their Japanese maple prior to leaving the farm. He had missed their nightly song this past winter. He was amused, though, that she hung them out where no breeze could blow their music into being. Only the brush of a hand could elicit their melody in this windless hall. Standing in front of the painted door, he was tempted to smash his fist into their tiny bells, breaking them from their precarious post at the top of the door. That would make for a grand entrance, but his impulse was subdued by the sound of her voice, talking to a student, on the other side of the door.

At least he could knock with some fervor and rhythm to amuse her. He chose *Beethoven's Fifth* as his pronouncement. Wishing he had brought Clare some flowers, Nero listened to the silence on the other side of the door and then the movement of her tiny, wooden clogs coming toward him.

"Nero, what are you doing here?" She looked smaller than he remembered. Perhaps teaching had erased some of her prideful stature.

"Clare, I'm here because you called and asked me to come." Her eyes were the same, though, reminding him of an ocean of stormy gray and blue like Joseph Turner's seascapes. Plenty of foam upon those waves; he could see the sea churning and he felt a surge of desire to ride her tumultuous waves.

"You said you were coming this afternoon."

"No, I actually said my plane would land at ten this morning. I was expecting you to be at your apartment, but you weren't. I've been wandering around this cozy little suburb ever since."

Disarmed, she invited him in and changed the subject. "This is Clive Serkin, one of my students. Clive, this is Nero Cardiff."

Clive quietly moved his pale frame off the bench toward Nero and extended his hand. "It's nice to meet you, sir. Are you Clare's brother?"

"My pleasure to meet you too. I'm pleased to see Clare is teaching. Clare doesn't have any brothers. I'm her husband."

Clive abruptly stepped backward from their handshake, as though he'd been stung by a wasp, causing his hand to recoil. Nero watched him grow deathly pale before his eyes, almost transparent. Clive sank down onto the piano bench.

Clare turned away from Nero to sit next to Clive on the bench. With the careful touch of a mother ready to apply a bandage, she offered an explanation. "Nero and I have been separated since I came to Westdale. I never mentioned him because I thought our separation was final, but I invited him out for a short visit to help me with a few things. There is no reason to worry. I'm staying and he's leaving after the weekend. We have some unresolved business to address with each other."

Confused by Clare's need to explain anything to this young man, Nero stared at the frail boy, who looked to be diminishing with each passing second. As Clive crossed his arms over his stomach, Nero noticed the enormous size of his hands. They clung to his sides with the fierceness of a prizefighter protecting himself from searing body blows in the ring. He was bending over, with his head almost leaning on the piano's music stand, as though he couldn't bring himself to look up at Nero.

"Clive, why don't we talk further about this later? A break

at this point will serve you well. You need some time to reflect about where we are headed and how we are going to get there, given your father's response. You really shouldn't have come today. Now is a good time for a break."

Nero noticed Clare's arm around the withering young man's shoulder, physically easing Clive up off the bench. *Why is Clare coddling this boy like a child?* Then she helped him with his coat like a mother would do for a five-year-old heading off to kindergarten. *The boy can't be much of a pianist*, Nero mused. *He couldn't even put on his own coat. He's probably disabled or autistic. How noble of Clare to work with him—such altruism.* As he quietly closed the door, Nero heard Clive brush the wind chimes on the other side, followed by the pianissimo of his footsteps down the stairs.

"Are all your students so responsive?" Nero asked, chiding her with his best whimsical smile.

To his delight, Clare came forward, hugging and hanging on to him until the last chime outside the door became silent. Her touch had always been able to suspend time. The quietness of the conservatory's top floor allowed him to hear the morning song of the finches outside her studio window. His beautiful Clare made music up here in the trees, he reflected.

As they came apart from each other, Nero could see tears spill over her fine-lined lower eyelids. "It's good to see you, Clare. I've missed you," he confessed. "Truthfully, not much pottery has been made since you left. My life has drifted through days and nights of wondering about us. I often think about how we are going to exit this life and what we will leave behind; basically banal, existential musings occupy my days without you."

Like the student in her studio moments before, Clare now seemed unable to speak, incongruous with the setting and purpose of a piano teacher. The quietude of Clare's spirit disturbed him.

"Clare, tell me what is wrong. Why have you brought me out

here?"

She hesitated. "You are the only person I can tell at this point. I don't know what to do," Clare began, confessing her helplessness. She sat down on the small loveseat in her studio and patted the cushion next to her, urging Nero to join her. Clare let out a long sigh and then slumped forward with her chin in her hands. Nero could see she didn't want to share the burden of what she was carrying with him so he urged her on.

"Go on, Clare. You can tell me. I know you better than anyone else."

"Back before I even left the farm, I started noticing some changes. I felt different inside my head. I'm talking about my thought process and also what I was doing, you know, how I was doing what I've always been able to do. The music was mostly all there, but the everyday behaviors, like laundry, were not. I couldn't remember if I'd done laundry that day, and then when I'd see the basket of folded clothes in my bedroom, I wondered who put them there. I even kept finding my car keys in the freezer.

"After getting the name of a doctor from Bethany, I went in for a number of tests. The diagnosis he gave me was a bit vague, but he recommended that I see a specialist in the city right away to develop a Personalized Care Plan. I'm what he called 'potentially shortened,' not 'terminal.' He said I may have early onset dementia." Clare could only whisper the last three words. Saying them aloud placed her in the category of the indigent, which was a placement contrary to everything in her life she had worked for.

Nero leaned backward, sinking into the puckered fabric of the couch. Trying to say anything in response felt futile. What could he say? *Dementia? Clare didn't have any dementia in her family history.* Her mother died of a heart attack, and her father, although absent from Clare's adult life, faithfully took care of the farm, maintained the tractors, and planted the crops, into his eighties. Clare was a musical prodigy. A brain like hers shouldn't be susceptible to something as common and frightful as dementia.

Nero was glad that he hadn't stopped for a drink on his journey to find Clare, but he needed one desperately now. Summoning all sentiment and reason, he wasted no time in igniting his
campaign to get her back to the farm.

"Clare, you should come home for a while and rest. Restore
yourself. Like you told your student, it would be good for you to
reflect upon things for a time and then come back here. It also
would be prudent to get another opinion from a reliable doctor
at Johns Hopkins in Baltimore. We don't know anything about
these Midwestern crackpots. This guy, Dr. Templeton, could be
all wrong. Who is this doctor anyway? You might be fine or it
might be something else.

"I would be willing to help you go through those steps so you
don't have to keep track of everything. Continuing to live on your
own doesn't seem like the wisest thing right now."

Nero began to sense his upper hand. Their relationship could
take on a new dimension and depth because for once she would
actually need him. He implored her, "Come home for a time, long
enough to get a real opinion. Your students can make it without
you for a few weeks, right?"

Admittedly touched by Nero's earnest appeal, Clare imagined
the therapeutic benefits of his suggestion. As the farm blossomed
into spring, a few weeks with Nero could steady her anxious
thoughts. The time away from Clive would help him separate
from her by virtue of necessity. Clive could continue with Mr.
Koussevitsky, while she explored her options and eventually returned to him. It would also give Claude and Julia Serkin a chance
to recover from Clive's shocking news. Even the best mothers go
out of town every now and then, Clare thought.

"I will never stop loving you," Nero confessed. "I will try to be
the man you need me to be for as long as it takes. I know I've said
this before, but I can do it. I'm healthier now than when you left.
I've been working on it. You can lean on me for strength until we

know what is actually going on. Then, when you're ready, I will release you—free as a bird to fly back to this stale, concrete enclave—if that turns out to be what you want."

Trusting Nero was not a given, but believing in herself at this point was less reliable. "I agree. Another medical opinion would be worthwhile.

"Mother's piano is still at the farm, so I could practice in the midst of the dogwood blossoms while you work in the garden and your shed," Clare said. "I need to warn you, though, it will only be for a short time, because Clive—the student who left earlier—is brilliant. He is heading for the Tchaikovsky Piano Competition, and my responsibility is to prepare him for that endeavor. I would need to be back in three weeks at the latest."

Nero heard the commanding tone in Clare's voice and knew she had not slipped as much as he had hoped. He remembered their early days at the farm when her music propelled him to create sculpture and pottery. He wanted his muse back. His imagination still clung to those tenuous shapes of hope and future. Ephemeral and unformed, they might now have the chance to spin again upon his potter's wheel.

CHAPTER 17

Pathetique—With great emotion

Lengthening shadows from the setting sun on Brookline's wet streets cast a veil over the city, in what felt to Clive like a funeral pall. As he walked, Clive pondered Clare's marital status. *Clare married?* So little he knew of her, yet she entrusted everything to him in the form of her Folio, her *hochme.* Hers was a wisdom that was almost supernatural. *Clare married? How could she deceive me like this?* They had held hands, gone out for dinner. She appeared to be so full of joy in their time working together side by side. Clive was in love with a married woman, who transported him places his soul had never been. It was adultery of the mind, beyond distraction. Or maybe even more than that.

Walking without purpose, his steps took him on a tour through the memories of his childhood home. Clive passed the Academia Preschool, where he performed his first concert at age three. Onward, he strolled by Brookline Academy, with its inner-city artistic mentoring program, dear to his heart. He looked for comfort in these memories and found none.

Turning toward uptown, he reached Westdale College, where his adventures with Clare secretly began. His school years unfolded in darkening phases of limestone, leading him down the street to the Jewish neighborhood, toward temple. There, he had celebrated his bar mitzvah and learned Torah and Talmud—once important words, now forgotten. If it were not for his mother's insistence on placing music schooling first, Papa's religion and faith might have been a much larger part of his life. As he continued to wrap his thoughts around his predicament, he began to feel sick to his stomach. *Clare married? How could I have not known this? There must have been a hint somewhere, a photograph, something. What a fool I've been. I actually believed she cared about me.*

After stopping to throw up in a gas station restroom, he stood on the curb of Boynton Street across from Temple Bethel. He could hear his bar mitzvah music, still pounding in his memory. Papa was so happy that day. Closing his eyes, he remembered how they all were dancing the *hora*, even Mama, laughing as she circled the dance floor.

Tears began to pour down his hollow cheeks. Bending forward toward the curb, Clive felt like he was falling into the rivulet of water pitching its way down the curbside. Dizziness gripped him. He lowered his enormous hand into the water to steady himself, watching the stream wash over his fingers. He gently placed the other hand in the runoff. Both hands, magnified in size because of the water, took on the appearance of clear glass. The chill of the spring rain illuminated his delicate blue veins. Kneeling on the curb, Clive felt paralyzed, unable to withdraw his palms from the gutter.

Round-toed, black leather shoes came into view in the street, only a step away from his bent-over frame. A warm, gentle hand reached under his chin to lift his head. "Clive Serkin. What are you doing out here in the rain? Come inside and get warm." Rabbi Sherveen inserted his strong arm into the damp crook of Clive's elbow. He escorted him across the street and up the steps of Temple Bethel.

The oaken wood of the floor and seats mixed with the twilight. The smell of the ancient room was familiar and warm, like a blanket. He was surprised how much he missed this room of his youth. Rabbi Sherveen walked down the aisle, leaving Clive alone. In front, the Ten Commandments, carved into walnut, looked down on him with their angular Roman numerals proclaiming each law. *Thou shalt not commit adultery. Honor thy father and mother. Thou shalt have no other Gods before me.* Every word penetrated his soul.

Rabbi Sherveen returned with a wrapping of towels, two of which he placed around Clive's shoulders and over his lap, and the third towel he wrapped around both of his hands. Sitting next to each other for an inestimable time, the two waited in silence. The twilight eclipsed into shafts of darkness. The only sound— the high-pitched hiss of radiators churning heat—caused the floors to crack and groan in accompaniment.

Once again, the rabbi reached out to take Clive's now warm hands. His steely beard gave him the appearance of Moses. "You have been blessed with the gift of these hands. Today these hands were in the gutter. Why?"

Unable to look at the rabbi, Clive felt his silent authority and gentle presence extract the words he did not want to say. "I have fallen in love with a married woman. A musician. My teacher. She did not tell me she is married, until today."

Rabbi Sherveen's eyes took in Clive's limp, broken frame, capable of such beauty and rendered unto ashes. "King David loved a married woman, and he killed her husband, yet he was God's anointed."

Clive remembered the story. "I have not killed her husband. I only met him today."

"I certainly hope you don't kill her husband," the rabbi said with an empathetic twinkle in his eye.

"You need to leave this woman, your teacher, and cling to

the God of Israel for strength. Return to him as David did when Nathan brought him to the awareness of his sin. It has been too long you have been away in the world of music. Come to temple. Seek the Lord and he will restore you. One day, Clive, you will be able to say as David did, 'Who am I, O Sovereign Lord, and what is my family, that you have brought me this far?'

"You must leave this teacher and hold fast to what is good. Your music is at home, Clive, with your father."

Studying Rabbi Sherveen's face, Clive saw no judgment, only wisdom and compassion. How long he had been absent from so many things dear to him. He rose and extended his hand to the rabbi. "Thank you for seeing me out in the street today."

Rabbi Sherveen smiled as he took in Clive's full height, remembering him as a small boy coming of age. "Your bar mitzvah was years ago, but today you must become a man in a different way."

Clive felt he should bow to a great teacher, like he did when his studies with Clare first began. He resisted doing so. Instead, he firmly held the rabbi's hand in both of his, lingering in the sensation of his steadfastness and wisdom, before turning toward the door.

X

Papa and Saul were having the time of their lives, stepping outside to smoke cigars together and then yelling from the porch, "Let it sing, but with limpidity." While he pressed his way through Scriabin's *Etude in D-sharp minor,* Clive wondered, *what does limpidity mean?* He didn't even bother to ask.

They often sat in the two chairs of Mr. K's front room, listening for an hour before they would say anything. Rarely would they interrupt his music. When they did, the two of them propelled each other, playing off their combined insights.

"Good. That's good, but inhabit the music more," Mr. K would exhort. "Put all of yourself into it. There seems to be something you are holding back. Hold nothing back."

Papa would counter, "The repertoire for the Tchaikovsky is not for the faint of heart or those with extreme technical precision. Technique is not enough. You must give yourself to it fully—body, mind, and soul."

Then Mr. K would follow, "Yes, Claude is right. This is mostly Russian music for a Russian audience. You're speaking to them in their own language. You must be more Russian than they are. Russian first for this jury. Jewish second. They can sniff in an instant when the soul is not in it."

Together, the two men were determined to deliver a fully prepared Clive to Moscow. From the time he was fourteen and won the Michaels Award in Chicago, Clive suspected his father began dreaming about the Tchaikovsky Competition, although Claude Serkin never mentioned it. Instead he often suggested otherwise to Clive. "Better to leave your dream in the hands of time rather than place a burden of expectation. There have been many great musicians, even prodigies, whose lives were destroyed by their parents, Nyiregyhazi being the worst. No one is going to let that happen to you, Clive. You will go only if you want to go and when you are ready."

Beneath Claude's confidence in his son's ability, Clive knew there was a shred of concern about his physical stamina and age.

"Van Cliburn was twenty-three when he won, but Clive, you are younger. There can be no poor eating habits. Pumping you up with vitamins every day will only carry you so far, and we have repertoire still to be learned. We haven't even started Rachmaninoff's *Etudes-Tableaux*, and you are already practicing almost eight hours a day."

Claude's concerns were tempered by Mr. K's practical, philosophical side. "Moses wasn't looking to win. He was being obedient to God's voice to bring deliverance. This isn't about winning, but honoring the composer and giving life to his intentions. Breathe into the music who you are. Honor the gifts you've been given," Mr. K would say.

Apart from Julia and under Mr. K's influence, Papa became a more patient listener than Clive observed in him as a conductor. Papa had often told his son, "All orchestras prefer the tyrant to the empathetic gentle hand, the Bernstein over the Mitropoulis. Dimitri Mitropoulis was a brilliant conductor, but he was humble. Orchestras don't want humble. They want to be controlled."

However, Clive saw his father change amid the comfortable furnishings of the old country, with his dear friend and colleague. Papa restrained his need to give direction first, often yielding to Mr. K's thoughts before expressing his own. The two of them were learning from each other, while Clive gained valuable insights from them.

His father's willingness to relinquish control for his son's benefit motivated Clive to exercise his will in favor of this pedagogical arrangement. Yet, his longing for Clare continued to burn inside him. He attempted to quench it by repeating Rabbi Sherveen's words, "Your music belongs at home, Clive, with your father."

During the week, Clive chose to skip his scheduled lesson with Clare. After leaving a message and not hearing a response, he hoped she was not offended. On the way home from Brookline after school, he summoned his courage and decided to stop by her studio. Clive wanted to tell her that he, on his own, had resolved that it would be best to take a break from their working together. He was part of a musical line of great teachers, but also a line within his own family, which he had wrongly disregarded. He needed time to repair the breach.

With his determination intact, Clive ascended the stairs and approached her painted studio door. The wind chimes were no longer hanging above the door, but there was a lavender note left behind with his name on it. All of his courage evaporated with the sight, as he slid down the wall and sat on the floor to read the carefully scripted words.

Dearest Clive,

First and foremost, you must keep working and in no way take this letter as a message of abandonment. I will be returning shortly, possibly within a week or two. Nero is taking me to New York for some medical tests and a second opinion. It's nothing serious, so don't worry about me. Please know that I have every intention of being with you in Moscow. Neither my medical condition nor any act of God will prevent me from sharing this momentous event in your life. Focus your energies on the Mazurka of the F minor Concerto and the Bach. Above all, trust the Folio, Mr. K, and your Papa in my absence.

All my love,
Clare

That's all she wrote. *A week or two. "All my love, Clare." Does she really love me? Medical tests? For what?* The empty hole inside him, temporarily filled by his meeting with Rabbi Sherveen, began to expand again. He felt like he was spilling out onto the floor. *What if she doesn't return? What if Clare has cancer?* He couldn't help but dwell on the phrase, *All my love.*

What kind of love did Clare feel for him?, he wondered. They had never spoken of their love, but it was there between them. When they were together at the piano, it felt as if the physical laws of nature were suspended, and there was no age difference between them. Clive felt an unmistakable freedom that caused his music to soar when he was one with her, by her side.

At that moment, Clive decided this precious note would go in the Folio next to the exchanges between Robert and Clara Schumann. They too at times must have felt this way. Fortunately, despite the battle, they endured. Robert and Clara always knew where they were and who their enemy was—both of which were presently unknown.

Clive didn't even know where she'd gone, but one person would know: Bethany.

CHAPTER 18

Crescendo—Becoming gradually louder

The cuplike flower of the dogwood appears to hold all of spring's freshness in a single blossom. Paper-fine pink petals surround the earthen-brown stamen with a supernatural gift of patience. These flowers, whose buds form in the fall, wait through shortened days and snow-driven nights to explode, turning the landscape into a quilt of new life. Clare closed her eyes to picture the memory. The farm was about to come alive again.

Sitting at her mother's piano and looking out the bay window, Clare could see Nero spreading mushroom compost on his raised flowerbeds. He too seemed to be coming alive. The piano was badly out of tune, but the scene out the window brought harmony to the dissonance. She entertained the thought of going out to help Nero. *Why not?* She left the house. With her bare feet upon the still-cool ground, Clare wrapped her shawl tighter around her shoulders as she strolled down the path of newly sprouted grass.

The feeling of her bare feet being planted in the soil lent new meaning to the farm. When she was touring, she rarely had walked the gardens in the early morning. She didn't have the time nor the desire for the freshness of the earth underfoot. Now she did. Nero saw this in Clare. A peace had come through forgetfulness and fear, unexpectedly in the waiting.

"Would you like some help spreading compost?" Clare asked.

Leaning on his shovel, Nero admired his wife, still in her nightgown, for it was early and dew glimmered on the grass. "If you get some proper gardening clothes on, yes, I could use it." Despite her age and apparent mental insecurity, Clare looked like a nymph in the garden. Nero wanted to take her to his potting shed and lay her on the floor, but the flowers were not blooming yet. It was not the right season for such a tryst. More time was needed, and understanding.

"Oh, I hear the phone ringing. Let me answer it, and then I'll get dressed and be back out in a minute," she volunteered.

"No need to answer; just let the answering machine pick it up."

Noticing her thin frame through the gauze of her Victorian lace nightgown, Nero marveled at how her body did not seem to age. Clare's mother, who also looked more like thirty when she died in her fifties, came from the hearty stock of the Great Plains. Aging slowly was in their genes.

As the sun climbed above the Snowdrift crabapple trees, Nero noticed Clare had not returned to the garden. Almost an hour went by, and the only sound was the mourning dove calling for its mate.

Keeping an eye on Clare was becoming a necessity. She often forgot what she was doing or where she was going right in the middle of the action. "Now what was I doing with these tomatoes?" Clare would say while making homemade marinara sauce, the connection lost in her mind. He often wondered whether it was safe to let her drive the car, for fear she would end up in a different town and not remember how to return home.

Spinning his wheelbarrow back to the compost heap, Nero

walked into the silence of the living room. She wasn't at the piano. "Clare! Are you coming out? What are you doing?"

He moved through the rooms, accidentally bumping into the arrangement of forsythia that she placed on the round front hall table, causing it to tip to one side. Fortunately, he was able to catch the vase before it went crashing to the floor. Curving up the stairs, past the wall of their wedding and honeymoon photos, he heard a cat whining in the distance, reminding him that he hadn't fed the goats yet. After such an endless winter, it was a miracle they were alive. He had lost count of the number of times he forgot to feed them.

As he walked into their bedroom, Nero heard the cat's whimper again, this time from behind his cedar closet door. The sunlight now stretched across the carpet, reaching the threshold of the closet, a bright edge fronting the darkness.

Lying on the closet floor in a tearful heap of nightgown and blankets, he found Clare. She was next to the trunk where Johannes slept within his little nest. A dread came over Nero as he feared she had discovered their little child without explanation. "What are you doing in here on the floor? Are you all right? Why didn't you come back outside?" Nero asked.

She looked pitiful, her face a mess of tears and her body convulsing in the blankets. He pulled his wife's limp body to its feet. "Tell me what is going on in here," Nero demanded. "Stop hiding things from me. I don't want to play games. Did the doctor call? Who was on the phone?"

Looking directly at him, Clare cringed under the pain of his tight hold on her forearm. Nero reached out to slap her across the cheek to provoke a response, but she withered away from him before he made contact.

"That was Katrina who called earlier. I was unable to answer the phone in time, but she left a message for you, saying she wouldn't be able to come over tonight for your usual get together. How could you? Why did you do it?"

They were separated as a couple, Nero thought. What did she expect him to do, remain in solitary confinement at the farm, while she trotted off to begin a new life upon the lilting Midwestern plains?

"She means nothing to me," he huffed. "She's a drugstore worker in town, who delivered my medicine in the evening, on her way home."

Clare could feel Nero's piercing eyes. She yanked her arm—red and burning as though bound by rope—away from him. All of a sudden, she remembered the day he locked her inside his potting shed until dark without food or water.

It was the weekend before the opening of Nero's new gallery. He had built the addition to his potting shed by hand over the previous summer, and he finally had fulfilled his dream of a home to display his work. Everything was in place. The invitations had been sent out and responded to; his beautiful goblets and plates were illuminated by newly installed track lighting. The caterer had planned an early fall harvest cocktail reception and word came through the town newspaper that reviewers from Concord would be attending the opening.

Clare knew it was a mistake, but when her agent called the night before the big event, she decided to answer it. There had been a cancellation in London; the pianist had fallen ill, and Covent Garden was asking for her to fill in. She agreed to take it. When she told Nero, he did not say a word.

In one swift tackle he rolled her on the floor into a ball and attempted to carry her to his potting shed. Clare fought back, and as she kicked his legs and scratched his face, he lost his grip on her. She ran for the car to try to lock herself inside and almost made it. Just as she went to swing the car door shut, he reached his arm inside and jerked her off the seat and onto the ground. The next thing she knew, she was locked inside his shed.

She was overcome by memories of her bruised hands from pounding on the door which were clouded by those of her father's gentle demeanor with horses. They were never without hay or water, yet she didn't have any food in the shed that belonged to her own husband.

"I'm not afraid of you," Clare shouted at Nero as they stood in the closet. "Daddy will take care of me. He won't let you hurt me again."

Stunned, Nero had no idea what was going through Clare's mind. Her departure from reality confused him. Could she be delusional? Trying to bring her back to the present moment, Nero controlled his anger and grabbed hold of Clare by the waist, whispering in her ear, "I am not 'Daddy' to you. I am the man you love, remember? It's me, Nero. Get dressed and come out of the closet."

Turning away from Clare, Nero slipped on his Wellingtons at the bottom of the stairs, preparing to head back out to the garden. He hoped she would come out of the cedar closet and get away from Johannes. *How unpredictable her mind is, and how frustrating*, he thought. Once outside, a single question stopped him in his tracks: Had he remembered to lock Johannes in the trunk?

CHAPTER 19

Arioso—Lyrically, expressively

Clive felt like he really didn't fit on the west side of town. Most of his friends lived in the east-side neighborhood, closer to Brookline Academy. This was foreign territory. *What's with all the picket fences and little gates?* Noting the address—935 West Street—in flowery tile letters underneath a front porch roof, he ventured through the gate and was careful to latch it behind him.

Despite his current height of six feet four inches, the ceiling of the Victorian front porch made Clive feel diminutive. The doorbell, framed in brass by small Ionian pillars, was both fancy and frivolous. After waiting a moment, a young girl, no more than four years old, was visible through the front door glass yelling, "Mommy, there's a big man here with scary eyes. He wants to talk to you."

Through the beveled pane, Clive could see a small, stout woman laughing as she approached the door. "Genevieve, that's not a very nice thing to say," she rebuked in a firmly amused tone.

Once she opened the door, he immediately saw a resemblance to Clare, particularly the Roman nose, but Bethany had the body of a miniature weight lifter. From what Clare had told him of her sister's burgeoning family, she looked like she could handle herself in any situation.

"Hello, Mrs. Taylor. I'm Clive Serkin, one of Madame Cardiff's students."

Bursting with an expulsive laugh, Bethany opened the door for Clive. "Sorry, hearing you refer to Clare as Madame Cardiff caught me off-guard. It's a pleasure to meet you. Clare has spoken fondly of you. Please come in. What can I do for you?" she asked.

As Clive selected a rocking chair from the circle in the front parlor, he felt nervous. Maybe this visit was utterly inappropriate, but here he was so he might as well persevere.

"I received a letter from Madame Cardiff, saying she had gone back East for medical testing. I'm preparing to audition for an important competition and want to ask her a few questions about my repertoire. I don't have a phone number for her so I thought you could help me reach her. If not, even an address would be helpful."

Clive kept rubbing his enormous hands against the rocking chair's knobby arms and looking around the room at the pictures on the walls.

"You have a big family. How many of your children play the piano, if you don't mind me asking?"

"Oh no, we have the three oldest taking lessons now—Jeremy, Jessica, and Devon. It's a lot of work, keeping up with everything they need to learn, but I don't need to tell you that," Bethany said with a knowing smile.

"Clare told me about your amazing talent. Even I know what an honor it is simply being allowed to audition for the Tchaikovsky Piano Competition. You must be thrilled." She waited for Clive to respond, but he only nodded in agreement.

"I'd prefer not to give you a phone number," Bethany continued. "I don't think her husband would approve, but I can give you their address. She shouldn't be gone much longer, but some mail from you might cheer her up. Wait here for a moment."

The sound of several children cascaded down the stairs. They were arguing about who had the longest hair. Clive was delighted to hear Clare had spoken "fondly" of him, but he wondered why Clare needed some encouragement. Well, he would certainly send mail her way to contribute to such an effort.

Bethany came back and extended a floral note with the address: 6W459 Wisteria Lane, Newport, New Hampshire 75645.

"You mentioned that your sister might need cheering up. Is she doing all right?" Clive asked timidly.

"Clare is doing as best as one could expect under the circumstances." Bethany didn't go into further detail. "Clive, I appreciate your concern for her. Truly, I'm honored to meet you. You look so much like your father. I saw him conduct at the most recent Westdale Artists Series. It was Mahler's *Titan Symphony* and absolutely gorgeous. I can't imagine the degree of strength and stamina your father must have to lead an orchestra night after night. It must be very demanding."

"Yes, it is. Thank you very much, Mrs. Taylor. I appreciate your help."

"Think nothing of it. Now I have to get back to my homework table with the older children. They're working on, or should I say struggling with, fractions. You remember common denominators, I'm sure."

Since Bethany was a part of Clare, Clive wanted to reach out and embrace her. Holding her in his arms might bring some of Clare back to him, but he resisted the impulse.

"Thank you again for making time for me, Mrs. Taylor. If you speak to Madame Cardiff, please extend my regards for a quick recovery and a speedy return to all of us."

Bethany watched Clive stride through the daffodil-lined path with confident steps and youthful determination. "Best of luck in the competition," she yelled through the screen.

Clive turned back with a quick flick of the hand and lightness to his step. "Thanks so much, Mrs. Taylor. You remind me a little bit of Madame Cardiff," he yelled from the gate.

"Oh, thank you. I'll take that as a compliment, but she got all the musical talent in our family."

And so much more, Clive thought to himself with a satisfied feeling inside.

X

Sitting at his desk, Clive thought about what to write in the Folio. A love letter would be premature, although he wanted to pour out his heart to Clare, telling her every detail of his life, including his visit today with her sister. On the other hand, an informational letter filled with questions about current challenges with his repertoire might require too complicated of a reply.

"Anna, could you come here? I need your female intuition." Clive trusted Anna's instincts, but he would not tell her too much for fear she would blab to Mama and Papa.

"My piano teacher, Clare, went back to New Hampshire for some medical tests. Remember when I told you she was acting forgetful? I suspect the tests have something to do with that, but I don't really know. She left me a note, explaining she'd be back in two weeks. I want to do something to brighten her day. I have her address, so I'm thinking about sending a letter and some flowers to Clare. What do you think of that idea?"

Anna giggled at Clive's earnest concern for this older woman. "That would be extremely kind, but it seems more like a boy-friend-to-girlfriend gesture and a tad too intimate for a piano teacher. If she is ill, why don't you send her a card and something healthy, like a box of herbal tea?"

"Herbal tea? Please! She lives on a farm in New Hampshire and probably makes tea out of her own herbs. Do you have any other ideas?" Clive asked.

"Why do you want to do this? You aren't even studying with her anymore. Is this some sort of thank-you gesture?" Anna's curiosity was getting the best of her.

Clive desperately needed Anna's help. Not sharing his emotions was distracting him from the competition. Doubt was creeping in, when he should be conquering Liszt. *Just tell her,* he decided. Doing so would make him feel better and gain some focus at the same time.

"Anna, please don't laugh when I tell you this. I'm in love with Clare," he confessed. "She means everything to me personally and musically. She is like my soul mate in the pursuit of art. The book you found is her Folio. She gave it to me as a way of grafting me into her gene pool and musical line. I'm a part of her, and she is part of me.

"The Folio is a collection of wisdom handed down through a line of her teachers, dating back to Brahms. She entrusted it to me, her only student ever to see it. Her thoughts are also included, about challenges as her career was being launched, back when she was doing what I am doing now.

"We approach Rachmaninoff, Chopin, and all of the Romantics in the same vein, but Clare catalyzes in me a life I've never had before. This life is a richness of color and expansiveness that comes through me and into my playing. Because of Mama and Papa, I am not studying with her anymore, but I'm not sure I can do this competition without her. On top of all that, I'm concerned for her health and well-being. I don't even know what's wrong with her."

He couldn't bear to mention that Clare was married. Clive could see on her face that Anna was already thinking he'd lost his mind. "I need some connection with her until she comes back. Studying with Papa and Mr. K is going well, but it isn't enough to get me there. I need more. I need her."

Clive could see Anna's ears burn red and her face flush at this untoward revelation.

"Okay, you need help, professional help, beyond my feminine intuition. Guys your age do not fall in love with women that old. I mean yes, maybe in the movies. I saw one like this once, *The Graduate*, weird, don't watch it. Clive, this isn't a movie. This is real life."

Clive waited while Anna considered his situation. Looking at Anna, he had nothing less than complete confidence she would get over the shock of it and come up with something.

"I do have an idea. Papa is going with Mama next week to a conference for a few days over our spring break. Why don't we go see Clare? You need some sort of exorcism over this infatuation, to be free of her as you go into these final months of preparation. If she is ill, she might not come to Moscow, so you must know in your own soul that you can do this without her. You need to break it off and be in control, be the man you are.

"We will drive out there together. The trip should only take a day. You see Clare, say what you should, which is goodbye, and get on with your life. That way, she isn't haunting you while you are waiting for her return. We'll be back before Mama and Papa even board their flight home from New York." His younger sister's craftiness often startled him. He wondered if her scheme was possible. Clare might not be home. He should let her know in advance they were coming. What would Nero think?

"Let me think about it. Anna, you are always on my side. Thank you," Clive said with sincerity. "You're right. I want to do the Tchaikovsky Competition with complete freedom, but I'm not interested in 'breaking it off,' as you described. A visit out there would give me the peace of mind I need to go on, but I also can't afford to lose all that practice time. Let me sleep on it."

After she left, Clive pulled out the chair from his desk and sat down to study the Folio. He read a thread from the past, a personal note pointing him to the future.

"Love me well ... I ask for much because I give much." Schumann said it, but is it true for us all? We shouldn't expect love in return

for our offering of music. Giving without reservation and expecta-
tion is our duty. Perhaps Schumann could demand love because
of his position as composer and his wife as performer. Theirs was
a relationship grounded in the give-and-take of a marriage of two
sharing the same work at its deepest, most intimate level of cre-
ation. If I were a potter or a sculptor or Nero a musician, would we
be engaged in a creative partnership as kindred spirits, producing
a more fruitful result? Probably not. Better to be free of the expec-
tation of love through the giving of art. It is all a gift and should
be treated as such.

Clare wrote about Nero in the Folio, in an entry from nearly twenty years ago. *How much more about their relationship might be in here? Nero, a potter? Were they sharing art at its "deepest and most intimate level of creation?" What else were they sharing at this "deepest and most intimate level of creation?"* He closed his eyes and pictured Nero sculpting his model Clare. His rough, silt-laden hands, shaping her figure from the earth ... Clive cut himself off before he imagined too much.

How he desired to be close to her again, even if only seated on a piano bench. He closed his eyes and remembered the intimate feeling of her hand in his. Despite the difference in size, they shared a hand-in-glove fit.

Since she had bestowed the Folio upon him, he rarely had the nerve or the need to write in it all these months. Now he might have a reason to start as a way of corresponding through it. He could jot a note, send the Folio back to her, and trust her to return it to him. She could not resist sending it back, could she? Such a massive tome would need a heap of packing material, but it was worth a try.

With courage, Clive took up his pen and wrote his first note toward what would hopefully be a future mode of correspondence with Clare.

March 21st (J. S. Bach's Birthday)

The competition is only a few months away. We are building repertoire faithfully and polishing the first- and second-round pieces. We are going to finalize the concerti last. The four etudes of Liszt, Chopin, Rachmaninoff, and Scriabin are in fine shape. The struggle right now is with the G-sharp minor Prelude and Fugue by Taneyev. This was Papa's choice for its technical showiness and emotive power. I like it, but it is so intricate in its difficulty. Any help you could give me by jotting a few thoughts down and sending them back to me would be so appreciated. Studies with Mr. K and Papa are going well in your absence, but I do hope you return soon. My lessons are far too quiet without your fire. Here is a quote to encourage you in the trial which you are facing, of which I know so little. I found this in an earlier section of the Folio, in Brahms's handwriting, but I believe he attributed it to Francis Bacon. "There is no excellent beauty that hath not some strangeness in the proportion." Please know, Clare, that I feel this is true for you and me. While we are disproportionate in so many ways, there is beauty between us.

All my love,

Clive

Not overly romantic, but with enough professional probing to prompt a response, he decided. Clive still had to prepare the Folio for its journey to Wisteria Lane. He would ask the archivist with Papa's orchestra for some advice, so this treasure could reach Clare without crumbling into shards. If the Folio stayed intact, perhaps his heart would also.

CHAPTER 20

Allegro—A fast, quick tempo

In the twilight of the spring garden, Nero pulled the folded receipt from the back pocket of his jeans. It was the fourteenth time he had done so since they returned home from New York.

P038775—Early Onset Dementia.

A diagnosis number, a description. He replayed the words offered by Dr. Christensen over again in his mind, trying to let them sink in, trying to let himself be encouraged.

Her astute musical ability could keep her brain growing new connections, as long as she keeps at the regimen of learning new things. Help her learn a foreign language. The origins of music and language work together in your brain. Because Clare's musical memory is so well developed, learning a new language will be relatively easy for her. The learning process will keep the brain's memory centers—like the hippocampus—healthy and working. Studies show that this important part of the brain can actually grow, so anything that forces her brain to continue to learn is es-

sential in keeping Clare as sharp as possible.

Dr. Christiansen's smiling face annoyed him. All he had to do was give advice and walk down the hall to the next patient while Nero was assigned the project.

Since Clare already knew several European languages, but did not know Latin well, she and Nero began to learn Latin words. *Barrenwort—Epimedium grandiflorum.* Nero would flash the picture of the plant on the card and Clare would say the words between sips of Chardonnay. Russian Sage—*Perovskia atriplicifolia.* The garden was such an obvious starting point, Nero thought. It was the place where life began.

"Let me show the pictures and you say the words this time. I want the fun part too," Clare requested, reaching out to snatch the cards from him.

"Oh no you don't; be careful, you're about to knock over my drink." Nero guarded his gin and tonic with a protective vengeance, managing to keep Clare from knocking it over and ruining their homemade flashcards, which he had illustrated to the quality level of a Dutch masterpiece.

Giving up coffee and alcohol was impossible for them, even though Dr. Christiansen recommended it would be best to keep Clare's mind free from chemical alteration. During their consultation session, he had warned Nero, "Alcohol especially can play tricks on the brain, causing her to see things that may not be there. Try to keep her diet as clean as you can, no chemicals, everything organic." After completing three cycles of flashcards and three glasses of wine, Clare cleared her throat, sat up straight in the wrought-iron chair and pronounced, "I need to be getting back, Nero. We've accomplished what we set out to do. We have a second opinion and a plan to deal with my condition. Now I have responsibilities back home to my students."

"Oh, really, to whom are you responsible?" Nero's soiled hand began to tighten on the glass as the topic of Clare's departure agitated him more than he expected. Having her around inspired a healthy vigor that gave him energy. The garden was taking shape, and his potting shed door was open and visitors were coming to the gallery again.

"I have a student who is preparing for the Tchaikovsky Piano Competition."

Yes, this is at least the tenth time she's told me that, Nero thought.

"You met him in my studio that day, didn't you? His name is Clive. Do you remember him?" Nero could see that Clare savored the moment, making Nero feel like he was the forgetful one for a change.

"Yeah, he was the stooping Jewish boy with the big hands. He looked like a crane and made about as much noise. There's no need to rush off. You're doing well here, and we're working together in some new ways. I would have never imagined you as a gardener. Why don't you stay and rest a little longer, at least until the lilacs finish blooming? This Clive must have other teachers working with him."

"He does, but none who are as close to him as I am."

Nero wondered how close to him Clare was. He watched her carefully as she directed her gaze out toward the garden. Working in the dirt had been good for her, and it was better and cheaper than seeing a doctor. *There's so much fear when one is losing their mind,* he thought. He noticed that when fear began to creep in about her future because she couldn't correctly count the money in her wallet, Clare would walk outside, kneel down, and feel the soil. Dirt had a calming and centering power. It was the origin from which beautiful things grow.

"Do you remember the day when we first bought the farm? We ordered at least ten different varieties of lilac bushes. We took those knee-high little sticks and encircled the backyard with them. Look how they've grown and spread, nearly down to the river. When they bloom, their fragrance and color is like a crown upon this land." He knew how Clare loved to clip the blooms and create arrangements, watching their single, starry flowers fall onto the top of the piano, propelled by the vibration of her playing. "Why don't you stay until the lilacs bloom?"

Clare waited a moment to respond, glancing in the direction of the river. "Nero, I can't. It wouldn't be right. I have to get back. I have a professional responsibility to Clive to get him to Moscow and beyond. He is a piano teacher's dream."

"Clare, you are not a piano teacher. You are a pianist. I'm amused by this sudden passion for your students. You've not exactly excelled in the nurturing instinct over the years."

"Time is running out for me," Clare admitted. "With Clive, I have the chance to accomplish what I myself have never done, to go to the Tchaikovsky. He is so good that he has a chance of winning."

Listening to Clare, he recognized the familiar "*I*" refrain. Like the rest of her life, this student was providing the path for her to accomplish something *she* wanted. How much of her desire to return to teaching was truly about Clive? How much of any of her desire had ever been about him?

"I want to show you something I made while you were gone. Come inside for a minute," Nero pleaded with Clare. If he couldn't keep her at the farm, perhaps Johannes could.

Making their way past the circular table in the foyer, Clare noted the forsythias in the vase had faded away, a reminder that she had been here longer than planned.

Once they reached the top of the stairs, he brought her into the bedroom they once shared. The lavender light cast fading shadows on the cracked planks of the floor.

"Have a seat on our bed while I bring it out." Nero appeared enthused, like a child about to bestow a handmade present on Mother's Day. Exiting the cedar closet, he carried a large bundle wrapped in her mother's lace tablecloth. He hoped she recognized the cloth, which added a sweet, ceremonial touch of nostalgia.

Sitting beside her, he put his arm around Clare in preparation for the viewing of his clay creation. It was the only time he had touched her with love since bringing her back to the farm. There was a comfort and gentleness in his touch that gave her pause. A few days ago, he almost yanked her elbow from its socket, and today he was caressing her with the sweetness of pure maple syrup.

"Clare, you know I have never forgiven you for not telling me you were carrying our child before losing it. You know how much I wanted that baby. While you were gone, my yearning for you and our baby became tangible, like a taste in my mouth that wouldn't leave. It hovered over me like a cloud, forcing me to think about what we could have done and might have been. So I made something. I imagined if our baby lived, what he would look like, and he is very beautiful. I want you to meet him, so I'm going to show him to you now. Please don't say anything at first. Just look at him, let your eyes take him in, and see him as our child."

Nero gently unwrapped the lace tablecloth. Then he unfolded the baby blanket he had used to secure Johannes. Clare recognized it as her favorite pink childhood blanket, saved by her mother and packed by her father into the trousseau trunk for their wedding day. Nero had swaddled the blanket around his treasure, with the deftness of a first-time father who had learned this skill at the hospital.

The crown of the baby's head emerged first. Clare could see a crop of golden curls like a Renaissance cherub. Its face was glazed a milky rose, the color of the climbing roses around their trellis. Its vivid, gray-blue eyes were remarkably alive, conveying the appearance of tumultuous waves in a Turner seascape. Tiny arms crossed over each other with the posture of contentment. She could see it was a boy. Everything about him was perfectly formed, as though Nero learned from the Italian masters. *How could he, a potter of leaf-stamped trays and lighthouse lamps, have made this?* Clare asked herself in silence.

"I named him Johannes after Johannes Brahms, because I know you love his music. He looks like the two of us, don't you think? He has your eyes and my chin. Do you like him, Clare? Would you like to hold him?"

There were no words to describe the pain Clare felt at the barrenness of her life, coupled with her pity, love, and admiration for Nero. He was a talent, a wonder with his hands. "I can't hold him, Nero," she said, as an eruption of emptiness tore through her from womb to vocal cords. "He's beautiful, but he's not real."

In the recognition of the lifelessness of Nero's handiwork, she remembered Clive. He was real, not fake, and he needed her now. Churning in her mind, the memories of the cold bathroom floor where her unborn child bled out of her body commingled with the blood of the calves she watched being born on the floor of the barn back home. The smell of straw and warm blood became palpable in the air, making her feel ill. Her guilt at not telling Nero she was expecting their child returned as a tidal wave ripping through the shore. She ran for the bathroom to retch in the toilet, falling to the very floor where her baby was left behind.

Leaning over the toilet, she thought of her daddy. How she missed his sure, strong hands, which once tucked her into bed at night. Some of the calves he delivered didn't make it, but because of Daddy, many survived. He knew the precise moment to reach with his hand up into the struggling mother to help her safely deliver the calf. The calves were so innocent and vulnerable as they turned to look for their mother instantly after birth. Turning away from the toilet, she saw that Nero had placed the clay child on the bathroom floor right next to her.

Instinctively, Clare pushed the statuette away and sprinted toward the comfort of her mother's piano downstairs. The lowing of the newborn calf, searching for his mother's milk, increased in volume in her mind, blocking the pathway of the words she wanted to say to Nero. Her mouth couldn't form the words her mind was preparing. Something like a rigid wall was blocking them. *I'm sorry. I'm so sorry.* She could think them and hear them, but they wouldn't come out. If she could manage to get to the piano, Nero might hear the words he desperately longed for. All her life, music had released her unspoken thoughts. Even when the pathway of her words was cut off, music had the power to unleash them.

"Clare, stop running from me!" She could hear his boots trailing her down the stairs. Feverishly, she grabbed the side of the piano and steadied herself on the bench. She attempted to play an apology for him, a reverent hymn of her past which he would understand. It might communicate what she was trying to say, but her father's voice overcame the music. "Clare, look at this little one. She's a beauty. Look at those big eyes."

Nero heard no apology, only the playing of an ancient hymn she was using as a foil to shut him out, to escape conveying her true thoughts and feelings. How he hated the way she always put the piano first, a dead instrument before his own heart. While she feverishly worked the keys, he determined to pound an apology from her, to manually extract the words from her with his bare hands if he had to do so. If he could get her to say she was sorry, he would be justified and they might survive.

"Say it! Say you're sorry for cheating me out of the child we never had!" With all his strength, he pushed her backward off the piano bench. She crawled to get away from him, but his boot pressed down on her and held her body beneath him.

As his hands stretched toward the straining cords of her neck, lines of Shakespeare learned in college flooded into his memory. With his full weight forcing her to stay still on the carpet, Nero bent down to whisper the words in Clare's ear:

"Orpheus with his lute made trees, and the mountain tops that freeze, bow themselves when he did sing: To his music, plants and flowers ever sprung; as sun and showers there had made a lasting spring. Everything that heard him play, even the billows of the sea, hung their heads and then lay by. In sweet music is such

art, killing care and grief of heart. Fall asleep or hearing die."

Crying and choking, fearing for her lack of words, Clare wanted to reassure this man that everything was all right. "The straw is in the barn, Daddy. I'll be home to help you with the calving this spring."

Straining her neck to the right to look over her shoulder, Clare could see her father out of the corner of her eye, dressed in his flannel work shirt and smelling of earth and manure. His face, chiseled by the sun, was filled with an intense anticipation. His hands were covered in soil.

With an instinctive release, he let her go. Looking into her confused eyes, Nero knew that Clare was losing her ability to see him, and he in turn the ability to reach her. Her mind was transferring her own father upon his very image.

Nero shuddered to think he was almost willing to kill for an apology from an apparition. She was dangerous, a love that existed in body, but not in mind. He would have to free himself from her in some way, and like his creation of Johannes, it would take time and great care to figure out the right method.

CHAPTER 21

*Interlude—A short piece that is played
between sections of a composition*

The path to the Japanese bridge felt rough underfoot. As Clive raced his sister to the island, slivers of red gravel cut into the soles of his bare feet.

"Come on, Anna, catch up to me. I can hear Papa playing. It's starting."

Anna's laughter came closer as they reached the bridge, but he arrived one step in front of her. "Ladies first," he said, deferentially ushering Anna forward.

She ascended the steep wooden arch ahead of him. Gripping the brightly painted railing with both hands, the two pulled themselves up and over the red bridge toward the island. Grandma Serkin's tiny summer pagoda sat upon a circular promontory of land, with only a grand piano and benches inside. All the windows were tilted open so the music could be heard across the pond. As dusk drifted into the summer day, the time came for the family to sing together. He could see all the rest of his relatives carrying their heavy picnic baskets, chattering in tandem with the sunset song of bluebirds.

"Be careful. Don't get too close to the pond's edge," Bubbe Serkin called out, while watching Anna and Clive tease the lazy goldfish amidst the lily pads with their long sticks. Bullfrogs jumped from the banks into the water, as they stealthily moved through the hedge grass that laced the pond. With frustration, Clive saw that his pole had become entangled just beyond the swampy bank. It was either stuck between two rocks or wedged amongst the murky water and tall cattails. As he tried to yank it free, it recoiled away from him and was camouflaged amidst the waving green reeds.

The rushing of the grass was whispering to him in the wind as he separated it with each forward step. Water now covered the tops of his shoes while he continued to inch on. Placing one foot on a slick moss-covered rock and the other upon a tuft of sea grass brought balance, and he could see the elusive pole more clearly.

"Anna, come here and help me get this," Clive cried out, but his sister had already entered the pagoda with the family and be-gun singing. A goldfish darted from beneath the rock, startling him. His weight shifted abruptly, and Clive pitched forward into the pond. The water was murky with slime-covered weeds and felt breathtakingly cold for June. Reaching for the grassy tufts to pull his body from the water proved futile. The grasses kept slip-ping through his hands.

Now totally submerged, he could see the sunlight through the green water but couldn't push up to the surface. The more he thrashed in the water, the deeper his feet dug into the mud. The grasses felt like they were grabbing hold of his legs, pulling him down, and a glazelike ice was skimming over the glassy pond above. *How can there be ice in June?* he wondered as he continued to hold his breath. *Stay calm. Don't thrash. Conserve your energy.* He freed himself from his shoes and swam up to the light-green ceiling, which separated him from desperately needed air. Placing the palms of his hands at the surface of the water, he could feel the barrier was like thin, clear glass and frigid to the touch.

Above the water, the shadow of a woman picking away at the ice with a sharp tool came into view. Her voice cried out, "Hang on, Clive. I'm almost through." Her slender hand penetrated the hole and was now visible in the murky water. He grabbed hold of it. The force of her firm hand pulling him upward allowed his arm to fully emerge. Despite both her hands raising him, his head and body were still pinned beneath the cold, hard barrier between them. Oxygen was running out.

"You can break through, Clive. Don't let go of me," she cried out with an edge of panic in her voice.

Awash in sweat, Clive woke up. It had been years since his family was all together at Bubbe Serkin's summer music house in upstate New York. *Who was the woman rescuing him? Her voice sounded like Clare's, saying, "Don't let go of me." Did she set me free or did I drown?* When questions from his dreams went unanswered, he would often try to fall back to sleep immediately, hoping to reclaim the vision.

This time, more sleep evaded him. It was Clare's voice and Clare's hand—small, milky white against the algae ice, about the same size as his childhood hand. "Don't let go of me."

He was a child in the dream and yet she was there. Had she always been with him in spirit before their conscious encounter? Might she be trying to reach him through his dreams?

Several weeks had passed since Clive sent Clare's Folio to the farm in Newport, New Hampshire, but no response came. Wilson, the archivist at the Chicago Philharmonic, had told him exactly how to send it in a manner that kept the Folio preserved and protected, but allowed for express, insured delivery. Acid-free bubble plastic—who knew such a thing existed?—and he had received delivery confirmation so he knew it was in Newport. Clare had said she would only be gone two weeks, and it had already been five. *Why?*

Anna's idea of going to see Clare is beginning to sound like the best hope of reconnecting with her.

How could she not send back the Folio? he wondered, feeling a twinge of anger. It was a sacred trust between them. *She knows how much I need it.* Without the Folio, Clive depended on Papa and Mr. K to help refine the repertoire. They were master musicians, but not great teachers. There was no sharing, only instruction.

)(

Saul and Claude came bursting out the front door of Mr. K's bungalow, with Claude furiously waving a trifold piece of paper with a wax seal at the top. As Clive climbed up the crumbling steps, Claude proclaimed, "The participants in the Tchaikovsky competition have been announced. You are in, and you are by far the youngest. Next in age, but four years older at twenty-two, is Heinrich Niebuhr. I knew it. I knew Niebuhr would make it. There are a total of fourteen competitors, the majority being from Russia and China. The only other American is Norman Pobanz. Do you know him?"

Clive halted before going in the front door. "I'm in. I really made it. I'm going to the Tchaikovsky Piano Competition. I can't believe it."

"Yes, yes, yes, we are all going!" The three men jumped up and down on the tiny front stoop surrounded by a crumbling metal rail, looking like Mexican jumping beans encased within their little plastic box.

"We must now research our competition. Let me tell you what I know." Claude went on talking as Clive entered Mr.K's foyer and stooped low to hang his coat in the closet beneath the stairs. "Niebuhr has the biggest reputation. He is already known in his home country by winning several prestigious competitions, and you know his teacher, Saul, none other than the great Sviatoslav Richter." Mr. K sat down in the tattered easy chair by the window and let out a long whistle. "Yes, Saul. Slava Richter, one of the greatest Russian pianists of all time. Richter rarely accepts students, so that means Niebuhr is something special. Niebuhr is an aggressive, superior technician. He likes to devour pieces and spit them out at the audience with sagacity. He is not pretentious and doesn't flaunt his talent. Instead, he uses it like a razor's edge upon the ears of his listeners. Like Richter in some respects, that veracity. While his playing is not known for its lyricism, it is truthful, intellectually honest."

Claude could see the concern flush his son's face, and he didn't want to intimidate him. "Now you, dear boy, being young and every bit as talented as Niebuhr, you have something he doesn't have. You communicate with your listeners in a way that is personal. When you play the Tchaikovsky concerto, a message comes through that is uniquely yours.

"This can only come from the joy or the sorrow inside of you and your own love of the music. It's deep down and you bring it out with freshness and innocence. Niebuhr doesn't do that. He is a machine and the pieces he performs will complement this. All you need to do is stay true to yourself and believe." Claude's enthusiasm grew with each sentence. "We are at a point now when we need to hire your concerto accompanist to play the part of the orchestra while you practice. I know a number of these types, but one in particular would be my recommendation, Walter Lipman. He, like Saul here, is a little man with a huge heart and a master at orchestral accompaniment. You will love him. He reminds me of a bird, the way he moves, always darting about and rather low to the ground. He's full of energy and at his age is able to keep going without coffee. I don't know how he does it."

"How old is he?" Clive asked.

"Oh, I'd say eighty-four, but he doesn't look a day over fifty. He gets up every morning at six and runs through Grant Park, trudging along in his Keds. Yes, Keds. Clive, you don't even know what those are. People wore them before we had all these expensive running shoes. Lipman is very particular and he knows what he likes. He's been invaluable to our visiting artists in rehearsal before a concert and he's in better shape than most of them," Claude said with pride.

𝕏

Word spread that Clive had been accepted into the Tchaikovsky Competition. As such, the perks of this honor began to manifest themselves.

"Clive, I have good news for you. The Steinway dealer in Langston Grove has agreed to allow you and Mr. Lipman free practice time in the store basement, where their inventory is stashed," Claude relayed.

"Since Saul doesn't have side-by-side grand pianos in his home, you and Mr. Lipman will meet at Steinway each evening around eight. This is going to be a wonderful arrangement for you to focus and carry on without interruptions of any kind. I'm so pleased Walter has agreed to accompany you. Saul and I will come by once a week to see how you two are getting on." Claude Serkin beamed. "Things are coming together, Clive. Can't you just feel it?"

Mr. Lipman turned out to be feisty, gracious, and talented, but he didn't like heat. This proved to be challenging when the air-conditioning system turned off at nine. Each evening, Clive took the old iron stairway down to the basement because the freight elevator was turned off at that hour.

"Mr. Lipman, are you down here?" In the poor light, Clive maneuvered his way through the maze of Steinway pianos, shedding his Chopin T-shirt immediately.

"Yes, yes, Clive, I'm over here. Come and take a look at this beauty. It must be from the turn of the century. Look at this walnut finish. I could have sworn they were all mahogany. I don't think we dare use this one, but what a treasure. Have you ever seen a piano like this?" Mr. Lipman put dress gloves on before running his hand across the flawless lid.

He is quirky, Clive thought. *Who has gloves in their pockets in July?*

Even though they practiced for four hours each night, Mr. Lipman would remain in his suit and tie. Despite steadily climbing temperatures—often within striking distance of one hundred degrees—with sweat pouring down his face and dripping onto the keyboard, he never removed a single article of clothing. "Why don't you at least take off your suit jacket, Mr. Lipman?" Clive inquired.

"Not to worry, Clive. We are here to make music, not to take off our clothes"—which is exactly what Clive would do. With each passing hour, he removed a layer of clothing until there was nothing left but his Israeli-flag boxer shorts. "Surely your mother doesn't allow you to practice in such undistinguished attire at home. Have you no sense of decorum? You act as if you were born in a barn," Mr. Lipman would say, mopping his brow with his fourth handkerchief.

"Perhaps tonight we could stop at midnight. I have an important test tomorrow in my AP Literature class and I can't be late for school in the morning," Clive suggested.

"Late for school, utter nonsense. If you are going to do this, Clive, you must live like superman. Increase everything, pursue high-level health. Compromise nothing but a touch of sleep. Are you drinking your nutrition power shakes every day at school? They do wonders for my stamina. What about the wheat germ I gave you and the curry and cayenne powders for your juicing? All of this will make a difference. If you practice these measures, you will not have any trouble missing a couple of hours of sleep a night. *Measures,* ha, no pun intended. Sometimes I am so funny, I surprise myself."

Clive sized up Mr. Lipman on the piano bench across from him. He looked like a Doberman Pinscher in human form: compact, bent over, and ready to strike.

Despite his penchant for sweaty fashion, Mr. Lipman proved to be a blessing with his adept knowledge of the concerto score for both the Chopin and the Tchaikovsky, coupled with his confounding endurance. When Papa first suggested him as an accompanist, Clive couldn't imagine an eighty-four-year-old man would be able to keep up with the rigors of preparing for a competition of this magnitude.

Not only did he keep up, Mr. Lipman exhorted Clive to press on after midnight, when he sensed Clive's spark going out. "You're almost there. Stay with it, Clive. One more time, *prestissimo!*"

He sounded like a track coach, encouraging his boy to the finish line with a bellowing voice and a stopwatch.

Everyone was behind him—Papa, Mama, Mr. K, Anna, and even the Brookline Academy community—relishing that one of their own was soon to compete on the world stage. All of them were there except Clare, the sole indispensable person he relied upon to lead the charge. The lack of the Folio rendered him totally cut off from her. In her absence, it was his lifeline to her, a lifeline he himself had chosen to sever by sending the Folio to New Hampshire. Why did she not send it back? In the dream, she had said, "Don't let go."

※

"Clive, there's a letter for you," Anna pronounced after sorting through the mail one Saturday. The postal stamp indicated it was from New Hampshire. After pocketing it swiftly so Mama and Papa wouldn't see, heart pounding, he ascended the stairs to his room. *Take a deep breath, relax; she's reaching out to you. This is a good sign.*

Sniffing the letter first to see if he could capture Clare's floral perfume scent and hoping she had sprayed some on the envelope, there was nothing. Looking at the handwritten address, the writing appeared to be cursory and rushed. The envelope was white, not lavender, her signature color. The image of the lavender calligraphy advertisement first seen on the Westdale Conservatory bulletin board flashed through his mind. *Perhaps her illness is affecting her ability to write*, he thought.

Almost trembling, he read the terse letter in his hands.

Clive,

Your book arrived and Clare will not be able to return it. She is not doing too well right now, and I am going to be taking care of her for an unspecified period of time. She asked that I encourage you to keep working toward the full attainment of your dreams, which she regrets she will not be able to participate in at this time.

Best of luck,

Nero Cardiff

Crushing the letter between his fists, Clive stopped to look at his mammoth hands. *He's such a liar. Ask Bethany what she thinks? No. Find out for yourself, enough of this mystery. Confront the brutal facts.* Clive's mind raced.

Newport, New Hampshire. There it is, about nine hundred miles away. That's more than a one-day drive there and back.

If he took Anna, they could share the driving. But then who would cover for him at home with Mama and Papa? *But she may not even need to do that because they would probably be at the conference. It will be better for me to go alone,* Clive concluded. *She doesn't need to get mixed up in this any more than she is already.*

I have the address. That's all I need. If I listen to recordings on the way, I won't be wasting too much time. Taneyev. Where's the Taneyev recording?

"Anna, could you come in here?" Clive shouted toward his sister's room. "I need your help ... again. I'm becoming dependent on you, which I am sure you are enjoying immensely. Don't worry, it won't last."

CHAPTER 22

Sforzando—Forced; a strong, sudden accent

There it was before him, the wide-open, unscripted land along Interstate 65, as seen from the freedom of a hunter-green Ford Fiesta. Clive felt like he was single-handedly writing a great love story across the American heartland. *Young Musician Flees to Rescue Piano Teacher from Demented Husband*, the headline read.

He pulled off at Exit 21 and noticed his gas meter reaching the red zone. Ahead was rural Route 10, the road to Newport, New Hampshire. After traveling a few miles, he decided not to risk waiting on the next station. It was almost dark, and there might not be another one before he ran out. Pulling into the small stop, only two gas pumps, Clive looked around and felt like he was in a 1950s sitcom. Off to the right of the entrance was a rusty pickup, the entire back bed planted full of petunias. The convenience store looked more like a general store from *Mayberry*.

"Hey, there, are you lookin' for somethin'? You look lost." Approaching from the other side of the gas pump, the man was wearing overalls and a "Go Whippets" baseball cap.

"I'm trying to get to Newport. How much farther might that be?" Clive asked.

The weathered gentleman looked at the boy quizzically. "Newport? You don't look to be from around here. What business do you have in Newport? That's a little tourist town, ya know, the kind with cute shops, a covered bridge, craft fairs and all. You hankerin' to do some shoppin'?"

Clive laughed at this man's unabashed curiosity, to say nothing of the fact this town still had gas station attendants. The hand-painted sign over the door proclaimed, "Gus's Garage."

"Are you Gus?" Clive asked.

"Nope, Gus was my father. He started this station when there was nothing here. After he died, I took it over. We have food inside too, if you want a snack." Evidently, the man was lonely and in search of some conversation.

"I can't stop right now. How much farther is Newport?" Clive persisted.

"Newport is about another fifty miles on Route 10. Once you cross the Sugar River, you'll know you're almost there. Who d'ya know in Newport?" His nosy demeanor seemed out of character for New Hampshire, which Clive expected to be more circumspect.

"I'm going to visit some old friends," Clive volunteered.

"Are they artists? A lot of artists live there and make things for the shops. If you have time, take a look around. You might find something you want to bring home to your mom. All right, you're set. Have a safe journey." With a thump of the car roof, the owner sent him on his way.

Clive could see the man in his rearview mirror as he pulled onto the road. His suggestion of a gift for his mother was unnerving. *Do I look like a runaway? What if he calls the police?* The velvety descent of darkness brought the chiming of crickets, which he could hear through the open car window. The airy nighttime moisture, laced with the scent of fresh-cut grass, trickled down his windshield. He would never find the farm at this late hour. Besides, there wouldn't be anyone milling about in town to direct him to Wisteria Lane. If only he could find a piano, he could use the late-night hours for practice.

After fourteen hours in the car and without someone like Mr. Lipman pressuring him to stay awake, Clive was at risk of falling asleep and missing the morning. A dangerous risk, he knew, for the morning would be the best time to catch Clare before she went out for the day. *What does a pianist do in New Hampshire? Would she have taken on other students? Where would they come from? There aren't many people here.*

"Your music is at home, Clive, with your father." Rabbi Sherveen's words repeated themselves, entwined with the Chopin nocturne playing in the car and the twisting pavement of Route 10. All the great composers fought for love. He learned this in the Folio. Chopin. Schumann. Even Beethoven, in his own cryptic way, had his Immortal Beloved. He would be no different.

The road undulated like the sea, lulling him into a drowsiness that he fought off with the music. He popped in a CD of Liszt's *Hungarian Rhapsody.*

Attempting to stay alert by playing along on the steering wheel worked well, but it was distracting. He didn't see the small black shadow emerge from the woods and dart straight out into the road. Desperately swerving the car across the yellow line and right into the oncoming lane, he saw the shadow stop dead in its tracks. Headlights came toward him over the crest of the hill. Clive had no choice but to head directly into the shadow to escape the oncoming car.

In slow-motion stillness, Clive swerved onto the shoulder and then brought the car back into his own lane. The shadow was gone. The oncoming car passed by.

Could he have imagined it? The shadow looked like a large cat, definitely black. Did they have panthers in this part of the country? The old wives' tale of black cats crossing in front of him was one his mother used during his childhood, but the animal didn't cross in front of him. He didn't hit it and Clive was now fiercely awake. He spent the next forty miles listening to Taneyev and questioning the ominous shadow. Could it be an omen? A dark presence coming between him and Clare? Or the shadow may have been a warning of something even more dangerous ahead? As the miles clicked by, his mind mulled the possibilities while his fingers pounded out the music on the steering wheel.

Newport—Population 1,571. The sign indicated he should have no trouble finding Clare in this country village. Gus's gas station attendant wasn't kidding about the cute shops lining Main Street. One after the other, their illuminated windows showed handmade quilts, paintings, and pottery. At the end of the street was the town hall, surrounded by a white rail fence. It looked like Popperville from the *Mike Mulligan* picture book his nanny read to him when he was young. *Hard to believe towns like this still exist*, he marveled.

Pulling the car over, he imagined Clare walking from the farm into town for her groceries. This was her town—or was it? With her touring schedule, how much time could she actually spend here? Not a single car was parked along Main Street. In the middle of the night, he didn't have a chance of finding their farm.

Sleeping in the car before the sun comes up will clear my mind and help me prepare to see Clare and face Nero tomorrow, he reasoned. The drive had allowed plenty of time to prepare for their conversation and divest the burning desire to punish Nero for his thoughtless letter.

Closing his eyes, Clive pictured the soon-to-be scene in the morning: Nestled within the prolific blooms of the apple orchard, a small farmhouse with a front bay window rests, visible from the end of the long driveway. He cautiously strolls up the gravel path to the front door. The strains of Brahms's *Waltz in A-flat Major* drift out the open window. With the ringing of the doorbell,

the music stops. The quiet spell of the humming bees is punctu-
ated by the sound of clogs against the pine plank floor. The door
opens. Reaching up, Clare throws her arms around his neck in
a joyous hug. "Clive, what an unbelievable surprise. What are
you doing here?" Walking hand in hand with Clive through the
front foyer, Clare calls out, "Nero, come and say hello. You won't
believe who is here." The apple blossoms on the table in the front
hall fill the room with the freshness of new life.

Startled by the sight of a policeman tapping on his window,
Clive wrested himself out of sleep, disoriented by the strangeness of awakening in a car. "Rise and shine. Shouldn't you be off
to school by now?" The town hall clock read five after nine. Clive
had slept much longer than he planned. "Thanks for waking me
up, officer. I'll be on my way now."

"You're not supposed to park on Main Street overnight, but
since you're not from around here, I can make an exception this
time."

"Thank you, sir." Had Gus from the gas station reported him
to the police? That was unlikely, or the officer would have been
much more curious.

"By the way, I'm going to visit some friends on Wisteria Lane,
but I'm not sure where that is. Could you point me in the right
direction?"

"Wisteria Lane. That's right down on the river. Follow Main
Street along the curve until you get to the mill. Cross over the
covered bridge and Wisteria is the first right after the bridge. You
can't miss it. Do you have their address?"

"Yes, sir, I do. Thanks so much."

As he approached the Sugar River, he saw the big mill wheel
directly beyond the covered bridge. The scent of apple blossoms
drifted up from the banks of the river into the hills. The entire
scene appeared to be lifted from a fairytale. He half-expected to
see woodland nymphs and elves waiting for him along the river
bank, to show him the way to the farmhouse.

Turning into the driveway past the mailbox covered in vines, Clive could see the house, surrounded by meadows and orchards. It was exactly as he had pictured it in his mind. *With all this blossoming color and life, Clare must love it here.* Even if he couldn't convince her to come back, he would always have this image of her here in his mind. With a shift of the car into park, he sat and listened. There were plenty of birds singing, but no notes from a piano.

A tinge of fear came upon his hands as they held on to the steering wheel. *You can do this. Go forward. Just go. What's there to lose at this point?* But the unnatural stillness and beauty of the scene held him in place.

"Bethany believes everything happens for a reason," Clare had told him. The looming sense that he was about to find out the reason held him back. Now, after coming all this way, he wasn't sure he wanted to know. He thought of Rabbi Sherveen, and for the first time since his bar mitzvah, he prayed. "God of Jacob, help me. Give me strength." He waited, hoping to feel something in response to his prayer, some wind of releasing or a confirmation to keep going. Nothing changed.

Stepping out of the car, it occurred to him that no one might be home. There were no cars in the driveway. The silence coming from the house could mean a long drive back empty-handed.

The house sat slightly elevated above the orchard, and the path to the front door was lined with bulbs in clay pots, their shoots cresting above the dirt. He could see his hand trembling as he stretched it toward the doorbell. Hoping for the sound of her wooden clogs, he waited. After what seemed like an entire day, the door opened.

The man was unshaven and disheveled, having a vague resemblance to the man he met in Clare's studio one afternoon. *Could this be the caretaker?*

"Hello, I'm looking for Clare Cardiff. Might she be here?"

"And who are you?"

"I'm her piano student, Clive Serkin. I was hoping to speak with her. I've come from a very long way."

The man stared at Clive and rocked back and forth in front of the glass door, arms crossed. Clive thought he might lose his balance and fall backward. "Her piano student, huh? Come on in."

Standing in the foyer, which gave the impression of Monticello with its rotunda ceiling and circular table in the center, Clive noticed a stale odor, as though the windows had not been opened all winter. In a vase on the circular table, an arrangement of dead forsythia branches gave off the stench of fetid water.

"What can I do for you?" the man asked Clive with a slightly sick grin.

"I'm sorry. I don't know who you are. Is Clare here?" Clive asked.

"No, she doesn't live here anymore."

"Do I have the wrong address? This is the address I was given for Clare and Nero Cardiff."

"Yes, this was once their house, but she became ill. She now lives somewhere else with people who care for her."

"What kind of care? I had no idea her condition had deteriorated to such a degree. That seems unlikely. It hasn't been that long since I last saw her."

"Yes, and with sick people things can change quickly."

"I'm sorry, who are you?"

"I'm Nero, Clare's husband, and her caretaker."

Clive wondered what could have happened to this man that he changed so dramatically since their meeting in Clare's studio. He looked bedraggled and torn. What could have happened to Clare?

"Could you tell me what is wrong with her? If you are her caretaker, why aren't you taking care of her?" It seemed like a reasonable question.

"She is demented, you know, crazy, as in losing her mind. She became violent and dangerous, so I put her in a safe place. She is free from harm there, and so am I."

"What are you talking about? Clare was fine when she left Brookline. Where is she? You are making this up like the fictitious response in the letter you sent me. She's here, isn't she? Tell me where she is."

Clive was growing increasingly frustrated and he considered physically confronting Nero. The man appeared withered, almost feeble. It didn't seem like the right move.

Before Clive had a chance to decide his next course of action, Nero grabbed Clive's arm and began to usher him out the front door. "I think I've already told you more than you need to know, so let's end this conversation before things get difficult."

In a whirl, Clive spun back at him with a sudden energy and ferocity. Nero was startled and lost his balance, breaking Clive free of his grasp. As Nero wrestled to pick him up and throw all one hundred and forty-five pounds of this boy out of his house, Clive groped for the closest weapon within his reach, the statuette on the hall table. It was the perfect size for him to grasp within his mighty hand and hurl it at Nero with all his force.

"Tell me where she is," Clive screamed. All of his anger toward Nero manifested itself in his giant hands. He didn't know whether to lunge forward and try to tackle him to the floor or hurl the statuette at him. He chose the latter. The statuette just missed Nero's head, went careening into the front room, and smashed into the side of the piano. The piano groaned with the crash, creating a hollow cry of strings, hammers, and ceramic shatter. The carnage immediately diverted Nero's attention. He ran away from Clive, toward the piano, and knelt down near the broken pieces. Clive watched Nero cowering over them in an attempt to join the clay statuette back together. Whispers and tears followed.

"Johannes, Johannes, my dear little boy," he cried out over the broken pieces, pathetically attempting to gather them together. With his bare hands, Nero swept them into a pile, then placed both bleeding palms over the top of the lifeless heap and burrowed his forehead into them.

"Are you going to tell me where she is now?" Clive asked from the hall, his voice echoing in the rotunda's emptiness. This time, he kept his distance from the mournful old man.

"She's gone. Johannes is gone. They're both gone. Leave me alone. Get out of here," Nero hissed through his tears. Clive could see the man was disarmed and grieving over the broken statuette, so he felt safe enough to search the house for Clare. Racing from room to room and screaming her name louder with the opening of each door, he came upon a bedroom in which every piece of furniture was covered in white sheets. The room had a large double bed and floral wallpaper. In this preserved room, there was a hint of the familiar. Despite the closed windows, the room smelled fresh, like the first cut of summer grass mixed with honey. This was Clare's room. Her scent was here.

With renewed courage and determination, Clive ran back down the stairs. He found Nero still in a pile over his statuette. Not only was the statuette broken, but the man was visibly shattered. *If anyone is suffering from an illness, it's him.* Keeping his distance, but with calm articulation, Clive spoke his parting words: "I will find Clare, and when I do, she's never coming back to you or to this farm or to New Hampshire. I'm going to take her far away from here. Forever. "

Nero didn't move. He sat still on the floor, kneading the broken pottery with his blood stained hands.

CHAPTER 23

Anacrusis—Upbeat, the pickup note

"Saul, Clive, come along. We can't miss this bus. There is so much to see and this might be our only chance to see it," Claude exclaimed, motioning to them like a conductor. Climbing aboard, the Russian tour guide was already giving the history of Bolshaya Nikitskaya Street in romantically accented, broken English. "This street is named for the Nikitsky Monastery, founded by the grandfather of the first Romanov Czar, Mikhail I. The monastery has long since been replaced by electrical substation for Metro. Here at corner we see little Church of Resurrection. Built in 1634, the church was one of handful to remain open under Communism. If you have time, you must visit because interiors are original, very old, beautiful." Claude leaned over to Saul and Clive. "We won't have time for that stop," he said with a wink.

"Now we come to crown jewel of Nikitskaya Street, Moscow Conservatory. Look at this palace of music. Today, this is where adventure begins. Dreams will be made or broken. Moscow Conservatory, truly is a palace. Originally home of Princess Yekaterina Dashkova, who was close friend of Catherine the Great. Princess Dashkova was intelligent and knew many famous people, like French philosophers Diderot, Voltaire, and American, Ben Franklin. The building still looks like home, magnificent. Music soaring from every open window. Here you must get out and take photograph."

As the little band of tourists descended the bus stairs, a flock of Muscovites, who had been following the bus, surrounded the group. "We take photo for free," they offered, competing for the opportunity.

"Clive, Saul, let's get a picture here with Tchaikovsky," Claude suggested. Out in front of the building, the statue of Pyotr Ilyich Tchaikovsky welcomed visitors and students, cast in bronze, arms raised for the downbeat. "I will do the same for the picture; let me conduct with Master Tchaikovsky," Claude said as he positioned himself in the center of the trio and imitated the pose of Tchaikovsky. Allowing one of the locals to take the photograph was likely to be a scam, but they took the risk. Fortunately, the group did not ask for money. With interlocking arms, Clive, Saul, and Claude proceeded up the circular drive.

Attempting to hold back tears, Claude was nearly overcome by the emotion of sharing this moment with his son and dearest lifelong friend, Saul Koussevitsky. He had always dreamed of Clive being here. Now he could admit this to himself. *We are now all here, together. From Haifa, to America, to Russia, together.* He looked over at his son, who was now three inches taller than he and recognized that the next five days would shape his entire future. *He will be a different man by sundown on Saturday, hopefully a man who can take defeat or victory with humility and honor.* This would also be a test of how well he had fathered Clive.

"I can't believe I am actually here, Papa," Clive said as though reading Claude's thoughts.

Claude reached out for Clive's hands and looked down at

them with reverence. He remembered the chubby feeling of his hands when he was three and the lengthening line of his fingers when he was thirteen. He closed his eyes and prayed he would remember what they felt like today.

"Remember this moment, Clive. You are entering a school of your great history. Tchaikovsky and Nicolai Rubenstein, two of the founders, have passed through these doors. Richter. Van Cliburn. Rachmaninoff. Scriabin. Arthur Rubenstein. Taneyev. Shostakovich, and now, you. Many of them were Jewish and given safety here for the sake of their art. May this be a safe haven for you, son, as you pursue your dream." Claude stopped at the door to give Clive a big Russian bear hug before they crossed the threshold.

Claude knew he had to memorialize the moment for his young son, who had been very quiet since they arrived in Moscow. Pre-competition jitters, he assumed. "And here before us is the grand staircase leading to the Great Hall. And at the top on the landing, you will see the bronze bust of Mussorgsky illuminated for dramatic effect."

"Papa, how many times have you been here?" Clive wondered, impressed by his father's knowledge of the details.

"Oh, more than I can count. But I do remember the first time I came here with your great-uncle Rudolph. I was no more than twenty and he gave me the tour. Not much has changed since then. Listen, do you hear that? Rachmaninoff's *Etudes-Tableaux.* Your competition is practicing," Claude said with a satisfied smile.

There was so much more he wanted to tell Clive, but he feared overwhelming him with an abundance of his perspective so he called upon Saul to take over the tour. "Saul, give Clive just a bit more history before we release him to his practice room."

"My pleasure, Claude." Saul was pleased his old friend had brought him into the teachable moment. "You know most of this, Clive, but perhaps there are a few things you don't know. The Tchaikovsky Competition is one of two piano competitions with an impact felt around the world. To the other, the Van Cliburn, we owe a great debt. Because of Van Cliburn, we come here without the expectation of our music being the first to change the world. He's already done that in a way which only he could do. At a time when the Cold War was raging and no American had ever played in Russia, Van Cliburn conquered the hearts of the Russian people, even Khrushchev's. Against all protocol and expectation, the Russian ruler agreed to give him the first prize because as he said himself, "Van Cliburn was the best." That was 1958, and the first Tchaikovsky Competition won by an American pianist. So you see Clive, you are free of the burden of expectation." Now it was Saul's turn to wink at Clive.

"I remember reading that the line for tickets to that competition snaked around many blocks. Is that true, Papa?"

"The excitement of this competition is, in part, due to the audience. The Russian people have a love affair with the piano, due to their heritage in composition and performance. We Americans have sports heroes. Russia has its artists and they are treated like royalty.

"It is true that the ticket line for Van Cliburn's first round snaked around the block and that was only for the first round. Being the youngest competitor by almost four years will work to your advantage. You will not have the pressure of expectation and reputation like your fellow competitor Niebuhr. He has all the pressure. He's good, but everyone is looking to him to make Mother Russia proud and keep the prize at home. In comparison, you are a relatively unknown American Jewish boy whose father brings his orchestra to Russia every few years. If they know anything about you, it is only because of me." Claude delivered this statement with a mocking hand upon his heart and a nod to the heavens, causing Clive to laugh for the first time since they arrived. Claude hoped it would not be the last.

"Clive, come, they are giving us the tour of the Great Hall now. It's not to be missed," Saul insisted. Upon entering the Hall,

Mr. K drew a sharp breath and sighed deeply as though in pain. He abruptly took the nearest seat, uncharacteristic for someone so enthused about experiencing every moment.

Claude sat down next to him. "Saul, are you feeling all right? Like Clive, you've been surprisingly quiet on this trip thus far. I figured you were transfixed by a state of awe, but now I'm wondering if it is something else. The flight over and all this touring immediately might be too much for you. Maybe it is time for us to head back to the hotel."

"No, no absolutely not. You go on the tour with Clive. It is better for you two. I want you to share every moment of this experience. This is more important for the two of you than the three of us. I will rest here until you return," Saul said.

))(

The Great Hall reminded Clive of Boston's Symphony Hall in its dimension, rather narrow and very deep, with only a Steinway concert grand on the stage. Surrounding the perimeter were portraits of every great Russian composer. Framed in a scrolling neoclassical relief, they looked like a pantheon of gods presiding over the present. "The gods of music," as Clare would say, "the gods of music are watching over you, Clive." Her voice was still singing in his ears, a hopeful prelude to the days ahead.

Looking at their portraits with black and white bearded faces, Clive felt a kinship with them because of the Folio. He was one of the few people who knew some of their personal thoughts and struggles, and what others descended from them actually thought about them. Rather than imposing figures, they were more like brothers, cheering him on. It felt like they were inviting Clive to join them, to become an agent of culture with them.

As the tour meandered back to the starting point, with Claude trailing and distracted by a portrait, Clive saw that Mr. K was still sitting in his seat. He looked pale and haggard.

"Mr. Koussevitsky, are you sure you're all right?" Clive questioned.

"Being in the Great Hall with you, with this huge endeavor before us, is a bit overwhelming; I had to sit down. Forgive me, my boy, for not walking with you on the rest of our tour. Sitting here makes me realize my life has come full circle. When I was a boy in Israel, we didn't have these opportunities. Oh, yes, we worked hard hoping for a better day, but the Russian school was out of reach for most of us. People did not come and go then like they do today. I longed to be here and would listen to my friend Sasha talk about this place, wishing for the day when I might be here."

"There are legends in these halls," Mr. K recalled. "Like the day Mr. Tchaikovsky himself stopped the orchestra in the middle of a concert, because someone in the audience was crinkling paper. He turned around, crossed his hands over his chest, and waited. Imagine the silence falling as the orchestra stopped. Once he was satisfied, he turned around and picked up precisely where he left off."

Mr. K's eyes misted over as he patted Clive's knee. "You are now here with them, living amidst these legends. This week, you will make your mark."

"Mr. Koussevitsky, I'm so grateful you made this trip with us. I thank you for all you have given me since I was a little boy. I hope you will be honored by my playing, that in some way, you will be repaid for your investment. Please know how much I appreciate your sacrifices for me. You could have gone back to Israel after Rachel died. I'm so glad you didn't."

Mr. K breathed in the moment, with a visible wince but without complaint.

"Let me see your hands." His withered hands lifted Clive's palms up toward the ceiling. "I pray such a blessing on these hands. May the God our fathers, the God of Jacob, accept the offering of your hands. Not that I am honored, but may He be honored." With true softness and love, visible through the thick lenses of his glasses, Mr. K reaffirmed his blessing. "This is what is most important. Clive, you must understand this. It is not about you, or me, or your papa. It is about bringing glory to God. This is something I have always tried to teach you because if I didn't, well, who would?" Saul held on to Clive's hand and gave it a filial squeeze. "Let us go now and find your father. He will be anxious to meet your competition at the reception tonight and he'll be anxious to get this old man to our hotel."

CHAPTER 24

Bravura—Spirit, skill on the part of the performer

Clive sat with Claude and Mr. K at the opening reception dinner in Rachmaninov Hall. In keeping with his eating habits, he pushed his borscht around in his bowl and his beef around his gold-trimmed dinner plate.

"If you're not going to eat anything, at least put Mr. Lipman's remedies in your water glass and drink up," Claude commanded.

"Papa, it's hard to eat until we know the order of play," Clive explained.

Claude tried to put his son at ease. "Drawing lots is done differently here. Most of the competitions you've played in have used the coin toss, but with fourteen musicians, that's not possible at the Tchaikovsky."

The official administering the lots was an enormous man. He looked like a combination of Khrushchev and Uncle Sam—bald head meets long, skinny beard. After dinner, all of the musicians waited in line to be handed a slip of golden paper. Once everyone had drawn their papers, the numbers were announced aloud.

Heinrich Niebuhr, 13. Clive Serkin, 14. Clive had the fortunate spot of last to play, but the unfortunate position of following Niebuhr.

As the participants returned to their tables, Clive noticed Niebuhr staring him down like a gunfighter in an Old West corral. "He's trying to intimidate you. Don't let him," Claude whispered. Niebuhr's black eyes, in the candlelight of a formal dinner, appeared to glow like a sacrificial flame. He looked stocky, built like a fire hydrant. As he turned to shake hands with one of the judges, his hands appeared massively disproportionate to his body.

Clive sensed his father perceiving his thoughts. "You and Heinrich are a study of contrasts in every way. Remember, this is not a beauty contest. The judges are listening, not looking. This contest is not about hands or the color of your hair. In the end of the day, the outcome will be determined by the heart," Claude said.

"Papa, how could I not be intimidated by him? Since everyone arrived in Moscow, a few competitors have said they've run into Niebuhr leaving the practice room at four in the morning. The rumor going around is he doesn't sleep at all. Instead, he seeks a state of harmony in whatever he is doing, be it performing or going to the bathroom," Clive joked.

"Harmony as a state of being is very important to Richter. No doubt, this quest has rubbed off on Niebuhr, his student. We're talking about much more than musical harmony. It's a total state of being, the attunement of one's life to what makes life worth living. Richter believed this 'necessary harmony' was attainable through the arts, beauty, and love, but there's no need to spend time thinking about that now. You stay focused on your own preparation and let Niebuhr focus on his."

X

After dinner, a bus shuttled the participants and family members to their hotels. Clive's hotel, the Hotel Savoy Moscow, looked similar to many of the buildings on Rozhdestvenka Street—only five stories tall with a façade covered in tall, thin windows. Inside the lobby, a pianist played *Moscow Nights* on the piano as everyone checked in. Norman Pobanz, the other American pianist, waved a confident greeting and sauntered across the inlaid tile floor to introduce himself. As usual, he recognized Papa.

A bellman accompanied the trio to their rooms and Clive noted that the hotel hallways were very narrow. They had to walk behind the gentleman with the brass luggage carrier in order to pass through the hall.

"Mr. Koussevitzky, you will have this room here, and Maestro Serkin and son will be right across the hall," the bellman directed. *Thankfully,* Clive thought. *I won't be able to hear Mr. K snoring.* After inspecting the room and deeming it satisfactory, Papa began the second of his motivational speeches. "This telegram came today from your mother. She wishes she could be here with us; you know that, don't you? She chose to stay home to be with Anna and allow this time of music together for the three of us."

Somewhat pleased that Mama remembered, Clive proceeded to rip open the yellow envelope.

> *Dearest Clive,*
> *I know you are ready. Be at peace and give it your all.*
> *I love you,*
> *Mother*

"Well, that's a pleasant surprise. How sweet of Mama."

"Even though she hasn't been there for you whenever you needed her, you know she loves you very much," Papa said, sticking up for her as usual. *You didn't see me at age five writing messages to her and sticking them under her office door after dinner, hoping she would write me back,* Clive thought, but responded, "Yes, Papa, I know."

"I too have something for you." Claude walked over to his leather suitcase and withdrew a small wrapped gift from the top pocket. "This belonged to your great-grandfather Yitzak. When he came to America from Israel, he arrived at Ellis Island. The journey was long. He was sick and alone, with very little money. Due to his illness, he was detained in an emigrant hospital where he became even sicker. He would sit in his small hospital room all day, looking out at the Statue of Liberty, and rub this between his fingers, praying for health and a happier life.

"The God of Israel provided for him. As you know, he recovered and became quite a successful business man. He came over with this and gave it to me when I made my debut with the New York Philharmonic. It has been in my pocket ever since. Now I want you to have it, for good fortune and success. I know you will keep it with you, always."

The coin, a ten-shekel piece from 1888, was large and shining gold. Although marked as only ten shekels, its weight made it much more valuable.

"Ten shekels must have been a lot of money back in that day, right, Papa?"

Mere words could not express the gratitude Clive felt for his father's willingness to part with this treasure, a piece of his heritage and family lineage. "Is it valuable?" Clive inquired.

"It is not valuable to this world, but it is priceless to the Serkin family. When you had your bar mitzvah, you became a man. Over these past several years, you have become a man in a different way. You have served your art with all of your being. Your spirit has been broken. I have seen it, but like your great-grandfather Yitzak, you did not let that stop you. Now, my son, you are ready to soar. Bring all you have learned to the keyboard and then let go of it. Be you, and that will be enough."

After hugging Papa, the duo climbed into ornate single beds, covered in copious down pillows and embroidered blankets. Exhaustion took over, and Clive resisted the temptation to go to the practice room one last time. Instead he thought of Clare and guessed his father knew of his love and loss. Papa said, "Your spirit has been broken." He must suspect something.

X

At first light, the breakfast room of the Savoy was clamoring with activity. The three men were seated at a table next to a copper fountain with goldfish swimming, which reflected halos of light upon the ceiling. A Russian newspaper had been placed on Claude's plate. The dream of Clare reaching her hand into the pond to rescue Clive flashed through Clive's mind. *A good omen. She is not letting go of me even though she's not here.*

After returning from the breakfast buffet, Papa hunkered down to business. "Give us the rundown on your warm-up this morning and how you envision that going. I don't mean to be overbearing, but I do want to know that you have thought through every detail. Since I've been backstage at the Conservatory, I can give you some insight about what to expect."

"Well, I've decided to arrive backstage two hours before my designated time to focus on my warm-up and listen to Niebuhr's playing. In the first round, we are required to play the Tchaikovsky's *Theme and Variations in F Major*, as well as Bach, Mozart, and several etudes by Russian composers. I noticed yesterday on our tour, the backstage area is stuffy, not well ventilated, so I'd like to bring a fan. I am grateful for that in a way, because I hate playing with cold hands. My area has a large mirror, helpful for stretching, but I'll probably stretch on the floor."

"Good," said Claude "You should know the building is so old and well constructed that you might not be able to hear the other competitors playing their pieces, which I don't recommend you try to do. Lay out your warm-up mat, lie down on the floor, stretch, breathe, and focus. If you must listen, listening from the ground may be an effective antidote to those thick plaster walls. Remember when you were a little boy and you would come down to Symphony Hall and hide under the stage to hear the orchestra? You're already an expert at this. Your dressing room will be right on the back, stage right of the performers. You might be able to hear best that way."

Mr. Koussevitsky also chimed in. "Do everything you already know, but do not forget to breathe. Breathe the notes in and sing them out. The music must sing out. Your piano is your voice. Now finish your breakfast. We don't want to hear your stomach grumbling."

The shuttle bus carried a group of around twenty to the Conservatory. The bus was silent. None of the participants or their family members looked at each other for the duration of the fifteen-minute ride. A handsome, polished-looking young usher in a blue blazer with a harp patch on the breast pocket greeted each person as they disembarked and introduced the escorts. Each escort would be responsible for the needs of their assigned competitor during the competition. Clive's escort introduced himself as Sergey and showed the group of three to the assigned warm-up room. He shook hands with each of the men. "Good luck, Mr. Serkin. We look forward to your playing. Let me know if you need anything." With an efficient turn, he made his way down the hall toward the parking lot to attend to the needs of his next charge.

The room was similar to those shown on the previous day's tour—walls angled and steep, plain peeling paint, a dressing table with a mirror, and a metal locker off to the right. Unremarkable, except for the messages written all over the walls.

"To study music, we must learn the rules. To create music, we must break them."—Nadia Boulanger.

"Music is enough for a lifetime, but a lifetime is not enough for music." —Sergei Rachmaninoff.

It was now time for Papa and Mr. K to leave. They each shook hands. "Good luck." And they each turned quickly and walked down the hall toward the Great Hall seating area.

Closing the door was like isolating himself from the world. There was only Clive and a lifetime of preparation in the room.

Yundi Lao of China had finished playing. Now it was Niebuhr's turn. The footsteps of the competitors could be heard outside the door. Lao's little feet tickled the floor as she went by, while Niebuhr sounded like a determined bull charging past the door. The clapping began before he even sat down. They knew him and had been expecting him.

Reaching exercises, stretch the obliques. Reach for freedom of movement. Reach up. Reach out. Breathe. Rest. Relax.

Niebuhr was on stage, conquering the variations with a commanding and impressive tone. Clive pressed his ear to the wooden floor, but he couldn't hear his competitor clearly. Trying to get even closer to the music, he crouched against the wall on the stage side. There was a marked improvement, increasing the audibility by at least ten decibels.

Closing his eyes like a doctor listening to a patient's heartbeat, Clive was surprised by what he heard. Contrary to Papa's predictions, Niebuhr had chosen the largely lyrical *Scriabin* **Etude in B Major.** This piece conjured images of a lovely summer day by the river, not an attack piece at all. His technique was flawless as expected, his sound fluid, free, and unencumbered. It was Niebuhr's own sound, not Richter's style. The audience responded with shouts of *Bravo!* and it was only the first round. What would they do for the finals? Carry him off on their shoulders?

Clive became jittery. *Wait for his feet to pass by the door before leaving the dressing room. Avoid the black pits of Niebuhr's eyes. There is no need to have him looking into my soul before I even begin.* The jury had made allowances for those who like to bring their own piano bench. Clive's bench with "Serkin" written on it was right by the stage door. Sergey smiled at Clive as they met at the entrance, following him onstage carrying his piano bench. *Deep breaths. Take this moment of rest. How many great pianists have touched this Steinway concert grand?*

The Great Hall was jammed with people who had been allowed to sit in the aisles of both amphitheater levels. Before sitting, Clive acknowledged their welcoming applause. He looked to the right and the left at the portraits of great composers, fixing his eyes for a second on Chopin. Then he thought of something Clare had said when he started studying with her: *"Chopin is greatness, originality, invention, and purity of sound. We all bow to him. This humility must be there."* With humility, Clive bowed first right, then left, and then to the audience in the middle.

With one more deep breath, he gathered himself into Bach's ***Prelude and Fugue in B-flat minor*** from *The Well-Tempered Clavier.* He recalled a conversation with Papa after questioning his readiness to compete in the Tchaikovsky. He could hear his father's voice: *What is your warm-up? Chopin played through the entire Well-Tempered Clavier as his warm-up.* Before he began, Clive scanned the audience for his father's beaming face, nodded, and whispered to himself, "Papa, as a tribute to you today, this is my warm-up."

Clive had been told the acoustics of the Great Hall are unparalleled. Within four measures, he knew this to be true. The instrument, coupled with the sound, sang out and carried as though it would resonate past the audience, through all of Moscow, and into the dachas of the countryside. Clive's mind filled with these images of Bach's music, moving all the way across borders and oceans and into distant hearts, into Clare's heart.

It would be unsophisticated for an audience to clap before the conclusion of the program. This Russian audience did, fueling Clive's intensity, tenderness, and confidence. He closed with the *Tchaikovsky Variations.* He could hear the hearts of onlookers beating in time with the music. He could feel their attachment to every note, hoping each would last, but yearning for the next one. Clive's piano voice spoke to them, and through their emotions they were talking back in a sacred dialogue without words.

They were beginning to trust him. Before the final note resonated out of the Hall, the audience leapt to its feet. Boisterous shouts of *"Bravo"* for the American. *Touché, Mr. Heinrich Niebuhr,* Clive thought. *Hopefully, your ear was pressed against the wall too.*

CHAPTER 25

Bel Canto—Beautiful singing

"Leonard Bernstein said, 'Music is the only art which does not require the censorship of the brain before reaching the heart.' Did you know that Papa? Do you think he was right?" Clive asked, remembering the quote on the wall of his dressing room at the Moscow Conservatory.

"Of course I agree. I agree with practically everything Leonard said. Those years we had together at Tanglewood when it was just beginning, he taught me so much. Yes, he was talking about the purity of music to touch our souls. Our brains don't get in the way with music like they do with visual art or drama. Even with the jury today, a transforming moment of music can take their minds completely out of it. Music captures the heart, first," Papa said.

The reference to Tanglewood immediately brought Clare to the forefront. She had first soloed there when she was right about Clive's age. Tanglewood. Clive imagined himself and Clare performing there together as part of the summer series after the competition. What would they play together? Faure's *Berceuse, the Dolly Suite,* would be perfect.

The day of the finals, the performers and their escorts gathered together in the Savoy's fountain room for another enormous breakfast buffet. This time Papa exhorted, "You might not feel like eating until the competition concludes, so eat every bite of your lox, bagel, and eggs."

"So yesterday was quite an unusual day. Did you hear about what happened?" Mr. K asked, leaning forward and lowering his voice. "After the second round, a debate ensued about one competitor's unorthodox approach to a Mozart sonata; I believe it was one of the Chinese gentlemen. In unprecedented fashion, the anxious competitor was asked to come back much later in the evening, while we were all having dinner, and play the Mozart sonata again. After all that uproar the poor young man did not make the finals."

Clive brushed his mop of black hair away from his face as he shook his head in disbelief.

Mr. K continued, "I've heard of these horror stories. We are so fortunate nothing went awry yesterday. Wasn't that something last night when they announced the names of the finalists? I was getting more nervous with each name called until I figured out they were announcing them in alphabetical order. That was a long wait for S., and at that point we knew Niebuhr had made it. Clive, were you as nervous as we were?"

"Yes, I kept waiting for them to announce my name and there were some surprises so I wasn't sure I'd made the cut. I was surprised Fissler from Iceland made it, given what everyone was saying about his interpretation of the Bach. We expected Lao, Niebuhr, and Rimsky, but what about Pobanz? I heard he was tentative yesterday with the *Tchaikovsky Variations.*

"Papa, when I looked out at the table, it looked like you were about to jump out of your skin. Did you two see me look over at Niebuhr while we were waiting on stage? I returned the icy stare he gave me at the opening night reception," Clive said, smiling as he finished his last sip of black tea.

"Clive, you are the first American to reach the finals in the last two Tchaikovsky competitions and the youngest in its history. Given the Tchaikovsky is only played every four years, you are the first American in twelve years to reach this epic position, and with Lao making it, I believe it is only the second time a woman has made it to the finals," Papa said, unable to withhold a firm slap on Clive's back with his strong conductor's hand.

"News of your success has reached home. Mama and Anna have organized a party for all our Serkin relatives to watch the finals on television. Brookline Academy has called a special school assembly for everyone to view the finals together on a generously donated projection system," Claude bragged.

"Even Rabbi Sherveen is going to tune in and listen on his transistor radio," Mr. K said with a twinkle in his eye.

"How do you know this about Rabbi Sherveen?" Clive asked.

"Because I know the rabbi does not have TV, but he is a devoted listener of Jack Brickhouse and the Chicago Cubs. What he cares for, he hears on his radio, and he cares for you, Clive."

Yes, he does, more than you know. Clive remembered how Rabbi Sherveen rescued him from the gutter outside temple. *Without Rabbi Sherveen's kindness, I might not be here today.*

As they gathered their coats to leave the table, Papa couldn't resist one final comment. "Word on the street is that the President of the United States will be attending for the first time. President Johnson didn't come to support Van Cliburn, but LBJ wasn't exactly a patron of the arts. He was too busy driving around his ranch in a big Texas Cadillac with longhorns attached to the hood."

"Papa, no more pressure please. I'm glad everyone is excited about the competition, but this isn't really about the audience." *This is about Clare and what she has done for me,* Clive wanted to tell them, but wouldn't dare.

After breakfast, at eight o'clock sharp, the bus driver delivered the competitors to the Conservatory. People were lining Boshaskaya Street for five blocks waiting for tickets. Rather than believe they were all coming to hear people play the piano, they knew they were coming for something greater. For them, it was all about the great tradition of their music. A desperate need for the music could be seen in their somber eyes.

The night before, their hotel room was quiet. Mr. K had gone to bed early. He claimed he was still adjusting to the jet lag, but he looked pale, almost gaunt. Claude gave the needed space to Clive and withheld further motivational speeches. Instead, the wisdom of the Folio, Clare, Mr. K, and even Rabbi Sherveen's words provided peace and comfort. The words Rabbi shared in the dry quiet of the synagogue penetrated Clive's heart, words from King David, who knew what it was like to fight against giants. "Who am I, O Sovereign Lord, and what is my family that you have brought me this far?" An eighteen-year-old boy playing against these experienced, older men, a David against Goliath, but Rabbi Sherveen had said, "Today, you become a man."

))(

As Clive stood, staring in the mirror and rubbing the ten-shekel piece in his pocket, Sergey knocked on the door. "Five minutes, Mr. Serkin." As expected, Niebuhr played first. *No need to press my ear to the wall this time.* The only sound was the second hand of the wall clock sweeping along the minutes like a metronome set on the slowest tempo, largo. Five minutes felt like another fifteen.

Finally, Clive walked down the dark corridor toward the stage door. Sergey, standing beneath the single light bulb, offered a slight bow as he reached for Clive's piano bench. "Good luck."

Looking out, Clive could see that the stage was covered with flowers showered by the audience on Niebuhr. He had played his concerto of preference brilliantly. Single-stem roses were piled so thick, they blocked the path to the piano and through the orchestra, and were being swept up by the custodians. Clive waited at the stage door for them to clear, which gave him a moment to scan the crowd.

Three rows back sat Papa, with an empty seat next to him. *Where is Mr. K?* Clive let his head protrude from the doorway just slightly with the hope of catching Claude's eye to question Mr. K's absence. *How could Mr. K not be here? First Clare, and now this? Nothing short of death would keep him from this moment.*

Maestro Gilels nodded for Clive to come forward. The audience began to cheer, clapping, "Sear-kin, Sear-kin" in their Russian accent. *They know it will be a duel to the death.* Clive's feet froze in place with a sudden paralysis. He wiped his sweating palms on his tuxedo pants, waiting for his Papa to look over at him. *Something has gone wrong. How could God allow anything to happen to Mr. K when he has come so far? This is his moment as much as mine.*

Taking hold of the coin in his pocket, Clive heard Papa's voice in his head. "Your spirit has been broken, but like your great-grandfather, you did not let that stop you." *This is the only time I will ever be here. Seize it. And then let it go.*

Again, Clive bowed to the composers on his left, his right, and to the audience in the middle. President Clinton was seated in the center box with the Russian Prime Minister, Boris Yeltsin. Clive saluted them from the heart as a gesture of respect.

He chose the *Chopin **Concerto No. 2 in F minor*** as his first selection, a risky choice for a competition of this magnitude due to its delicate poetry and de-emphasized orchestral accompaniment. But this music of Chopin was his heartbeat and if he was to connect with the jury and the Russian people, he needed to invite them into his heart.

After majestically interpreting the opening movement, Clive

surrendered to the larghetto, finding it difficult to keep his composure. The music transported him back to Clare's studio, with the tingling wind chimes announcing his arrival at her painted door. Love born on a bench, lived out on piano benches through time by the Schumanns and Chopin himself, who could only play and not speak of his love. Small wet drops fell in slow motion through the movement onto the keys, his tears for what had been lost, but also for beauty gained.

With the quiet finish of the larghetto closing in, he paused to take a deep breath and collect himself for the Allegro Vivace. The orchestra receded and the piano emerged with new energy and conviction. With every facet of technique and artistry in his grasp, he played with all the grandeur Chopin put into his finish—unspeakable depth, mined out of ascending arpeggios, playing on air until the final note lifts off.

Exhaling, eyes still closed, Clive heard only the melody ringing in the silence. A tap on his shoulder by the bow of the concertmaster urged him to acknowledge the roaring applause. Rising from his bench, Clive heard nothing despite the deafening sound. Everyone was standing. Women pushed their way forward, reaching their hands up over the stage. Clive bent down to shake the few nearest to him. Like Clare's, they felt so small set into his own exhausted hand. He suddenly became aware of the cultural divide bridged by the music: an American playing music by a Polish composer in a Russian piano competition.

The jury frantically finished their notes as Clive left the stage for a water break. He waved and winked at Papa, who also was on his feet and throwing a kiss.

As Clive stood backstage waiting for the applause to die down, he thought about the famous stories surrounding Tchaikovsky's **B-flat minor Concerto.** How Toscanini forced Horowitz to rehearse over forty times, practically to the point of death, and yet his recording was the one he loved the most. How Gilels played this piece with thunder and Richter with determined force and nuance. Even Van Cliburn, with his shy edge to the Andantino Semplice, connected seamlessly with his competition audience. But best of all was Tchaikovsky's own story. On Christmas Eve, he tested out his concerto upon the ears of Nikolai Rubenstein, who tore it to shreds, dismissing it as impossible, unplayable. Instead of cowering in the corner, Tchaikovsky believed in his work and refused to make the changes Rubenstein suggested. "I shall not alter a single note," was his response to the condemning critique.

Now it was Clive's turn to speak to the Russian people in their own language. Without altering a single note, he gave them their national voice, the voice of Tchaikovsky.

X

Before the closing night dinner reception, the competitors posed for pictures with many of the Russian dignitaries attending. Clive left the audience whipped into a euphoria, showering the stage with flowers for him as they had with Nicbuhr. Claude was unable to get into the room due to the heavy security, which caused a long wait for their reunion and any information about Mr. K to be relayed.

After numerous broken English conversations with unknown Russian politicos, Clive finally found Claude in the lobby of Rachmaninov Hall.

"Papa!" He screamed, running to embrace his father. "We have done it. Our dream is real," Clive proclaimed, knowing Claude would understand that the dream was no longer just Claude's. Now fulfilled, it was Clive's as well. For once Claude found himself unable to speak. His teary eyes and quivering jaw spoke to Clive with an intimacy that words could not conjure.

"Where was Mr. K?" Clive asked.

"Mr. K suffered an episode of heart failure while waiting in line to take his seat in the Great Hall, but he will be fine. He is tougher than he looks. They brought him a television in the hospital, so he could watch the finals as well as today's outcome. I saw him early this morning and he is in high spirits after the way you played yesterday."

"I am so relieved," Clive said. "If something happened to Mr. K while we were here, I would never forgive myself. This trip might have been too much for him at his age." Clive reclined in a gilded chair while staring out the window past his father. He folded and twisted his program for the evening, trying to hold back tears. *Had I come with Clare, this disaster could have been avoided.*

"No need to harbor blame about this, Clive. Being here with you after so many years of working together would be worth any sacrifice to Saul, even if it resulted in death. In his mind his life would be fulfilled and he would be home with his beloved Rachel. I only wish he could have been in the Hall to see all the little details he couldn't pick up on TV," Claude shared.

"One of the jurors was crying at the end of your Tchaikovsky," Claude whispered, hoping others in the crowded lobby did not hear. "Take that as a compliment and do not fear tears, Clive. Tears are a gift from God."

Clive felt a deep emptiness at the thought of almost losing Mr. K, another beloved friend and teacher practically gone. "Papa, do you think I have a chance?" Clive asked.

"A chance?" Papa laughed aloud. "You have more than a chance. Everything was there, Clive. Niebuhr was good, but your playing carried an emotional weight that was preeminently alive. There is no other way to describe it. You played like a Russian, yes, like a Russian Jew, even more than the Russian himself.

"Something like a transformation happened to you on stage. Your performance was magnificent. During the Tchaikovsky, people seated around me were on the edge of their seats from the opening crash of chords up the keyboard until the finish.

"Do you remember when we would go together to the art museum and look at Renoir's painting of the lady sitting in her long gown at the piano? I believe it's called *Lady at the Piano.*

The painting is more beautiful than reality, with such richness of color and texture. That is how you played at the finals. Your music transcended reality."

"Thank you, Papa," Clive said with a renewed sense of pride. "Even if I don't win, I've already won, knowing that you and Mr. K are pleased."

X

The following day, the finalists gathered in Rachmaninov Hall for the announcement of the results. The Great Hall simmered with the intensity of a tea kettle spewing steam. The Khrushchev and Uncle Sam announcer, with a voice more barbed wire than honeysuckle, came to the podium and turned to the finalists who faced the audience.

"Welcome, beloved countrymen and women. We are here today to announce the winners in the tenth annual Tchaikovsky Piano Competition. The jury has reached their decision. We acknowledge the fine performances of all the competing musicians by showing our gratitude." The crowd applauded for about two endless minutes.

After taking a vanilla colored envelope from his breast pocket, the official tore the golden seal and removed a single card. He then made the entire Hall wait as he saluted the prime minister in the balcony one final time.

"Third place, the bronze medal goes to Mr. Joseph Fissler of Iceland." Clive watched as Fissler exuberantly shook hands with all of the jurists and bowed to the appreciative audience.

"Second place, the silver medal goes to Miss Yundi Lao of China." Niebuhr turned, looked at Clive, and smiled for the first time as he anticipated his victory. It would be unthinkable for the Russians to leave Niebuhr out of the top three finishers. As Lao hugged Maestro Gilels, the applause grew louder and rhythmic, the steady pounding of a 2/2 time signature calling out both of their names.

Clive felt calm. He closed his eyes and imagined the faces of the inner-city students of Orr High School, followed by the face of Clare. The Russians were now screaming out their names with competing fervor and ecstasy. *These people love our music and we have fulfilled a need in them, perhaps a hope that someone young, from far away, can unite with their countrymen and give them a beautiful gift. Could it be a tie? It has happened before.*

"First prize and the Tchaikovsky Piano Competition gold medal is awarded to Mr. Clive Serkin of the United States of America."

Clive felt all of the wind rush from his lungs with hurricane-like force. Doubling over, gasping for air like a finisher crossing the line after a grueling marathon, he heard his heart pounding in his ears in harmony with the chant of "Sear-kin, Sear-kin" coming from the audience. His heart and their voices beat in unison.

The other competitors rushed over to offer their congratulations as the cheering increased. Clive couldn't breathe because the middle of the huddle was stiflingly hot. To avoid fainting, he moved downstage to accept his flowers and the medal. Women at the lip of the stage attempted to hand their children up to him. Not sure how to respond, he kissed them and patted the top of each adoring head. After about a minute, Niebuhr walked over and shook hands. Clive could see the questioning disappointment register on Niebuhr's face. *What could have happened? Something must have gone wrong with his final performance. Papa didn't say anything.* No one this young had ever won before and never before had a Russian failed to place in the finals.

Looking for Papa, Clive saw him standing next to Sviatoslav Richter, who had both of his hands clasped together over his head. He was shaking them from side to side, sharing a gesture of triumph. His generosity in the face of his own pupil's stunning loss brought Clive to the edge of tears.

With a bow to the left, to the right, and to the middle, Clive acknowledged the many flowers and gifts the audience was throwing onto the stage. Grabbing a red rose from the floor of the stage, Clive waved to President Clinton, who offered a distinguished bow in return.

The crowd finally quieted as Clive sat down to play his encore of gratitude. Anticipation of the music brought sudden silence. He had not prepared for this tradition. In a moment, he knew what to play. For the audience, nothing but Russian fire and showmanship, Scriabin's *Etude in D-sharp minor*. *For my beautiful Clare, Brahms's* **Waltz in A-flat Major.**

CHAPTER 26

Al Segno—Return to the sign

Word of his victory reached home before it was announced on the Moscow stage, due to a jury assistant giving an inside tip to a reporter from the *Chicago Tribune*. Ironically, Mama and Anna knew even before Clive and Papa arrived at O'Hare airport. Mr. K needed to stay in the hospital for a week, and Claude agreed to fly back to bring him home after a bit of celebrating with family and friends.

Clive's home phone rang endlessly. Mama, of all people, was unable to keep up with the volume of calls. "Welcome home, Clive. I am now your agent. You'll need to pay me fifteen percent for every booking," Anna said, throwing her arms around Clive before the victor even walked through the front door. Papa always handled everything related to competitions in the past, but the calls for engagements alone were so numerous, Clive's schedule for the next six months was in place before the wheels of American Airlines Flight 363 touched down in Chicago.

Anna said, bouncing up and down, "It must be like living a

dream come true. You are now famous. Come inside and I'll go over your concert schedule with you for the next four weeks. You are going to be all over the place, and guess where your first concert is? Right here at Brookline Academy. Home court advantage, right? Our school is going to pay you. Lucky. Now I want to ask you a couple of things about venue preferences." Anna's enthusiasm for her new job was admirable, but overwhelming.

There was no manual that explained what to expect when you win the Tchaikovsky Piano Competition. *All I want to do is find Clare and tell her we've won, not come home and take audiences everywhere by storm.* After the third evening at home, Clive couldn't speak to one more media person or sign another autograph.

It was time to tell Mama and Papa everything and ask for their help. As usual, he enlisted Anna's strategic skills with this task. Confiscating all of the cordless phones and placing them in a pile, Anna strutted into the center of the living room and screamed, "Emergency Family Meeting is being called right now!"

"What's going on in here, young lady?" Mama whisked in wondering.

"Clive has something to tell you. It's a secret that I have known about forever, but you are about to find out right now. You'd both better sit down and make yourselves comfortable." In silence, Papa and Mama waited next to each other, appropriately on the loveseat.

Without a glimmer of fear, his plea for help began.

"Long ago, as you know, I responded to an announcement to study piano with Clare Cardiff, herself a famous pianist. She had come to Brookline to teach and live with her sister. Our professional relationship took another turn. I fell in love with her and I thought she was in love with me. We were very close, hugging, holding hands, going out to dinner, acting like people who are in love are supposed to act, as best I know.

"Then I found out she was married. She was diagnosed with an illness undisclosed to me. Before I could find out what the diagnosis was, her husband came and took Clare to their farm in New Hampshire. You remember I was losing so much weight? Well, I was growing despondent with no word from her. So I took matters into my own hands and drove to New Hampshire and back in two days, all in an effort to find her.

"I found her husband, but not Clare. He claimed he put her in a 'safe place.' I don't even know what that means. She could be rotting in an institution somewhere. He claimed she became violent, but that's impossible. He is the violent one. You didn't know I went on this trip because you were out of town and Anna protected me.

"Please, don't be angry with her. Anna needed to do this, in order to help me move ahead with the competition. Although it was painful, the trip allowed my body and mind to completely focus on the task at hand, but part of my heart is missing. Before I do anything else, I need to find Clare and tell her that we won. I need to thank her.

"Papa, you said you saw me crying during the second movement of the Chopin concerto. My tears were for Clare and all she taught me, and yet she wasn't there. Please, I am desperate for you both to help me. You have the connections; I don't. If anyone can help me find her, the two of you can."

"Well, it sounds as if Anna is the resourceful one you've been relying on. Why don't you have her help you?" Mama inquired, clearly hurt by not being brought into the dilemma sooner.

Clive slumped onto the couch, greatly relieved of the burden nagging his soul for more than a year. After Mama's quick retort, there was nothing but silence. They didn't even look at each other like parents usually do, wondering who was going to speak first.

"Um, Clive just poured his whole heart out to you. Well, aren't you going to say something to help him?" Anna inquired. The silence continued.

Mama softened. "Clive, darling, I can't believe you've been suffering with this by yourself all this time and yet you still won. This is nothing short of a miracle. You don't have to go through life alone. Yes, we will look into this. I can't guarantee it will help much, since medical records are private, but I know some officials in New Hampshire who are affiliated with care facilities or institutions, as you called them. We might be able to locate her through those connections, if that is where she is. You said her husband is violent. Might he have harmed her? Forgive me for saying this, but are you sure she is even alive?"

The jarring thought caused Clive to sink further into his seat. Despite his own terrifying encounter with Nero, he had no idea if Nero could kill his own wife. "I'm not sure."

"Papa, are you all right? You're not saying a word," Anna said. It was not like him to be this reticent in a crisis.

"I'm so sorry, Clive. I have failed you by being unaware of what was going on. I was so caught up in the competition and my own work that I couldn't even see what you were facing. Please forgive me. I will connect with all my East Coast music collaborators and find out if she has performed or taught anywhere. We will find her. Yes, you need to have closure on this, in order to embrace your new life."

"My new life? I'm still hanging on to the hope that Clare will be a part of my new life," he confessed. Papa left Mama's side and walked across the carpet to sit next to Clive on the couch. "Clive, this woman has done a great deal for you, and we will try to help you find her, but your life is your own now. You have an obligation to bring joy and music to the people of the world who will want to hear you play. Your audience is your new lover, so to speak. I'm not discounting what you and Clare had together, by no means. You must realize that your life as a concert pianist will not mesh well with a woman in her fifties who is ill. Please try to understand this. As I said, we will do the best we can to help you find Clare, but you must find yourself."

After a week of searching through every nook and cranny

of New Hampshire, the efforts of Mama and Papa led nowhere. Somehow, the world famous concert pianist known as Clare Cardiff had vanished. Mama suggested she could be in a hospital somewhere. Even with all of her NIH know-how, she could not get around the Privacy Act to find out which one. Clare had many friends in Boston and New York, none of which Clive knew, but she could have run away from Nero to any of them.

As a last resort, it was time to turn to Clare's sister, Bethany, and her husband, Tim. Bethany had given Clive the farm address. She was the only other person who might know where Clare was. After all, Clare came to her in the beginning.

Not knowing their last name, a phone call wouldn't do. The address of their house on West Street was still in his memory, so despite Clive's insecurity about going there a second time to obtain information on Clare, he decided to try.

What a different experience from the first time he strolled down West Street into this Gentile enclave. On that day, people hardly acknowledged him. Today, they were yelling from their cars, "Congratulations, Clive Serkin, we are so proud of you." All of Brookline now believed they owned a part of him. They even put up a billboard in the downtown area, *Brookline Welcomes Home Tchaikovsky Winner, Clive Serkin. Congratulations!*

All of the attention was embarrassing. Mama told Clive she received calls indicating that the city was planning a parade like Van Cliburn's. *Only his was in New York and thankfully, this is Brookline, so hopefully it will be low-key and no ticker tape, Clive thought.* He was a bit surprised his hometown cared so much about the piano.

After ringing the familiar little columned doorbell, the sound of someone inside practicing scales on the piano could be heard. The scales stopped and an older boy answered. He couldn't be but a few years younger than Clive.

"Hello, can I help you? Wait, you are Clive Serkin. Mom, Dad, everyone, Clive Serkin is standing at our front door! Come and see him!"

Within thirty seconds, the whole crew of seven inside the house was standing in the foyer, staring.

"Hello. I am Clive Serkin, one of your sister Clare's students," Clive said, directing his comments at Bethany. "You might remember we met some time ago and you gave me Clare's address. I'm still trying to find her because I would like to let her know about the competition."

A little girl with pink-ribboned pigtails asked, "Have you come here to play for us?"

"Not right now. I'm hoping to speak to your mom and dad."

"Yes, please come in. Children, you all need to play outside for a bit while we grown-ups talk to Mr. Serkin. Off you go and stay in the yard. No going over to the neighbor's house."

The young boy was heading past Clive, so he stopped him to ask his name. "My name is Jeremy. It's a pleasure to meet you, Mr. Serkin. Congratulations."

"I believe it was you, practicing those scales when I came to the door. Keep working on it. You never know where it might take you."

"Yes, sir," the boy said. Overnight, the whole community had catapulted Clive from unseen Jewish boy to adored hometown adult hero. It was going to take some getting used to.

Bethany and Tim showed Clive to their front parlor, where he sat waiting for them to reveal anything they might know. Their faces appeared compassionate and tense. "You don't need to play for the children. You must be asked that everywhere you go now. Congratulations. Even though we don't really know you, we feel a kinship because you were an important part of Clare's life, by all she told us."

"*Were* an important part of Clare's life?" *Oh, God, please no.*

"Let me tell you all that we know, and Tim, please add anything I might be missing," Bethany began after taking a deep breath. "This is a difficult story for us to share. You know that

Clare went back to New Hampshire with Nero. They agreed a second opinion was in order on her diagnosis. The doctors at Johns Hopkins confirmed she had early onset dementia.

"Nero believed he could take care of her, and he tried, but her decline was so rapid, she became difficult and unreliable, even delusional. One night, he found her outside in the fields in her nightgown with bleeding, bare feet. She was completely lost. Nero was devastated. He concluded she needed to be in a place where she would be safe and receive excellent care. She had quite a bit of money saved from concertizing, so money was no object.

"He found a place called The Hudson, reputed highly for artistic therapies with cases like Clare's, especially music therapy. She put up quite a fight against going there, to the point he could not visit Clare without her verbally attacking him. She was always screaming at him, 'I want to go home. Please let me go home.'

"The pain of losing Clare, both mentally and physically, was too much for Nero. He wanted to take care of her and he couldn't. Theirs was a complex relationship that brought Nero a lot of heartbreak. We believe he was overcome with a combination of grief and guilt, and sadly, we learned a few weeks ago that he … took his own life at the farm. Now we are handling the estate and looking for a buyer for the property."

Bethany sat in the still rocking chair, looking up at the family portraits which covered the walls. She appeared to be holding back more she wanted to say. "I feel terrible putting all that depressing news on you after you've recently arrived home from your victory in Moscow."

Bethany and Tim leaned forward in their rocking chairs, attentive to whatever Clive might say in response. "Yes, that is tragic about Nero. I can't imagine what he must have been feeling. I'm sure he loved Clare. I met him once at her studio and he seemed so casual, at ease, even comfortable with himself. It's hard to believe he would take his own life. But I must say I'm partly relieved. I was afraid you might tell me that Clare was the one who was dead. I had asked Mama and Papa to help me find her. Despite using all of their professional networks, they could not find a trace of her anywhere."

Tim nodded. "I'm not surprised by that. Given her stature as a famous musician, she is very self-conscious about people finding out where she is and what is happening to her. In fact, she is still hopeful she will 'recover' and return to her normal life."

"And so am I," Clive declared. "Is there any chance I could visit her in The Hudson? It would mean a great deal to me, to be able to give her all the details of the competition. I know it would bring her joy and maybe improve her health somewhat."

Bethany and Tim looked at each other with the look of two people who have been married for years and already know what the other is going to say. In a voice dripping with sweetness, Bethany spoke first. "You can visit her, but be prepared for the fact that she is different now. Like all of us, she has good days and bad days, and you might not catch her on a good day."

"Have you gone to see her?" Clive asked.

"Yes, I have. We had a wonderful visit," Bethany said. "She is in a beautiful facility that's perfect for her needs, where music is constantly encouraged."

Tim looked concerned. "If you do visit her, it's important that you go free of expectations. You don't know what you might find. Her type of dementia advances rapidly, so be prepared. She might not recognize you. For that matter, you might not recognize her."

"I want to see her, that's all. Even if I don't get to speak with her, I'll be overjoyed." All of the rocking chairs continued in their creak-filled cadence as the trio rose together and walked toward the door. The couple's generosity in sharing this information moved Clive. "How can I ever thank you? You've done so much for me when you didn't need to do anything."

"Well, we do need a new piano teacher," Bethany proposed with an imploring smile.

CHAPTER 27

Al Fine—To the end

O nce Papa and Mama learned of Clare's physical situation, they insisted one of them go with Clive. Papa wanted to make the trip. He looked at it as a rite of passage that Clive might be denied in the future, the trip they planned to take together after his high school graduation. At this point, they didn't even know if Clive would be attending his graduation given the number of concerts Anna was lining up.

The Hudson was in upstate New Hampshire. The drive with Papa felt like old times, when father and son would leave the city together after a rehearsal and talk about every aspect of the pieces the orchestra was preparing. On this trip, Claude spent the first six hundred miles telling Clive every detail of every competitor's performance at the competition.

When actually listening, he became grateful for how fortunate his competition rounds had gone. No travesty befell him, like a string breaking in the middle of his concerto, which happened to Niebuhr, or the entire pedal workings falling off the piano, which actually happened while Yundi Lao was playing a Rachmaninoff Prelude in the first round. During most of the drive, he sat silent for hours, starring out the window, thinking about Clare.

Dementia. A disease old people have in nursing homes. How would she live without the ability to play the piano? Once I save up enough money from touring, I could move to New Hampshire and start a piano studio there.

In Erie, Pennsylvania, Papa noticed Clive didn't say much on the drive. "Clive, I feel like I'm doing all the talking. What is going on in that head of yours?" his father asked.

Since Moscow, Claude had started to feel more like a friend than parent, an equal to be confided in, a peer who advises rather than judges.

"I'm thinking about Clare, about my life and where it is going. What do I want to accomplish with my life?"

"You are only eighteen and have done something no one has ever done before. You need some time to get used to that. Sit on it and don't rush into anything. After receiving the von Karajan medallion, my first big prize for conducting, I went on a rampage of sorts. I took every single podium offered to me to gain more experience. After one year, I sought refuge at Bubbe Serkin's home in upstate New York for some time away to recover. I was running on my own strength to achieve everything I could, as fast as I could get it.

"While we were sitting in her music house on the island one day, Bubbe said something I will never forget. 'Claude, you are talented, but not too wise. Don't let the applause of the audience determine your life. Applause can be deceiving. If it is all you are listening for, you can't hear the voice of your master, the God of Israel. It is his reward you should be seeking.'

"Bubbe Serkin was a wise woman. She was content, a real listener, and loved music with her very soul. I spent many hours in her music pagoda that summer by myself—listening, separating myself from other voices, and trying to hear His voice."

"And what did you hear, Papa? Did you hear His voice?"

"Yes, I believe I did. Not like Moses, but in a quiet way, like a whisper, you know, like the gentle singing of birds. Once I put away the cares of my own life, I heard a new song that became more important than the song of my own design."

The most fulfilling times for Clive were the field trips they took from Brookline to perform for inner-city kids at Orr High School—young, impressionable minds that needed inspiration.

Their hardened faces said it all: The music took them to a different place. It would have been so easy for them to resent classical performers—the suburban brats who had everything on a silver platter—but they didn't. They loved the music, many of them for the first time.

)(

The entrance of The Hudson was truly grand, a gray granite archway with bronze lettering. The lawn was pristine, dotted with large sugar maples and English oak trees. There was a formal-looking canopy over the front walkway to shelter the residents and visitors from the rain or bright sun. Today the sun was streaking across the lawn and playing shadows with the trees.

Once parked in the lot, Papa sat quietly, looking out on the lawn. He turned to Clive and asked, "Do you want me to go in with you or wait out here?"

Clive knew he had to make this part of the trip on his own. "Please wait for me. I don't know how long this is going to take."

"I will be waiting for you, my son." With a slam of the car door, Papa climbed out and came around to hug his son. "I'm proud of you. You're doing what you need to do to move on."

Making his way toward the canopy, Clive thought he heard music off in the distance. The Hudson's grounds were impeccable—a good sign. Clive checked in with the reception desk. "I'm here to see Clare Cardiff. It is my understanding she is a Hudson resident."

The receptionist didn't even look at her room list. "As we speak, Madame Cardiff is giving a recital in the Meadows room, the second room down the hall, on the left. Would you like me to take you there after you sign in and get a badge?"

"No. Thank you very much." *A recital? How sick can Clare be?*

Passing by a gift shop on the way down to the Meadows room revealed women shoppers who were all carrying their own purses and paying for their own transactions. Many of them looked young, a couple of them not much older than Clive. *Does anybody need help here?*

Just to the right of the door, there was a sign mounted on an easel, with heavily scripted lettering.

In Recital
Dr. Clare Cardiff—Piano
Sunday Afternoon
October 23, 1994
Music of Brahms, Beethoven, and Liszt

Listening outside the door brought a double dose of encouragement. Clare was playing the Adagio from Beethoven's ***Pathetique Sonata,*** her technique flawless as usual. Clive pressed his hands and head against the door as he'd done so many times against her painted Mount Fuji front door, back in Westdale Conservatory. Letting the vibrations of the music enter through his hands and into his heart, Clive listened. Unable to stand outside another minute, he pushed the heavy door open by a brass handle and quietly entered the hall.

Surveying the room, choosing to stay in the back, he noted that every chair was taken, with people standing in the back. Everyone looked to be in their fifties, some even younger.

A few of the women were crying. One woman was staring down at the carpet and shaking her head back and forth, in tempo with the music. A group of four sat on the floor, with their backs and heads leaning against the wall. There was an eerie air of disconnection between the listener and the performer. It was the opposite of the feeling he experienced at the Tchaikovsky Competition, where it felt like the audience was speaking to him without words.

Clare chose to skip the *Rondo* section and play an unfamiliar tune. She began singing along with the music while she was playing, something he had never seen or heard her do before. Clive could hardly see her face, so he closed his eyes and listened to her soothing and full voice. It was the voice he still loved, the voice of music.

"Great is Thy faithfulness,
O God my Father.
There is no shadow of turning with Thee."

Clare now had the complete attention of everyone in the room. They were singing along with her to lyrics they obviously knew by heart. Those in the floor group rose to their feet. Several residents who were sitting in chairs were now standing. A few of them were even raising their hands up in the air.

"Thou changest not,
Thy compassions they fail not,
As Thou hast been, Thou forever wilt be.
Great is Thy faithfulness!
Great is Thy faithfulness!
Morning by morning new mercies I see.
All I have needed Thy hand hath provided.
Great is Thy faithfulness, Lord unto me."

This must be some well-known Gentile song that's familiar to people, Clive imagined. Clare's audience was rapt as she played her own improvisation at the end. Wild applause rang out as the music concluded. Unlike her concerts, Clare did not move from her position on the bench, until someone stepped forward from the front row to turn her around to face the still-standing audience. She bowed, feebly—first to the right, then to the left, and to the audience in the middle. An assistant led Clare toward the door. People were reaching out to touch her arm or shake hands in gratitude. Clive tried to catch her eye, but she didn't see him.

"Was it good? Did they like it?" Clare asked the assistant.

"Madame Cardiff, they always love your music. You know that. Didn't you hear them singing? They love everything you play, especially when you play those hymns."

"Mama taught me all the hymns I know. She came over the other day and helped me with a few of the rusty ones. My mama, she knows her hymns. When is she coming back to see me?"

"Madame Cardiff, your Mama has always been with you. Every time you play, she's there."

"And Daddy too?"

"Yes, and Daddy too."

Clive trailed behind them the rest of the winding way in silence. As they walked, Clare was faintly humming a tune. The assistant moved slowly, not rushing her. When they stood at her door, Clive heard the assistant say, "Here we are, Madame Cardiff, back home again. Millie will be checking on you tonight if you need anything. I'll be here bright and early in the morning to take you down to breakfast. Let's get your TV turned on for the night." The door closed behind them.

Clive stood patiently and waited for the kind assistant to leave Clare's room. "See you in the morning, Madame. Good night and pleasant dreams."

The assistant smiled as she passed by Clive. "May I ask you something? My name is Clive Serkin. Here's my entrance badge. For many years, Madame Cardiff has been a friend of mine. I'd love to see her again. Does she receive visitors?"

"Oh, yes, she loves visitors. Don't count on her remembering you, but she'll act like she does."

"Thank you so much. One more question. If she doesn't remember me, how can she play music like that, like she's always played it?"

"Oh, all the ones who played and could sing when they were younger, they can still do it. She happens to be really good at it. Music is fixed in the brain. It's alive when the other parts are dying. You know, it really matters what goes into your young mind, because when you're old and can't even go to the bathroom on your own, that's what you're going to have left. Remember that now. How old are you?"

"I'm eighteen."

"Well, if you haven't studied any music yet, there's still time to make that happen, but you'd better get busy. You run along now down the hall and knock on your friend's door. She'll be glad to see you." With an energetic bluster, the assistant hustled off to the next resident.

The time has come. Face the door. "Be a man," *Anna would say. Take a deep breath and knock.* Listening for her wooden clogs and not hearing them caught Clive by surprise as Clare opened the door. She looked beautiful. Radiant. Her bachelor's-button-blue eyes flashed at Clive as she took stock of her young visitor.

"Hello, Clare."

"Have you come for a lesson?"

"No, I'd like to talk with you. May I come in?"

"I don't usually let strangers into my room, but you're a handsome young stranger, so please, come in."

The apartment was very small and filled with memorabilia from all her travels. Clive recognized the posters from La Scala and Carnegie Hall. In the corner of the living room was a distinguished vintage Bechstein, finished in black with carved legs. *It must be a family heirloom because she didn't have this piano back in Brookline.*

"I'm sure you remember me. I'm Clive Serkin, one of your students."

"I knew you were one of my students. What did you say your name was?"

"Clive Serkin. We worked together on the Chopin piano concerto and many other pieces. I played it at the Tchaikovsky Piano Competition."

"How did you do?"

"I won."

"You won! That's wonderful. Let's have some champagne and celebrate. Let me see what I have in the refrigerator. What did you say your name was?"

"Clive. Clive Serkin."

"I had a son once named Clive Serkin. I'm not sure what happened to him. Do you know him?"

As she rummaged through the cabinets for glasses, Clive walked over to the piano and began to play the second movement of the Chopin concerto. The piano was exquisite, with such a rich cantabile. The clattering of crystal glassware grew quiet as the music filled the small room. Clare came and sat beside Clive on the piano bench. Her face turned toward his. With a searching look into his eyes, she took his breath away.

Next, she raised her hands and placed them on the keyboard, playing the piece in unison with him. Four hands making music together as one. She looked at him again. This time though, her expression changed. "Clive. Clive Serkin?"

"Yes. That's me."

"I do know you. You are my student, my Clive. You're back from Moscow? Tell me everything. What happened at the Tchaikovsky Competition?"

He could see by her eyes that she was with him again, long enough to share his duel to the death with Heinrich Niebuhr, Mr. K's heart failure and survival, the magnificence of the Great Hall, and the unforgettable devotion of the Russian audience.

After they talked through all of these momentous events, Clive stood to demonstrate his bow. "I bowed to them, all of the composers, just like you taught me to do."

She clapped with great fervor and screamed "bravo" as he demonstrated. "What did you play for your victory concert encore? Wait, don't tell me. I should get our champagne first."

He played the Scriabin and the Brahms for her. As the final note faded away, she came over to the piano bench and sat down again. She held him tightly, crying as though the world was changing and she knew she would never be able to live this moment again. He held her, gently stroking her hair, rocking back and forth to the rhythm of silence. Over and over again, she whispered through her tears, "Clive, my son, my son. Take me home, take me home."

Minutes passed before she regained her composure. The embrace ended and Clive knew their relationship had changed forever. He had become the teacher and she was the student. *I will take what she has given me and pass it on to others.*

"Clare, I wonder if I might write something in your Folio, the big book of wisdom from composers and pianists down through the generations. Do you still have it?"

Clive hoped the name, Folio, would also jog her memory. She lit up like a menorah. "Yes, I do have a book like that, a Folio. Let me see, where did I put it?"

She wandered into the small bedroom. Clive could hear several drawers open and close. She returned with a wrapped package. Unopened, the Folio was still wrapped in the foam and plastic in which he sent it back to her. "This is the biggest book I own. Might this be it? Let's open it. It's all wrapped up like a present. I love presents!"

As she ripped the packing with such an indelicate hand, Clive watched in fear that she might damage it. "Do you mind if I help you open it?" he asked.

Gratefully, she handed it over. *It's unopened. Nero must not have shared it with her.*

"Look, it is crumbling on the edges like an ancient manuscript. What is it?" Clare asked, confused again.

Clive carefully leafed through the ancient pages, sharing passages with her. He read her his final note on the last page about his struggles with the Taneyev piece.

"Yes, I know that piece. Taneyev is such a sticky wicket, but judging by your outcome, you conquered it. Please, go ahead and pen something else. Write down a story—a true story—one that I can enjoy reading later. I love good stories."

Clive carried the huge book over to the Bechstein and laid it on top of the lid, using the piano as a desk. Then he wrote a final entry in the Folio.

In a faraway city there lived a boy and his piano. He loved his piano very much, but he couldn't breathe life into his playing until he met a beautiful lady, his teacher. She taught him to play the piano like no one else could. She set his fingers and his heart on fire. The boy grew up and went away to a far country. People there loved his playing and they threw flowers at his feet to thank him for his music, but he had not thanked his teacher.

So he traveled back home and found her. She lived in a beautiful music palace with many rooms. He played for her and told her how much he loved her, how she set his heart and his fingers on fire, and then he left and went off to give his music to those who needed it the most.

Thank you, Clare. I love you.

Clive Serkin, Tchaikovsky Piano Competition Gold Medalist, 1994

He handed over the Folio, "Will you read it to me?" Fearful of losing his composure, Clive hesitated, but managed to read it to her aloud.

Her enchanting childlike smile beamed like a blessing, filling their last moment together. "That is a beautiful story, Clive Serkin. Thank you. Mother and Daddy will love reading that story to me."

"No, Clare, thank *you*." With one last side-by-side hug upon her piano bench, he let her go, then turned and walked out of The Hudson to Papa—and the world.

Epilogue

The Serkin Institute for Music and Memory was founded by Claude Serkin and his son, Clive, in Chicago, Illinois. It is a not-for-profit research institute and care center that provides concerts, consultation, music therapy, and instruction for those suffering from memory loss due to all manner of misfortunes, from traumatic brain injury to dementia and Alzheimer's disease. Claude Serkin conducts orchestra performances in the Cardiff Auditorium regularly, with his son as soloist. Clive also serves on the S.I.M.M. Board of Directors, in addition to teaching piano at the Institute. This outpatient center serves the greater Midwest, and plans are underway for a second Institute to break ground in New York City during June of next year.

The Folio was recovered by Bethany upon Clarc's death and donated to the Serkin Institute for Music and Memory, where it is displayed and available for public viewing on Tuesdays throughout the year.

Author's Note and Resource Guide

Martin Luther said, "Next to the word of God, the noble art of music is the greatest treasure in the world." Music is powerful. It brings transformation, catalyzes healing, and imprints itself upon our lives and souls when we are often unaware.

Much research with dementia patients is being done today, demonstrating prolonged improvement of memory when music therapy is used to activate the hippocampus, allowing neuron pathways to connect and, in some cases, regenerate. There is tremendous hope for those suffering from memory loss that their brain function can be improved, anxiety and agitation reduced, and positive attitude enhanced with the use of music therapy.

For readers seeking help and further information, please consult the following resources:

Alzheimer's Association **www.alz.org**
ARTZ **www.artistsforalzheimers.org**
Institute for Music and Neurologic Function
   www.musictherapy@imnf.org
Music & Memory **www.musicandmemory.org**

My hope for this work is threefold. For all of us with loved ones suffering from memory loss, may we bring music to their minds in a loving, awakening manner, which unlocks lost memory and releases hope from despair. Second, may the medical and compassionate care communities pursue and apply the therapeutic benefits of music ever more vigilantly.

Finally, may all of us guard our hearts, minds, and the likes of our children by pouring into them good music, quality literature, and images that bless each other and build one another up. In the end, the music may be all we retain.

Discussion Guide

1. Clare reflects on her belief that, "Pain gives birth to art." Do you agree? In your experience what are other catalysts for artistic creation?

_____

_____

_____

_____

_____

_____

_____

2. How does Clive come to accept the significance of his true family lineage, rather than Clare and the Folio?

_____

_____

_____

_____

_____

_____

_____

_____

3. Despite Clare's apparent lack of faith, she tells Bethany, "All our lives have transcendent value." How does this come to fruition in Clare's life, in your own life?

_____

_____

_____

_____

_____

4. Clive quotes Leonard Bernstein, "Music is the only art which does not require the censorship of the brain before reaching the heart." Do you agree? Is there any other experience in life that fulfills this description?

_____

_____

_____

_____

_____

_____

_____

5. A significant theme of the book is the role of the audience. Claude tells Clive, "The audience is your new lover," yet he himself had to learn from Bubbe Serkin that our passions are best pursued out of our own love and devotion. How has the role of those on the outside, or "the audience" influenced your own pursuits?

_____

_____

_____

_____

_____

_____

_____

6. A secondary conflict in the story is the impact of God pre-determining the events of our lives as opposed to ourselves as the controller of our own destinies. How do the main characters come to terms with this dilemma? Upon which side of this idea do you subscribe?

_____

_____

_____

_____

_____

_____

_____

7. Much has been written on the power of memory to color the lens of our own life experience. How has memory influenced your view of yourself and others? Do you have personal experience with dementia or Alzheimer's through relationships? Describe how the aspects of Clare's descent into dementia seem familiar or dissimilar to you given the person you know who is dealing with memory challenges.

_____

_____

_____

_____

_____

_____

_____

8. Clare sees the necessity of preserving Clive's innocence for the sake of his art. Did she make the right choice? Is innocence still valued by American culture?

_____

_____

_____

_____

_____

_____

_____

9. Think through the role of hands in the story. What memorable moments in the plot revolve around the use of hands?

_____

_____

_____

_____

_____

_____

_____

10. What music do you love? How has music impacted your life with significance? Share a favorite musical memory.

_____

_____

_____

_____

_____

_____

_____

Q and A with author
Margaret Ann Philbrick

1. What inspired you to spend four years working on A Minor?
My children all play the piano, and our oldest son's teacher requested that a parent sit in on the lessons and take notes. We would then review with him during the following week. As he moved on to college, I was left with a notebook full of wisdom that needed to be shared, but I didn't have the framework for an idea. While I was having lunch in South Haven, Michigan, I started talking to my husband about what it would be like for a concert pianist to lose his or her memory. That question took me on a one year research journey to find the answer.

2. How did you go about your research?
I started with Dr. Oliver Sacks because he is one of the most well-known neurologists in the field. I read his books and watched YouTube videos of him talking about his patients. His work led me to many other experts and their writings. Once I completed that investigation, I embarked on several more months of research into the life of a concert pianist. Howard Reich's biography of Van Cliburn was one of the most helpful. Also, I interviewed many people who had been touched by dementia and Alzheimer's. Once I assessed all the research, I knew there was a story to mine out of that mountain.

3. Are you a musician yourself?
While in high school, I was a serious flute student and was accepted into a college conservatory, but my parents were moving toward a divorce at the time and I wanted to get as far away from their situation as possible. Instead, I became an English Literature major in Texas, which is why I have wrinkles today. I spent a lot of time lying out in the sun and reading novels.

4. Can you name a few of your favorites?
I tend to think about this question as a list of the books I wish

I would have written. The first ones that come to mind are: *Jane Eyre*, Georg Eliot's *The Mill on the Floss*, all books by Milan Kundera and Gabriel García Márquez, and recently my neighbors' books—*The Aviator's Wife* by Melanie Benjamin and *Sing For Me* by Karen Halvorsen Schreck. I also adored *Between Shades of Gray* by Ruta Sepetys. For teaching, I read a lot of classic YA novels. My favorite this year was Robert Louis Stevenson's *The Black Arrow.*

5. Talk about your creative process. How did you write the book?

I'm a pretty insecure writer having been a Lit major and constantly reading books that I feel are beyond my own creative abilities. I actually think this is a good thing because I relied on the discipline of prayer before I sat down to write each day, knowing I couldn't do this project alone. I'd spend time asking the Lord for creativity, original thought, wisdom, memory, whatever I needed to write the next ten pages. I'm disciplined when I get into a project, so I would write every day and then revise the next day what I wrote the day before and then move on. I always set goals for myself—another ten pages, finish the chapter. As I'd move along, another piece of research would be required, and I'd go off on a tangent for a day or so and then come back to the writing.

6. Did you use the notebook from your son's piano lessons?

Oh, definitely. In many ways the voice of the main character is the voice of my son's teacher. There are aspects of her in the work that I'm sure she'll recognize when she reads it, like her clogs. She always wears these precarious, high-heeled wooden clogs. I've never known anyone to wear shoes like this in the summer with bare feet. She's a fascinating conundrum.

7. Your book has some unique features, like a Discussion Guide in the back and recorded music in the ereader that anyone can hear while they are reading and live links to other resources. How did all that happen?

Well, I love Koehler Books because they are open to thinking outside the box of what a book can be. When I created *A Minor*, I thought about the music first. If you were only listening to the story, what would it sound like? Then I outlined all the musical works, and I'd listen to them while writing. It was important that the music told the story as well if not better than the words. Eventually, the idea came to me that I wanted the reader to have the same experience. Koehler Books was open to partnering with me in creating that experience. My husband, who is a lawyer, was an enormous help as well. The Discussion Guide is for the classroom or book clubs. As a teacher, it comes naturally for me to ask questions so people can learn more. The live links send the reader to the places where they can get help with memory issues in their own family or even for themselves.

8. *One of your questions in the Discussion Guide addresses the importance of the protagonist maintaining the innocence of her protégé even though she could have taken advantage of him. Why did you decide to go that way and do you think American culture has lost its innocence?*

Clare knows that the purity of Clive's imagination is tantamount to his artistic interpretation of the works; it is a competitive advantage he has and a winsome one. She chose to not compromise that advantage. Yes, the loss of innocence in American culture is negatively affecting the power of our imagination and ultimately our innovation, which has always been an edge for us. When everything is openly revealed it hinders our ability to create, to make pictures for ourselves and interpret through the lens of what we know and experience. Dean Koontz has just written a novel that addresses this beautifully. It's called *Innocence*. Making the choice to maintain one's innocence and even more altruistically, the innocence of another, is expanding the pure heart of the child in all of us, and that is a great gift.

9. *What were some of the disappointments along the way to getting published?*

Oh, all the "noes" that had been so close to being "yeses"—I never cared about the folks who were too busy to respond, but the ones where I had provided the entire manuscript and even changed things upon their request all to be told "no" months down the road. Those were tough, but I always believed in the story and knew there was a home out there waiting to bring it to life. I remember sitting on the edge of Lake Michigan, crying and praying that God would give my story a home. A few weeks later, He did.

10. Is it hard to raise a family and write a novel?

I can say my writing drives my kids crazy. My youngest son calls me the "bat." Sometimes he comes home from a piano lesson, and I'll be at my desk in the dark, writing by the light of the screen, too engaged to turn on any lights in the house. I try to write when they're not at home, during the school day. It's definitely not good for them if they feel like my "callings" are taking the place of them. Sometimes I've had to drop everything or step away from a project entirely, but raising children is a very short season and hopefully, I can write for the rest of my life.

11. What would your advice be to someone hoping to write their first novel or write anything for that matter?

Know your purpose, why you are writing what you are writing, and stay tethered to that vision. Write for the joy of creating and do not allow yourself to think about publishing, which is such a distraction, until you're done. Then let your work simmer for a while. Take long walks and think about it. Do you still love it? If you do, pray and turn it over to God. Ask Him to reveal the next step and then trust him to do so. In the Redbud Writers Guild, we embrace the truth of Psalm 37:5:

"Commit your way to the Lord, trust in him and he will do this."

Go at it with God. Writing is too lonely to do alone.

Acknowledgments

My deepest thanks to Dr. Oliver Sacks, Dr. Daniel Levitin, Dr. Paul Robertson, and Dr. John Zeisel, whose research on music and the brain served as the backbone of this story.

Blessings upon the numerous friends and family members whom I interviewed, especially my cousin, Dr. Christopher Dull. The thoughtful care for your loved ones and the loved ones of others is greatly appreciated and contributed significantly to the storyline.

Abundant gratitude to all the authors whose books deeply informed this work and were a delightful read for me—Howard Reich, Debra Dean, Kevin Bazanna, T. E. Carhart, Greg Dawson, William Trotter, Samuel Chotzinoff, Michael Steinberg, Alison Acheson (for your beautiful children's picture book on this topic), Chaim Potok, and Deborah Wearing.

Love and thanksgiving to my prayer partners: Katherine Ruch, Laura Tabbut, and the Redbud Writers Guild, especially Redbuds in the Chicago Manuscript Group. Without your prayers and insight, this book would never have come to fruition.

Forever love to my family, who always believed in my work despite growing tired of hearing about it at the dinner table, and special thanksgiving for my husband, Charlie, and his keen ability to listen, identify gaps in the plot, and provide legal expertise.

Unceasing gratitude goes to my first editor, Debbie Deloach, for her gift of taking my ill-formed manuscript and turning it into a readable piece, and to my second editor, Jodi Anne Steiner, for her wise insights, musical knowledge, and ability to ask the right questions. Thanks to my first readers, Messrs. Jim Bell, Mark Galli, and Ms. Sharla Fritz, for their experienced critique and encouragement. Armfuls of thanks and blessing bestowed upon all at Koehler Books for believing in and accepting my manuscript.

Love and thanks to the late John Fawcett, for his anointed worship leading at Church of the Resurrection and appreciation imparted to me of the music of Johannes Brahms. I wore your prayer shawl, knitted by the Catholic Women of West Chicago, the entire time I created this book. A deep bow to Bonnie and Trevor McMaken for recording *Great is Thy Faithfulness* and to Janna Williamson for her recording of Schumann's *Traumerei* and Brahms's *Waltz in A-flat Major*. For more of The McMaken's music go to **www.themcmakens.com**.

Thank you to Doug Jurs for your willingness to share your letter to Mahnil Fernando and to Addie Jurs, who encouraged me to not give up on this project, during her life and from beyond the grave.

Abundant thanks to our son Caleb and Dr. Karol Sue Reddington, for your inspired collaboration at the keyboard. May every student have such a gifted teacher, who can draw the purity of art and music from a teenager who doesn't practice nearly enough relative to his God-given ability.

Finally, thanks be to our great God for His gift of music. He is unchanging, the Alpha and Omega, the composer of every song and story. Lamentations 3:22-23: "Because of the Lord's great love we are not consumed, for his compassions never fail. They are new every morning; great is thy faithfulness."

CPSIA information can be obtained at www.ICGtesting.com
Printed in the USA
BVOW05s1020070414

349946BV00001B/1/P